I0595856

Also by S.L.Mason

KILLING GODS

ALETHEA

CALYPSO

HERA

FATES

UNDERWORLD

ELYSIUM

POSEIDON

THESE HALLOWED HILLS

TRICK OF FAE

TEST OF FAE

THORNS OF FAE

TWIST OF FAE

TRAITS OF FAE

ALETHEA

KILLING GODS I

Quick Quill Publishing

© 2019

This Book is a work of fiction.

All of the characters, organizations, and events portrayed in the novel are either products of the authors imagination or are used fictitiously. Its not about you.

Copyright 2019 Quick Quill Publishing, LLC

The distribution of this book without permission is a theft of the author's intellectual property. If you would like permission to use material from the book (other than for review purposes), please contact us at www.Quickquillpublishing.com Thank you for your support of the author's rights.

DEDICATION

~ 5 ~

To my husband, Jude.

With you, anything in the universe is possible.

TABLE OF CONTENTS

PROLOGUE

~ 10 ~

Mock me if you will, but everything I did, I did for love

Pythia

CHAPTER 1

SYDNEY

My mouth had gone dry, eyes burning. No one had ever called me a whore before. I've always been able to talk to any of my parents' friends. But my father propelled me, by the arm, down the hall, to my room. All this time, my mother was trailing behind, staring blankly ahead in silence.

Fingers laced into my hair, using it to throw me face down on the edge of the bed. Jarring pain shoots through my knees as they crack against the hardwood floor. My jaw slams shut, causing my teeth to dig into the tender flesh of my lower lip. The taste of blood from the tip of my tongue was followed by a whooshing sound of leather being pulled from the belt loops. This is always accompanied by the slapping of leather on flesh. All these are causing my heart to race due to the adrenaline that fills my veins.

Instinct screams at me to get up and run, but my upbringing has trained me to take my punishment. I accepted this because I knew that my parents loved me, and they wanted me to become a better person.

Father's words fill my ears. "I only do this because I care about you. Count!" A lash of pain lands across my back and wraps around my torso, stinging the side of my breast. I arched in agony at the attack on my tender flesh. I respond to it with a scream that roughens my throat. Before my face is smashed into the bed, a river of tears runs down my face and drips off my nose.

"COUNT!" Father shouts.

Choking, I coughed out. "ONE!".

The leather slices the air creating another lashing sound landing on my upper legs and wrapping around my quads to my thigh. Every one of my nerve endings screams. I automatically cough out. "TWO!" He hits me again, but this time, it lands on my butt, curling around to sting my hip and lower belly.

"THREE!" Drool drips out with the next number. As my skin glosses with sweat, the hit makes a burning cut.

My upper back and shoulders come next. "FOUR!" Instinct overrides my upbringing. Survival is more important. I push myself up and try to crawl away. My arms are shaking from the pounding pain. The nails from fingers scrap on my scalp as a hand grasps my hair and pulls me back.

"Girl, you need to learn not to be a whore. Stay still, or it will get worse!" He growled

Worse? Hot sweat ran from my forehead and underarms.

AGAIN! I couldn't count anymore. I was sobbing so hard that my throat was raw and horse. Snot streamed from my nose onto the bed. AGAIN! My hips and hamstrings arched in agony.

AGAIN! Why? Why? Why? I laid there every limb shaking and my mind reeling. AGAIN! Part of my back and my right arm took the brunt of the blow. Every hit was burning a path across my body ripping through to my core. I turned my head, rubbing my face into the salty tears that were running down my face burning my lips. Slime covered my upper cheek with the warm snot my nose had deposited on the blanket. But it was enough to see my mother standing off to the side. She was blank, empty, like a house with no one home. My eyes pleaded with her for help.

"Turn your face back to the bed, girl! Don't look up again until I tell you." AGAIN! And AGAIN!

Where did I go wrong? I ran through the actions from the previous day, racking my brain to figure it out.

Darkness descended.

CHAPTER 2

SYDNEY

BANG

"Syd, get up!" Tobias is such a pain.

I rolled out of bed. My feet hit the floor, and I jumped up, heading to the bathroom in one smooth motion.

"Don't wash your hair. It won't dry in time, and you will freeze your tail off, sis." T hollered through his door at me. T, that's what I call my brother Tobias. I clipped my hair up off my shoulders and hopped into the shower.

I would say the day dawned, but dawn was way off. The sun wouldn't rise for another two hours at least. It was all I could do to contain myself. I didn't know how to ski. I didn't own skis or ski clothes. I grabbed a pair of jeans, a turtleneck, sweater, jacket, hat, gloves, and my backpack and hoped I wouldn't freeze my butt off.

I had 20 bucks to my name. That was a fortune for a 13-year-old in '89. T's friends showed up 20 minutes later, and we all piled into Charley's minivan. It wasn't the coolest car in the world, but it carried a ton of people, and that is why Charley drove it. T sat up front and I was in the far back next to Charley's sister, Katlin. She's a year older than me. Dark brown gleaming hair, green eyes with a perfect body. The only person of interest for her was herself. I hated her.

"So, Sydney, do you know what high school you are going to?" Miss Perky always had everything perfectly planned.

"Yeah. Washington, like T and Charley." I didn't bother to turn my head and look at her. She didn't care what my answer was. It was just an excuse so she could talk about herself.

"But that's a tech school for boys. Girls don't go there!"

Yes, I know. I won't run into you there. Thank God!

"I want to study drafting, so that's the place to go."

"I bet you won't get in. You don't have the grades for that school. You should stick to your local school. I'm going to St Marie's for girls. They have the best academy. Then I'm going to the design school in New York, and then I'm going to work for a top designer and make millions!"

She never shuts up. AND THEN. God, couldn't she find a better way to start a sentence other than "And then"? If she was going to St. Marie for academics, why couldn't she find another way to begin a sentence?

"Sydney, you should lose weight. You will never look good skiing if your outfit makes you look fat. Like what you have on now."

Not everyone can look like they stuck their finger down their throat in the bathroom thin like you Katlin!

Every time she opened her mouth, I wanted to shove my fist into it. At one point she looked at me and said: "You know you could be pretty if your teeth were straighter, and your eyes were a prettier shade of blue, like your brother's." She tucked her silky hair behind an ear.

Not knowing what to say was a constant problem for me. But I knew that on the ride home I would not sit next to her. And then the big kicker poured out of the gash in her face.

"It's so nice of you to come along and watch everyone's things while we ski."

My mouth formed a big O as my eyebrows shot up. Stunned was the only word for it. Pressure formed in my chest and heat covered my face. T said he would work it out and that we will find a way. I managed to look her in the eye with a fake smile. I heard the words fall from my mouth, but I don't know how they got there.

"Sure. No problem. I don't know how to ski anyway, so it's no big deal." Stretching my cheek muscles tighter across my face, I wanted to show my teeth for effect.

From birth, it's been pounded into me to always be polite. If things aren't going your way, don't make a scene. Talk about it when you are alone but be polite. There's no way I'm going to let that harpy think she got one over on me. I couldn't give her the satisfaction.

T's girl-of-the-week, Alison, turned and thanked me as did everyone else. Charley was T's best friend, along with Jim and Mark. Jim's girlfriend was Kim. I looked at all their faces and I smiled, trying to keep my upbeat attitude going. I didn't mind watching everyone else's stuff because I liked them. Most of them I had known my entire life. But Katlin? I didn't want to do anything nice for her. She didn't deserve any nice gestures. I wanted to burn her things and not watch over them. So, why did I say that?

My chest burned along with my eyes. I turned to focus on the view out the window. I didn't want to fake small talk with the harpy anymore. The sun wasn't even up, and she already managed to ruin my day.

The further up the mountain we went, the higher the piles of snow pushed back from the road. At first, they were little humps of dirty white but grew to eight-foot-tall walls hedging us in and herding us up on the highway and to the ski lodge, just like rats in a maze.

Katlin started talking again, so I nodded and smiled. But deep inside, I was hoping she'd bite her tongue off, or swallow wrong and choke to death. Either way was fine for me. About fifteen of the longest minutes of my life later, the ice walls spread out like large arms welcoming us to the parking lot.

The parking area was enormous. You name it, cars, vans, trucks, they were all there. The ice and snow were so hard packed on the ground, I couldn't even make out the parking lines. Here and there, people headed in the same direction. I saw a man wearing rubber duck shoes and a giant Parka with its hood pulled up and cinched tight around his face. He held orange wands that he waved around in his mittens covered hands. His pants were black and padded and I bet that when he took it all off, he was three sizes smaller. We came to a stop next to another van.

T smiled at me as we piled out of the van. I grabbed my things and took up the rear of our group. Like a homing beacon, we followed the crowd heading to the Lodge.

The air was still and crisp, causing my breath to puff out in clouds. I put my gloves on, but after observing what everyone else was wearing, I wasn't sure if they were going to keep me warm. I had my doubts, but it was exciting.

People flowed toward the lodge with skis on their shoulders and big bags of equipment. I whipped my head in all directions to take it all in. I had no idea what I needed in order to ski down a mountain. There were bags of every size from huge to small. Some were being carried, others had wheels and dragged behind. Most skiers were young and fit, both men and women. Off to the side, I spied a few hip kids with snowboards slung over their shoulders. They were pushing and shoving each other as they went. Heads covered in hats of all kinds, bobbed up and down as each person made their way across the lot. It was icy crystal magic.

After walking through the maze of cars, I came face to face with a bunch of stairs. They led up to 4 sets of double doors and a sign that said, "Mount Hood Ski Lodge."

I was freezing, and it had only been five minutes. How do people do this all day? Inside, Tobias told me to pick a table close to the windows. Everyone else got in line to buy their lift tickets.

A giant window faced the mountain. In the cold pre-dawn, everything was covered by a misty gloom. The lights glistened off the snow but drowned in the shadows of the trees. I had never seen a ski lift before, but it looked like a death trap. Wide open seating with no safety bar to hold you in, feet loose swinging in the air. Yes, death on a cable. The sun chose that moment to crest the east face of the mountain, rising over the lodge and leaving a shadowy roof line in the snow. A light beam broke through the cloud, bathing one run in brilliant light. When it hit the snow, it sparkled, shooting little stars in every direction. It was man-made fun.

While I was day-dreaming, Tobias walked over and sat down at the table and coughed. I turned smiling at him, hoping Katlin was wrong, but his face said everything. He kept glancing down at the floor. He slapped his gloves into his right hand with his left, leaning forward to rest his hands on his knees. He was breathing heavy and lifting his head. So, I knew she was right even before he started talking.

"Sydney...I don't have enough money." It was tearing him up inside. T hated to be wrong and not keep his word. I didn't want him to kick himself over me. It wasn't that important. They were his friends, and I wanted him to have fun. I cut him off, "I don't want to ski. It looks scary. I hope you didn't already buy me a ticket, T."

He looked so relieved; he stood up and kissed me on the forehead, whispering: "I'll make it up to you!" He squeezed the breath out of me. "Don't worry, I will have fun no matter what." I didn't want T to feel bad. I knew he didn't have much money. He worked all the time, besides his school work. *It sucks being poor.*

Skiing is for middle-class people, and I was definitely not a middle-class girl. Most of my clothes came from the second-hand store. I rarely got anything brand new. When I did, it was a no-name brand. We bought the store brands for everything. It was cheaper. I wasn't old enough to get a job, and I didn't babysit. I wasn't old enough yet. There would be other ski trips.

T gave me another squeeze, went to Alison planted a kiss on her lips, then glanced back to wink at me.

"Let's go get our gear!" Katlin picked that moment to rub it in. "Since you are going to sit here all day, you don't mind watching my stuff, right? And, don't even get the idea of stealing the makeup from my purse." Her eyes were even more hateful than her words.

As if I would do any of that. I smiled and replied, "I don't want to get pink eye, so don't worry." I tried to sting just as bad as she did, and I think I managed to do so because the next moment, she pinched her lips and tossed her hair, storming away.

Looking back out the big window, it hit me. This is where I will be for the day. I wanted to ski, and T would have paid if he had the money. He would have sat out himself if I'd made a fuss. I couldn't do that to him. Selfishness wasn't my thing.

I loved my brother. Even though he was 3 years older than me, he never treated me like a little kid. He was always taking me along with his friends. Tobias made sure no one bothered me ever.

Tobias was 6'2" with big muscles. He lifted weights and played football. Tall, dark and handsome, that was my Tobias to a T. Girls fell all over themselves for him. But he wasn't all looks and no brain, he was a sweet talker too. 'T' could charm the panties off any girl he wanted, and he often did just that.

The girls I went to school with, drooled over him, always asking if they could come over on the weekend to hang out. I said no most of the time. I didn't need those kinds of friends. There was a girl who actually tried to walk in the bathroom while he was in the shower once.

Too much jabbering about T meant you couldn't be friends with me. He was the most popular guy in school. Everyone knew him and was friends with him. He had a friend in almost every school in three counties around.

Thinking of all this, I took the clip out of my hair, shook it, and pulled my brush out. I hadn't had time to brush it at home. My hair was my best feature. When I finished, I didn't put it back up. It was warmer with it down, so I left it that way.

I stood up. The ride had been almost 2 hours, and I needed to stretch. Treating the table as a ballet bar, I raised my leg and set it on the table. Then, I leaned over into the stretch, touching my head to my knee. My fingers grasped my insole, and as I was turning to the side, I raised my arm over my head, reaching for the same foot. The pull of the underside of my leg burned and energized me. I switched legs, then moved on to stretch my hamstrings.

How do you kill 6-8 hours with nothing but a book, a hairbrush, and a window? Two TVs hang from the corners with no sound. No one seemed stuck like I was. So, I chose the easiest possible activity. I started to stare out the window at all the fun.

CHAPTER 3

HERATHINA

Log Entry 1,784,652.32 ATD

I know people have always found me odd. Many say I'm the emotional one. My parents told me I felt things too strongly, and I should suppress that. Emotions have no place in the scientific fields.

Mother said that "to truly study something, you must remove yourself from the situation and your feelings. Your opinions have no place in your observations. You must be withdrawn and stand apart from all the data. You cannot use your gut."

However, none of these philosophies have ever worked for me. My gut has helped me through everything. I was not like everybody else. I do not have the precognition visions to show me what I should and shouldn't do. I do have control of the forces, but so do others. I have the hearing, and it's strong. I can hear anyone's thoughts I want within the 50 worlds.

But my real talent lies in the power of Dreams. I can send information and bend the mind with a dream walk. I could visit anyone I desired in a dream walk. I am a child born of a dream walk. We are rare and cherished.

Many whisper behind my back that I'm secretly an empath, and that's why I am so emotional. However, all known Empaths died in the cleansing at the Great Division.

Our people have titles for each phase of life: Young one, Old one, Ancient one. These are titles of respect. Though, when people call me Young one, they say it with a snicker. They don't mean it with respect. They are referring to me as if I were an underdeveloped species. They use it as an insult. I do not have this disdain for underdeveloped sentient beings as they do. Mostly when they attempt to insult me, I just ignore them. It's a sign of immaturity to offend someone by using double talk.

*****

Standing in the Citadel, I wasn't sure if they were going to choose me. If they did, I would be the youngest member of a team in two aeons. They might send me just to get me off the homeworlds. I've never been anywhere else other than the 50 homeworlds and this is my chance to finally make a real contribution to our society. To do something that matters to our science, to the understanding of our Origins. The big question is how did we become what we are? It's not like we hadn't been looking for the answers to these questions. We had, but after the Great Division finding information was difficult. So many minds were lost along with the knowledge they carried.

The Citadel filled with millions of people that wanted to hear the council's decision. It was an ocean of vibrant, beautiful minds, every face wrapped in anticipation. Many of them leaned forward, desperate for the correct answer.

I sat together with Athena, Artemis, and Apollo. We'd all gathered in the Citadel for the same reason, the council's decision. There were only three hundred missions per aeon. Some would last a few thousand years, others much longer.

"We have deliberated for this last century over who should go and participate in each project. All participants will receive an announcement on their bracelets in just a few moments but first, let me announce the projects." The High Council members were all were dressed in the traditional white robes. Simeon is our leader and speaker for the High Council, and he was the one person on the council I knew for sure would vote against me.

He listed about a hundred things that were utterly irrelevant to me. I couldn't care less about studying botany on a planet. Or going and visiting a gaseous Giant. The deep-space probes did hold some interest. However, being stuck for several thousand years inside of a spaceship following the edges of the known universe didn't. Always being around the same people, no, thank you!

I want to study the fascinating part of intelligence in sentient beings. I want to study their mind. Every person sitting in this room was a fascinating, individual, a powerful mind capable of incredible feats of intelligence and beauty. There is nothing more powerful than the brain, except maybe the heart. But, try convincing my people that.

The spokesman of the High Council began. "Several hundred years ago a planet was discovered with sentient life very close to our own. Its inhabitants are not only genetically but also mentally capable of reaching the level of evolution we have. It has been studied for the last 200 years via probes. The other members of the high council and I have decided that we will indeed go there. This will be one of our projects for this Millennium and many more to come. We are going there to find the answers to the original question. The project will be called Alethea. It shall be led by the revered Ancient One, Poseidon. All those who will go should be prepared to spend one, two or three hundred millennia on that world. Their job will require witnessing the development of the Homo sapiens."

I didn't hear another word he said. My bracelet had beeped, and my announcement had reached me. I was to be part of Alethea's team. At last, I had my chance to contribute to society and find answers. How did we get here from there?

CHAPTER 4

SYDNEY

The hair on the back of my neck stands up and a million tingling sensations run down my spine. *Turn around*

My eyes darted around. There are people everywhere, but nothing is out of place. As I turn to survey the room, a stabbing pain fills my head. My hands shoot to my temples and move in a circular motion until my eyes land on him - Adrian. He's with his father and he is staring right at me.

My cheeks curve up, lips curled into a smile, the heat of a flush moves over me.

Why am I blushing?

Brushing my awkwardness aside, I wave them over and watch as they weave their way through the crowd. Adrian's father, Tom, says "Hi!"

"Hello! Nice to see a friendly face." My breath remains caught in my throat.

"Are you here alone?" Tom gazed over my shoulder, looking for another person, an older person.

Tilting my head to the side, I could see how this looked.

"No, I'm not. My brother and his friends are out skiing. I'm watching their stuff," I said while waving my hands at both the window with the view of the mountain and the table with bags scattered around.

"Why aren't you skiing?"

Cause I'm broke, duh!

Why do people ask questions they already know the answer to? My head turns, eyes darting to the most exciting thing in the room - Adrian.

"Oh, um" I start to stammer but manage to continue "I don't know how and well...it's not a big deal. I've never been to a ski lodge before, so this is fun."

Tom doesn't look impressed by my answer. I'm sure he knows I don't have the money. It's not a secret that my family is poor.

Smiling, I turn the conversation to Adrian. "How long have you been skiing?" I wanted to appear nonchalant about everything, but I rushed the words a little too much.

"I started three years ago. It's cool. We try to come up here on weekends for both day and night skiing. I'm skiing Angels Fall for the first time today!" He leaned over, raising his hand to point out the window at the side of a cliff.

I felt like all the air from the room was caught in my throat. I didn't think I could ever do anything like that.

What did you do? Jump off and pray?

His black jumpsuit and green Columbia sportswear jacket hugged his lanky frame. His goggles sat high on his head, causing blond hair to stick up every direction leaving no hair to cover his pink ears. Blue eyes beamed back at me. The look was hotter than the devil himself could manage.

At 14, Adrian was almost as tall as his father. That means at least 7" taller than me. He looked more like a man than a kid. This is definitely something that could not be said about me.

Dragging my eyes away from Adrian was more of a chore than keeping your hand warm in the snow.

"Tom, are you guys going to be here all day?" My heart speeds up, and a tingling fills my belly.

"Yes," Tom answers and his penetrating gaze drills into me.

Cool. That means that I would get to talk to Adrian a few more times, or he would hang out with me when he got cold!

"Do you want me to watch some of your things?" My reasoning was simple - if I watch their stuff, then he'll have to hang out. My heart was pounding like crazy because I knew I was pushing it.

"No thanks, Sydney, we have a locker."

The excitement that had been growing in me deflated like a hot air balloon at the end of its trip.

"Oh, okay. Well, if you get tired and want to warm up and chat, I'll be here all day."

Tom smiled down at me, then looked at Adrian. They said their goodbyes and tromped away in their bulky ski boots.

At least he spoke to me. Maybe now we can be friends again.

Adrian and I had been friends since we were babies. Our mothers always put us together to play, even after my younger brothers were born. I spent more time at his house than my own.

My favorite thing to do was riding the rocking elephant. The trunk was made with graduating wooden disks. Each one was attached through the center with the rope and knotted underneath. As you rock back and forth, and the nose smacks against the frame, making a loud noise.

We had sleepovers. Our minds took us everywhere. We built forts and achieved Spaceflight. We traveled on safaris, crossed oceans and climbed trees. We took turns on a slide in the backyard and played in the sandbox. He had been my best friend.

Had been.

A couple of years ago, his family changed church congregations. I wasn't asked over to play anymore. Adrian seemed aloof. I called a few times to chat, but his mom answered and said he wasn't available. Soon after, we didn't see each other at all. Sometimes, I would notice him going into the church, as my family was leaving, but he never said 'Hi'. I didn't have any other close friends at church or school. It was an ache in my chest that took a long time to go away.

I turned and sat back down to look out the window, watching the skiers jump off that cliff and thinking that they are completely crazy. I guess it could be fun, but it wasn't going to be fun for me. I was stuck here. Time inched along. No matter how many times I checked my watch, it never seemed to move.

I spied Alison walking back to our table. Her nose and ears flushed pink.

"Hey, Syd! How is your day going?" There was snow on her back and in her hair.

I got the feeling she had taken a tumble.

"It's okay. I saw a friend of mine a while ago."

She glanced around the room, opened her coat and shook the snow out of her hair, yanking her scarf off her neck and fluffing everything.

"Al, can you watch the stuff? I want to use the restroom." I was dying to get away from the table for five minutes.

"What? Oh, yeah sure. Just don't be long." Her distracted mind barely noticed my departure.

I took my bag and headed toward what I thought was the bathroom. But when I looked up, I saw the sign across the room. I turned and ran face first into a chest. Adrian caught my arms as I bounced back.

"I'm so sorry! I did mean to run into you. I was looking for the restroom."

A deep chuckle issued from his broad chest.

"I was looking for you!"

My tummy filled with that tingly feeling again! "You were looking for me? Why? I thought you would be on the slopes by now." He shook his head.

"My dad wants to talk to you."

"Oh! Am I in trouble? Do you want me to watch your stuff?" I know I sounded too hopeful, and needy, but I was bored. "Na. Nothing like that"

"Well okay, but lady's room first."

"Sure. This way, my lady" said Adrian, trying to act like a knight or something.

The heat from my blush stained my face. No boy had ever called me a lady. His eyes sparkled as he extended his right arm, inviting me to go first.

The crowd of people in the lodge pressed me all around, but Adrian stayed behind me with his arms out to help push people to the side. It was like being in an Adrian bubble. The last time he and I had been together, I was taller than him. But now, he made me feel small and protected.

I entered the restroom and looked in the mirror. My face was bright, and my eyes were shining. My hair was in a tangle, but I worked it into a braid. I thought I looked a little prettier.

As I exited the bathroom, I could only see Adrian's broad back. His big shoulders blocked most of the door and from behind, he looked like a man. If I didn't know he was the one blocking the way, I'd have never recognized him from this position.

I reached up and tapped him on the shoulder. Turning to me, he smiled, and for a second, I thought I'd melt because my legs felt like jelly.

"Come on! My dad's over there," he lifted an arm and pointed to the left.

"Okay, but let me tell Tobias's girlfriend," we threaded our way back to Alison.

"Hey, Alison! My friend's dad wants to talk to me. I'll be right back. Are you ok with that?"

She looked at me and at then Adrian, releasing a big smile. "Does T know this guy?"

"Yes, he does. You can ask him yourself if you want. This is Adrian Shipman."

She winked at me. "Okay. Are you sure it's his dad you're going to talk to?"

I rolled my eyes.

"Yes," God, why did she have to say that?

We replayed the crowd parting back to Tom, who looked me directly in the eyes. As unnerving as his gaze was, it reminded me of Adrian's. The clear, penetrating blue that made you feel as if they could look right into your soul. I always felt that if I lied to Tom, he would know.

"Do you have the money to ski?"

My cheeks were flaming, "No, but it's okay. I'm fine. I really am" I thought that if I underlined the fact that I was cool about everything, I would not only convince him but also myself.

I took a step back. Tom's question threw me. I wasn't used to people asking me about money. I toyed with my fingers lacing and unlacing them.

"Do you want to ski?"

Oh, God! Please don't embarrass me.

"It's okay. I don't need to. I brought a book with me. Anyway, T needs someone to watch everyone's stuff."

He shook his head as he pulled out his wallet.

"Here is a hundred dollars. If you want to ski, take it." I started shaking my head as I raised my hands, taking a step back.

"I can't do that. I can't pay you back and I ... I... Thank you... Adrian! Thank you, Tom! You are both too kind. I can't pay you back, so I can't. But, thank you."

I backed up again, ready to walk away. I didn't like to admit that I was poor. It is always embarrassing to make someone understand without having to spell it out.

Duh, I'm broke!!! And by the way, so is the rest of my family.

My face was hot; I must be the shade of a tomato. Why would they embarrass me like this? I hate it. I can't take the money. What would my father say?

Adrian wrapped his large hand around my bare wrist, holding me in place.

"Sydney, stop! Look, my dad is giving it to you," he looked straight in my eyes and then continued, "You will not owe him anything."

The touch of his hand on my skin sent shock waves through my body. Fear filled me as blue flashes ran over the room. Everything froze. I locked my eyes with his crystal-clear blue orbs. My heart was beating with his, our chest rose and fell in unison. But when I blinked, it was all gone.

"But I can't take it. I don't know what to say, I..." the feeling of needing air was crushing me.

"Do you want to go skiing?" he released my arm and quickly the world snapped back like a rubber band in the original position. I shook my head to clear my mind and looked over at Tom.

"Yes, but I can't. I mean, I'm fine here. I'll ski next time." I schooled my face in the fake smile I had learned over the years. For the first time all day, I was hot. Not from the temperature, but from shame.

Tom spoke in a low controlled tone. "Sydney, T and his friends can watch their own things. They shouldn't drag you here and leave you to watch their stuff, while they run off to have fun." He took a deep breath, but there was no muscle moving on his face that could imply pity. He looked me straight in the eyes and added "Take the money! It's a gift."

At that moment he had taken charge, so I stopped fighting it.

I'll find a way to pay him back.

"Adrian, go with her and buy her a ticket. After that, take her down for her gear. Make sure they give her good stuff." A smile broke over Tom's face. He looked relaxed for the first time since I laid eyes on him today.

"Go and have fun! Also, put your things in a locker." He stiffened as I latched on to him, hugging him, with all my might and excitement.

"Thank you, Tom! I'll pay you back." I struggled not to cry from joy and with a whispery voice I let go of him, "I promise!"

CHAPTER 5

SYDNEY

Adrian grabbed my hand. As he pulled me along, there weren't any blue lights or crazy feelings this time. I was floating and laughing; it was old times again, but different.

We talked about school.

"I fell on every run my first day. I had bruises from head to toe." He chuckled.

My belly ached from all the laughter.

At the main counter, Adrian asked for all the equipment I would need. Every item was fascinating. Long skis, poles, boots with all those crazy bindings that clamped you into them. Adrian argued with the rental guy about the ski lengths. I didn't even understand why the length mattered. After we got all my things and were outside, I figured he was going to find his dad, and I'd be on my own.

So what? I'm going to have a great time.

"Adrian, thank you again! I don't know what to say. I would still be sitting in the lodge trying to read my book." As I said that, I felt the invigorating crisp air biting my nose.

He just stood there smiling. I felt that it took him ages to talk, but my rational part was aware that only a few seconds passed. "Well, did you know that your ticket comes with a free lesson?"

"Good! I'm going to need it, so where is the trainer? I don't know what to do, and I don't want to break anything." I looked around the trampled snow to see if there was a sign pointing to lessons.

He continued to smile at me and said, "It's right here. I'm your teacher."

I cocked an eyebrow in disbelief.

"What?" and with this, his smile turned into a smug one. "Yea, I'll teach you. It' not hard, and you're a fast learner." He waved his hand in the direction of a lift.

"Okay, but you can't laugh if I fall" I clutched at my ski poles with my eyes darting to my ski tips. The last thing I wanted, was to fall before I even made it to the lift. Worse yet, cause someone else to stumble.

"You won't fall." For some reason, he held his head high confident in his assessment of me and my abilities.

I didn't manage to say anything because he continued. "Lesson number one: Keep the tips of your skis apart at all cost, or you will fall!" He looked at me to see if I was following him. Well, how could I not? I nodded to let him know I am all ears. "Lesson number 2: If you keep your skis parallel, you'll go faster."

He droned on, I listened, but after a point, I lost interest in the mechanics of skiing. We joined the lift line, and my heart sped up. Our turn came, the chair arrived and scooped us up like a hot spoon in an ice cream bucket.

I couldn't help but look around. Every time my eyes wandered back to Adrian, I was shocked to see that he was staring at me. High up in the air, the bench swung backward, then forwards. It was terrifying. My body lurched forward, sliding into the protective bar and then pushed back. My heart pounded with exhilaration.

"Lift the tips of your skis before we get off, or you'll hit the drift at the top and flip over. Then, you need to snow-plow for your life and don't hit anyone." He tapped the side of his boots together, knocking snow off both skis and boots.

I did everything exactly as he instructed and slid to a stop at the top of the run.

"You look like a pro, Syd!"

Huffing, I turned my head to glance up at him. "Thank you! I'm actually more glad that I didn't kill anyone." After saying this, my vision met the edge of the bunny slope and I turned to face it.

"Go ahead! I'll be right behind you. Okay?" He waved me on while pulling his goggles down over his eyes.

Clamping my lips shut, I took a deep breath and plunged over the edge.

The wind rushed in my face, blasting the hair back from my face. Without an actual explanation, my feet knew what to do, turning side to side while remaining parallel. I reached the end of the run and slowed down by turning to the side and came to a stop.

I heard a slicing sound that filled the air. Adrian pulled up behind me.

"You are a natural Syd. Bet you can do it all day."

I didn't know what caused my heart to speed up. It could have been the adrenaline or Adrian, but pressure filled my chest.

"Thank you! It was great. Can we go again?" holding my breath, I should have held back but then again, who wants to live life holding back?

"Yes, you can. I have to get back to my dad." And with that, the heat in my chest ceased as if the cold around had reached down into my marrow.

"Oh, okay. Yeah, you don't want to stay on the baby slopes. You've got that Angle to fall off the side of." We both laughed. "Thank you, Adrian and your dad too. I... I will pay you back." My eyes searched for anywhere to land other than his face. I didn't want him to see my disappointment.

"Don't worry about it. Have fun!" He patted me on the shoulder and winked like I had seen my brother do to his friends a thousand times.

He gripped his polls and pushed off for a lift on the far side. I wished he would stay, but I didn't think he wanted to. He was kind to me. Just like a friend would be. But, I didn't want him to be a friend or look at me that way. Not anymore. Katlin was right; I'm not pretty. Not like her. I was the girl that you were friends with or didn't notice at all. He hadn't noticed me in years, so why this bothered me now, I don't know.

Shaking it off, I skied for the rest of the day. I was actually late returning to the lodge, where I found T. Pissed was a very soft way to describe his reaction.

"Sydney, where have you been? You disappeared. I looked everywhere for you." His eyes were wild, and he had both hands on my shoulders, shaking me a little.

"But, I told Alison. I told her that I was with Adrian and asked her to tell you." I moved to shrug him off, but he didn't let go.

"She didn't say anything. Where did you get the money to rent skis?" he became even more nervous.

With a shaky voice, I said "Adrian"

"Adrian Shipman. So, all this time you were with a boy." His words were cold and cutting.

"No. I mean yes, but hold on rewind. Tom, his dad, gave me the money, Adrian just taught me how to ski and then he went skiing with his dad, and I went on my own."

God, what's the big deal, honestly?

His voice grew, "So, you were alone out there?" and with it, tears threaten to fall from my eyes on my burning face.

The tension between us was cut by a deep voice that made its way to us through the surrounding noise.

"Tobias, Sydney was left alone, here, in the lodge to watch everyone's things. Does that sound like fun to you?" T turned to stare Tom down.

Under Tom's hard glare T's shoulders slumped. He knew he'd lost.

"No, it doesn't."

"Thank you for taking care of my sister; she deserved a good time too." T's eyes searched the floor as he ground the words out.

For a moment, I forgot about T's anger because Adrian waved, as he and his father left for the long drive home. But that moment soon passed due to Katlin's appearance.

"Who was the Greek God you were talking to?"

In my mind, my fingers curled around her neck as I squeezed the last breath from her harpy-like face. As I do this, her eyes are bulging from her skull just before she gives up the farm.

But we live in the real world and not in my dream, so I simply said, "A friend of mine." I didn't forget to grit out a smile.

"I'm sure he's 'just' your friend. Introduce me to my new boyfriend."

Duh, didn't she see them walking away? How thick can you be?

"Katlin, he isn't your type." Charley loves to tease his sister and save me, thank God.

"What would my type be, Charley? And more importantly, what type is he?" She rubbed her hands together like an evil cartoon character.

"A gentleman." Charley nudged T and high-fived the others, all the while laughing.

"What?!!"She sputtered for a few minutes searching for a comeback but came up dry in that shallow mud puddle of a mind.

"He would want to be your friend first," Charley was still laughing.

God, I love Charley!

T jumped in "Yea, Adrian's a good guy, not a snake."

Charley laughed, "Kat, he's your age. Too young for you, Hun."

She had said that she liked older guys. Katlin hmphed and did that quick turn every bitchy girl on the planet learns at bitch school then headed to the car.

The ride home was better because we slept, and I didn't have to hear Katlin's annoying voice. Every muscle ached from overuse. It was about 11 PM when Charley dropped us off and went home. My head was ringing from the altitude change so I collapsed on the bed.

*****

My parents are very religious. At 10 AM sharp, each Sunday, we attend church. There were no exceptions unless I was ill. Sometimes I was invited to visit other families after church, but mostly I would go home. Today, we went straight home. Tobias talked to dad for 30 minutes and then took off.

"Sydney, come to the living room!" My father always carried that devoid of emotional tone.

"Yeah, dad. What's up?" His face spoke of trouble, and I was going to get it.

I didn't think anything was wrong. Why would I. After all, the day was much like any other Sunday?

"Did you spend time with a boy yesterday?" Something about him whispered wild and it frightened me. I heard a low humming in the background and the closer I got to him, the louder it grew.

"Yes, I... talked to Adrian Shipman and his father." My voice faltered,

"Was his father with you the whole time you were 'talking'?"

The hum turned up to a light buzz.

"No, he wasn't. His dad gave me money to ski, and then Adrian took me to get the skis and the lift ticket and taught me how to ski. Then, he went back to his dad." My head vibrated with the hum.

"So, you were alone with that boy." His voice was hard and clipped. The buzzing became a light ringing.

"No, there were people everywhere."

What is his deal? You can't be alone in a crowd, can you?

"But you didn't know any of those people, did you?" his jaw snapped shut at the end of his words creating a cracking sound.

The ringing in my ears turned into an angry mumbling.

"No, I didn't. I knew only Adrian and his father, Tom. Did I do something wrong?"

"Yes, you did, Sydney. You can't talk to boys. Not to mention being alone with them. That is what a whore would do. I won't have you become a whore too." He breathed the final word out low and seething.

CHAPTER 6

HERATHINA

Log Entry 1,784,652.32 ATD

Athena and I, along with the twins Apollo and Artemis, had all been chosen for the Alethea project. Apollo and Artemis were annoying because they kept finishing each other's sentences. They always played their mental connection to the fullest, but I found it to be an irritating childlike habit. Only the young in our society behaved this way.

*****

All children born are twins. Always one boy and one girl. Children are rare in our world and are treated as great prizes, not coddled, but cherished. The parents of every child are always viewed with awe. Especially children that come from dream walk. They are usually extremely powerful.

Our kind has intimate interludes throughout our existence, but children were only produced through a mating. Our species evolved to automatically search for the perfect genetically compatible persons and only reproduce with them. Over time, matings evolved. Now, genetic compatibility is not enough. The mate has to also be intellectually compatible. It has to be a perfect meeting of minds and bodies. Though many partners would live for thousands of years separately, they are never truly far apart; the meeting of the minds is a constant connection. Unless one consciously blocks their partner out, they share all things, living each other's lives in unison. Meeting again and again in a dream. We call it the dream walk.

My brother, Hyperion, and I were born of a dream walk. We are special, but I fear my parents are disappointed in me. My brother, they adore. He mated, in our three thousandth year, and soon became a father. Hyperion studied the movement of the universe, so he found his place in our society. He explained the mathematics to me, but I quickly lost interest. Because I loved my brother, I wanted to please him and be a good student, but the formation of stars, planets, and exo-planets bored me.

My parents called me over emotional, headstrong, stubborn, and irrational. I felt what others felt, however small. What I did feel was the pull of independence. I was more than happy to go my own way. Most twins spend all their time together in childhood, but I was pleased with or without Hyperion. The mental touch was all I needed. While Hyperion studied the stars, I studied the people.

In a lot of ways, I really didn't care what my parents thought about me. The likelihood that I would see them in the next thousand years was minimal. Now I was on the Alethea project. This meant that I might not see them for a million years or more. The only contact I would have with them would be through the dream world. Hopefully, by the next time I saw them, I would have achieved something so they could genuinely be proud of me. Something big, an accomplishment of epic proportions.

Log Entry 1,784,652.33 ATD

I brought my crates that were holding my belongings to the landing field. The suspender racks moved them for me.

Yes, I jumped the gun. I was so sure that they were going to choose me. I had packed everything worth taking even before I had an answer. I'd left it on the side of the landing field in anticipation.

I stepped out of the Citadel, allowing the bright Red Sun of our home world to wash over me. This was my first step into the future.

The warmth from the sun ceased as Poseidon blocked the light and my way, pulling me out of my dreamy musings.

"Greetings Ancient One! I'm most honored to be a member of your crew," I said in a tone mixed with gratitude and happiness.

His smile, wide with his broad full lips and his large gleaming teeth, met my greeting. His aqua blue eyes twinkled, as he reached out to place my hands in his own.

"So, you have finally been given your chance. I knew they would choose you. You have a most inquisitive mind. The insight you possess after studying one's psyche is most intriguing. It will be good to have you with us, Young One."

"Thank you, Ancient One! I only hope that my contribution will be worthy of the trust placed upon me. I now feel my life can truly begin," I responded while scrunching my shoulders then releasing them with a long breath of relief.

Poseidon released a booming laugh, turning many heads in our direction.

"There is no need for such formality. On this project, we will all be equals. I am merely a leader. By the time we are finished, you will be an Ancient One yourself, so please, call me, Poseidon. We have no need for trivial titles among our people." He offered me a warm practiced smile. I had seen him use it many times to put his subordinates at ease. I was surprised to realize it was effective, even on me.

"Thank you, Poseidon! I hope that I will be worthy of the trust you and the high council bestow upon me."

Poseidon is my father's best friend. I had spent most of my life thinking of him as an uncle, and I believe he also has a soft spot for me. Not that I am full of myself and I imagine something that I want to be true, but many times, he sought out my company in a crowd.

"Will you come to the celebrations? In three days, we leave, and we will not be coming back for some time. Do you not have friends you wish to say goodbye to?" Poseidon's polite demeanor made it difficult to ascertain if his inquiry was merely good manners or genuine concern.

"I came hopeful and prepared. I will store my goods on Alethea, and then I'll join the celebrations. I have been fortunate in the council's choices; many of my friends will accompany us on this project. There is no one special that I leave behind." I stopped for a second and looked at his face. I was probably cocky, but I had to ask "Poseidon, do you leave anyone?"

His forehead wrinkles and his countenance darkens.

"As you well know, I am not mated, and I lost my taste for lust a long time ago. I do not look behind but only to the future and that means, our study of the Homo sapiens. I attended many celebrations. You are welcome to accompany me if you wish," he smiled and continued in the same tone, "However, I've already moved my things to Alethea. Would you like me to get someone to show you to your quarters?"

"Thank you, Poseidon! You honor me with your invitation, but I think I will go solo tonight." I replied.

He smiled patting my shoulder, then turned, taking giant strides in the direction of the celebrations.

*****

Alethea is a grand ship. They had not launched her into the spatial void. The sound of anti-gravity suspenders around the edges of the circles are humming. She is kept in a perfect balance. Themia strives for balance in all things, and Alethea is balanced upon the tip of a rhombus. The main body of the ship is centered around the four corners of the rhombus, with three concentric rings, radiating out from the center. From the side, she looks like a four-sided pyramid facing up and down with blindingly white rainbows shooting in every direction.

Long ago, my people developed a composite of crystalline materials, and now all technology is embedded in the crystalline structure. However, she only looks white from afar. Upon closer inspection, you can see the various flecks of different micro crystals they used to create the internal circuitry. Because technology amongst our people grows exponentially, the moment this ship came off the line, she was already obsolete. But Alethea was designed to last.

Her internal functions work like an ecosystem. Having studied millions of worlds, over more years than my people can remember, we discovered the secrets of creating worlds. Even though we cannot create a planet, we have the knowledge and technological means to create a microcosm of a world inside a space-faring vessel. Or turn a plant into a habitable world.

Being inside Alethea was breathtaking, but I managed to find my quarters easily. Our people were not averse to straight lines. However, when building a spaceship that is circular, most things tend to be circular rather than linear. As long as you understood what ring you were on, you just had to keep going in that circle until you reached your desired destination. Rings were all colorized and the passageways were numerical classified. Luck was on my side. My quarters were on the outer ring and that provided a broad viewport. My belongings were shifted to my room, leaving me only with the task of unpacking them.

CHAPTER 7

SYDNEY

Blue, Azure, Sapphire are the kinds of blue that only exist in the warm waters of the tropics. The perfect kind of blue is far away on the horizon, where the sky meets the warm aquamarine of the ocean. Dividing the two is an island. Though I can't see the entire island, I instinctively know it is perfectly round. Right in its center is a mountain with a dome-like apex.

Wind whips the hair into my face. As I move in closer to the mountain, the humidity of a tropical rain forest replaced the salty dryness of the ocean. The entire mountain is covered in variegated shades of green. Large-leaved climbing plants trail down the slopes and cling to the trees. The thick scent of the flowers surrounds me, drugging my senses.

The mountain is cut down in the center by a shining White Palace. A massive plain pediment is held up by some Doric Greek columns. The building grows out of the mountain but is held together by stars, glistening in the sun. It's almost painful to watch it. My hand shields my eyes from the blinding glare.

My gaze follows the underside of my hand down to find a cloud. Mist lingers at the base of the building, and a torrent of water pours from it, giving the illusion it is floating on a cloud. The drop is longer than any waterfall I had ever seen. I was too far away to see the pool at the bottom, but it was there. I could feel it. The mist-shrouded it just as the roar covered the twittering of birds.

As if pulled by a string, I float up and away. Rings appeared to surround the mountain and the land ridged with water rivulets or channels. Everything had symmetry to it, a balance.

The roar of the waves rock me with its rhythm. I could almost taste the tangy salt on my lips. The wind caresses my face and throws my hair around my head and I could make out a murmuring. It came in rhythm with the waves. I know from the voice's cadence that the murmur comes from a woman. She is whispering something to me, but it's intangible.

Say it one more time. My ears strain to hear her.

A burning sensation radiates over my body. The wind picks up and whips past my face. Only later I realize what's happening. I'm falling. Terror grips me. A scream rips out of me, but it disappears along with the wind. I am clawing at the air with my hands, kicking and squirming with my legs.

I'm going to die.

Excruciating pain radiates from my back. I slam my body on something hard and that blasts me out of unconsciousness.

I don't remember when it stopped. I laid there on my belly for a while, whimpering. I couldn't move. My back muscles, along with every other part of me, are stiff. I think that this is how you feel when you are run over by a car.

My eyes are encrusted with salty tears that crack open to a blurry and strange world. There, but not there, intangible. I blinked several times in an attempt to clear it away. Muscles in my arms complain when I move them to rub my eyes.

I am squinting at the surroundings. It's too bright in this room. Earlier it was closer to bedtime and dark outside, but now it's almost painfully brilliant.

*****

I noticed that the bed has blood on it. What is happening? My arms won't move right, and as I run my tongue around my mouth, I encounter a sore. It tastes of tangy copper.

But what I found to be riveting, was the blanket. I could see all its threads and the blood droplets that were caught in the weave. Momentary fascination distracted me from the aching. I needed to get up, so I started shaking my head to clear my sight.

My eyes are burning, my head is pounding, and from my knees to my neck, everything is on fire. Planting my hands on the bed, I push with shaking arms that scream in protest while the muscles in my back are working overtime to do their job. My stomach is flexing while I am pulling one leg under me to gain a foothold. I feel my knee popping as I push up.

Who knew standing would be so difficult?

My left leg couldn't hold out without my right. The right leg had taken the worst of it. Every lash still burned. A film of sweat grew on my forehead and upper lip. The dip between my breasts itches with the grim of built-up sweat and salt.

I crashed back down on my ass with silent tears running down my face.

Someone had to have heard the slam of my body on the hardwood floor. And there it was - a sound of movement and heavy breathing coming from the hall.

How can I hear that?

I could clearly detect the shifting of feet on the floor creaking in the sub-floor before the knock happened.

My throat was raspy and raw. I swallowed, moving my tongue around to create spit.

"Yes," I croaked out, cringing at the sound. It was too loud.

"Syd?"

T. He must have come home. How long had he been here? Did he hear? The knot in my throat balls up as my eyes pricked.

"Can I come in?" His voice boomed through the door.

I covered my ears with my hands, but still, the sound of his voice rang in my head.

"Yes," I choked it out, softer this time. Even though I wasn't facing the door, I heard an intake of breath as he entered.

"Oh, my God!"

My back slashed with blood and parts of the dress were torn and hanging. Flesh peaked through ripped holes. The white and red polka dots was covered with blood drops making it look even more dotted. An overwhelming sense of horror filled me as I looked at myself. The sight made me choke.

I don't know how, but I was seeing through him. I was feeling his revulsion like I was him. His first instinct was to run. However, he curbed it, taking control of himself. I could feel the warring in T. He stopped the gagging reflex only seconds before puking.

I don't know what just happened, but whatever it was it came and went quickly. I had been in his mind.

"Can you help me get up? I don't think I can stand."

His large hand reached down and wrapped around my wrist as my hand mirrored his. He pulled me up.

"I think your dress is ruined, Syd." His voice came out raw and strained.

"Can I help you take it off?" He was trying not to look frightened, but I could feel him shaking.

I shook my head in assent. He unzipped the leftover tatters, then eased it off my shoulders. It drifted down into a bright screaming puddle of white and red polka dot splotches.

I never wanted to see that dress again. I wanted to die.

"Look, you need to lay down on the bed, and I'll get something to put on your back and legs. I'll get the first-aid kit and an ice pack, and… we'll see what we can do." He faltered.

"T, why?" there had to be some reason for what had happened. Fresh tears formed a trail down my face and neck.

"I don't know, Syd. Just let me help you." Tears fell from his face too.

I swallowed it back over a big lump.

"Where is Mom? Why isn't she here?" She hadn't done anything. She just let him hurt me.

"I don't know Syd… She, she's in her room." His voice was timid and disjointed.

"Where's Dad?" I asked, but T kept his head down. He didn't want me to see his eyes. He busied his hands with picking up what was left of that dress, then placed it in the wastebasket with his back to me.

"He went to bed."

He went to sleep after that?

Who sleeps after beating someone senseless? And what about her? She was in here with him, watching everything he did to me.

I was never going to take my eyes off of him ever again.

My hot tears increased, and a crushing vice screwed down on my chest, making it impossible to catch my breath. They left me here. She didn't even think to help me.

I needed to use the bathroom, but I was afraid of what I would find. My walking was labored and slow. Every muscle in my body screamed as I had, and every heartbeat in my body was a throb of pain. The sores on my back pulsed in the same rhythm as my heart.

The vanity mirror by my bedroom door showed only the blood on my arms and a swollen face with a rainbow of colors beginning to form.

I couldn't reconcile the girl in the mirror with the one I saw this morning. Even my eyes looked different. I'd always had the O'Dear blue eye but dark. Now, there was a crystal blue surrounded by a dark ring.

How is that possible? People don't change eye color in a few hours.

I was different, I could feel it. It was all too bright and too loud, not to mention all that blood.

I squeezed my eyes close. I didn't want to see the carnage he'd reeked on me. Lack of sight heightened my senses. It made me hear the breathing of every person in the house. Somewhere, someone cried softly. T shifted on his feet. I could also hear a soft, sleeping breathing that blended with the murmur of the TV.

I flashed my eyes open. I didn't want one more second of that. It felt like I was living a thousand lives in one incredible moment.

"Where are you going?" T's voice cracked. It sounded like it had 3 years ago before it deepened.

"Bathroom. I have to pee." I squeezed the handle with a shaking hand.

"Let me help you!" He moved swiftly to my better side and held my arm, then walked me to the bathroom door. Without T to steady me, I would have fallen. I took care of my needs then grabbed a washcloth to begin the process of wiping myself.

My arms refused to bend in the necessary ways. My hands were tender from my clasping and digging of nails. In those horrible moments, every muscle in my body strained preparing themselves for the next blow.

"T, can you help me?"

The door flew open. His eyes were wide, darting all around. He came up short when our eyes met in the mirror then widened with surprise. "Syd, your eyes are different. They look like mine." A heavy breath escaped, blowing into my hair.

"Yeah. Can you help me clean up?" I didn't want to bring more attention to myself than needed. "Please!"

He didn't say anything else. He just scrunched his brows together.

Watery blood rivulets ran down my back, dripping on the floor. The blood was thick and crusty, and it itched as it cracked before flaking off. T trailed the cloth across my back over and over and even though he didn't apply any pressure, it stung.

T's gagging and the sensation of too much saliva filling his mouth was back. I felt that I wanted to hurl myself.

Shaking my head back and forth, I attempted to clear the sights and all the feelings out. What was happening? I didn't need to be in anyone's head but mine right now.

The water in the sink became a darker and darker shade of red. "It's not as bad as I thought it would be." T attempted to sound light and dismissive "There are a few cuts that bled a lot. They got smeared around that's all. How does it feel?" But his words were lost on me.

I looked into the mirror and T stared back at me. The blankness of his question brought back to me how clueless he was sometimes.

"Like my father beat the shit out of me. That's how I feel, T. How do you think I feel?" My eyes pricked with fresh tears, throat knotted tight. "I feel like crap! Why, why did he…" I began to dissolve, I wanted to scream, but fear gripped me. I knew that if I raised my tone, 'he' would hear me and come back.

T managed to break his eyes away from mine. He opened his mouth to speak but seemed to think better of it. Therefore, he snapped his jaw shut and kept wiping.

When he finished cleaning me, we went back to my room. T rubbed ointment on my cuts and placed bandages over them. I pulled out a clean t-shirt. Not that it mattered anymore, but I turned away to put it on. I started pulling it over my head, and with every move, all my muscles screamed at me to stop. He covered me with ice packs and gave me a pill of some kind. The act of swallowing felt like I'd shoved a rock down my gullet, but soon after, I embraced sleep like the death I had wished for only hours before.

CHAPTER 8

SYDNEY

I didn't go to school for three days after, and no one talked to me. The lack of communication was a blessing in many ways. Noise overwhelmed me with my amplified hearing. People walking up the street outside hurt. A constant humming in the background filled the empty void in my mind. My telescopic sight allowed me to see individual threads in any piece of fabric. My eyes hyper-focusing on mundane items disoriented me. Because of this, I fell or walked into furniture.

Images and feelings coming from other people scared me the most. It was one thing to hear or see, but to feel precisely what someone else was feeling was terrifying.

The day of my return to the real world marked a change in my fashion sensibilities. I started wearing anything to cover my bruises - turtlenecks, sweaters, high-necked shirts, jeans, long-sleeved shirts. If it covered, it was in style. I learned to sew so I could alter if needed. I learned the art of layering, buying two to three sizes too big to make sure to conceal as much as possible. Dowdy and matronly. These were the only words to describe my fashion showings.

My world had transformed overnight. All the household chores were now solely my responsibility. I wasn't the only one who'd changed, my parents had too. I didn't notice it at first because I was locked in my own world of pain and disbelief, but there were a lot of little things.

I didn't realize they had stopped talking to me, but it dawned on me. Every time I walked into a room, the conversation died. If I inquired if everything was alright, my father instructed me to return to my room.

He didn't say 'please', nor 'can you excuse us', no 'thank you', nothing. The only thing that I heard was just 'leave'. As soon as I was gone, they continued where they left off, but retreating didn't change the fact I could hear everything they said. What would they say if they knew?

However, it wasn't only my family that had changed. I was different in little ways. Every time my father looked at me, the connection was strong. I saw myself how he saw me, with pure unadulterated hatred, but there was an undertone of fear. There was more there, but I couldn't make it past his hate to the core of the problems pouring out of his mind. He has an unshakable belief in the rightness of his actions.

A couple of weeks went and by, and the incident started to fade into the past. I hoped that whatever had caused it would blow over and life could return to some kind of normalcy. As much as there was ever going to be for me. The changes hadn't lessened. Deep down inside, I knew I would never be normal again.

When I asked my mother questions, she shrugged and turned away. She didn't answer me. Instead, she walked away. My brothers didn't talk to me either.

Father informed me I had a bedtime. I had to be in my room at 8 o'clock every night. One night I needed to use the bathroom. All my family was in the living room laughing, playing cards together. It sounded like fun and I wanted to be part of the family fun.

"Can I please join the game, father?" I was hopeful until his malevolent gaze met my eyes.

"No, go back to your room, and don't come out again!"

Turning to return to my room, the relief rolled off of his mind. Why didn't they want to be with me anymore? What had I done?

The next day, I confronted my mother about it.

"Mom, I know father is mad at me. What can I do to make him forgive me? I don't know what I did, but I will do anything he wants. I want things to go back to the way they were before."

She was cold as ice. She didn't even look at me. She just responded, "A woman should know her place. Be quiet and subservient."

That was the dumbest thing I had ever heard. The only place I had ever heard stuff like that was in the bible, or medieval books. It sounded more like the Scarlet letter type drivel, than a way to earn their trust again.

Was I so unpalatable, they couldn't stand to be with me? I cried sometimes because loneliness left me hollow and desperate. What had I done, for them to hate me so much?

A month had passed until the moment when my father next came to my room on a Sunday evening.

"It's time," he said just like he would announce dinner.

What does he mean?

He reached out and filled one of his large hands with the hair on the back of my head and forced me face first into the bed.

"What did I do?" I cried.

He shook my head before letting go and answered, "You're a woman now. Your mother told me your time had finally come. I can't allow you to become a whore. I didn't stop it last time, but I won't fail this time. I only do this because I care. It's the only way to keep you from being a whore too."

What does he mean 'didn't stop it last time'? What last time? This happened before? To whom?

He didn't use the belt this time. He just hit me open handed.

"I don't want to disfigure you."
Isn't that a laugh?

He didn't want to scar me on the outside. No one worried about the scars on the inside. I was supposed to lay there and take whatever they gave me.

AGAIN, AGAIN, AGAIN.

I had hoped that the beating was a one-off, but it was not. It became a pattern. Every other Sunday, my father would come to my room to keep me from being a whore. Unless I made a mistake and that list kept getting longer. I constantly walked on tiptoes hoping I didn't fuck up. If I didn't meet his standards, he would teach me a lesson with the belt. He never told me what not to do. It was trial and error. Every error came with a new set of bruises.

Curiously the dream came after every beating. It repeated what I had seen before. I tried to recall every detail, but it went by in a blue flash, like a movie on repeat with the fast forward on. Another strange change was that the humming in my mind turned into an intermittent mumble.

Rumors went around the church. I was a whore, and my daddy had to beat me for it. I heard them from across the hall. Everyone talking, whispering. It didn't matter how low a voice they used. I overheard every word. Every time, I had to sit in church and listen to the nasty, mean things these Christian people said. Who could believe in God?

The kids stopped talking to me. I didn't receive any more invitations to visit for lunch or invites to parties or picnics. They snickered as they went by me with noses in the air.

It felt like I didn't exist for any other reason than to torture. My brothers were allowed to have a normal life. To have friends and have fun. I didn't.

At weddings, my father would tell me to play the piano for everyone. The piano was always off to one side, so no one noticed or spoke to me. When I finished, people didn't even clap. Somehow, I had disappeared before their eyes. I was invisible. The kids even walked into me, pretending that they didn't see me. Snickering, they never said sorry.

I didn't understand how or why everyone thought I was a whore. Only my family knew what happened in our house. I didn't believe that they would tell anyone about what happened. How did everyone know? As I was thinking about all these a voice spoke loud and clear.

< Your mother told them. >

< *What?* > I was whipping my head around to determine the source of the voice. But no one was near enough to have spoken to me.

< She told everyone! >

< *But why would she tell anyone?* > My eyes were still searching for the source of the voice.

< Attention. She likes it. >

< *She likes it?* >

That is just sick. Is everyone I live with fucked in the head?

The person who spoke to me had to be nearby, but there was no one!

No answer… great, I am talking to myself.

The voice was new. I heard it in my mind. When it had started out as a mumbling in the background, it didn't bother me.

< I don't want to mow the lawn. >

< *What?* >

It said things that I didn't understand like it wasn't talking to me.

Talking back wasn't an option. All I needed was for my father to find out I heard voices. He would cart me off in the patty wagon. I was already in prison. I didn't need a straitjacket or a padded room to go with it, not like my crazy aunt.

I tried to ignore it, pretending it didn't exist. Just like me. I wanted to vanish. If he didn't notice me, then he wouldn't want to beat me. It was a he, the voice. It was a tenor, like Pavarotti.

I was assigned scriptures to study. The one person I didn't want to have contact with, my father, was the only person who did talk to me. All interactions were curt and laced with a heavy dose of hate. He became an unfeeling and cold bastard. He'd never been warm and fuzzy, to begin with, but the man I interacted with had taken it to a whole new level.

When I was near him, any sudden movement caused me to flinch, raising my arms to cover my face and head. I didn't want to cower, but fear filled me being in the same room with him. My heart rate spiked along with trembling and stomach clenching. I didn't want to sit down or turn my back on him. I felt safer if I kept close to the door of a room with my back to the wall.

I watched his every move as close as my eyes were able to. I became able to detect when his heart rate went up, along with breathing. They were a sign of irritation, and it was time to leave the room.

His reading assignments were related to the facts that 'God wanted good obedient children and wives' and that 'Rachael gave her maid to Abraham to have'. I wanted to know how giving your maidservant to your husband to fuck wasn't turning her into a whore? How was that okay? But, I was too afraid to ask.

Religion became this big question mark for me. If God loves us and protects us and wants to help us and answers prayers, why doesn't he answer mine? Why, when I prayed, did no one come to save me? Why doesn't he tell my father not to beat me?

How was it okay for Mary Magdalene to be a whore? Jesus forgave her and welcomed her with open arms. But my father could barely stand to look at me. I was sure that she had sex with a bunch of men whereas I was a virgin.

I spent most of my time reading and playing the piano. If I was doing that, then I couldn't be a whore. Right?

I prayed a lot to God to help me, but I didn't feel like God was watching or cared. What if God is a voice that only a few people hear in their minds as I do? What if he isn't real? What if all those people in the bible were crazy?

All these questions ran on without answers or end. The best I could hope for was to move out when I turned eighteen. But, there were a few more years til' that moment. Other than that, I didn't see any end in sight.

On the outside, I appeared quiet and subservient. On the inside, I was screaming and hysterical. What was wrong with me? What could I change so that they would love me? I thought they did before. They used to kiss and hug me. I remember being told that I was loved. How did talking to one boy change all that? Why didn't they love me anymore? The same conversations ran through my mind over and over.

Safe to say my father was crazy, and my mother was complicit.

The summer was the hardest. My old swimsuit wasn't good enough anymore. Father said it showed too much skin.

Mom looked for a while for one that father approved of, but none of them would cover my bruises.

Finally, I settled on a pair of long gym shorts and a long sleeve t-shirt. It was ugly and made me look dowdy, but it was the only way I could swim.

I didn't like to swim at the local pool because the girls made fun of me and snickered behind my back. Being able to hear everything they said didn't help either. We went to the river, and it was better there. People from different age groups paid attention less to my outfit. T's friends said something a couple of times, but T jumped in and shut them up.

At least I knew that no one was leering at me. I mean, who could think that a baggy t-shirt is sexy?

CHAPTER 9

HERATHINA

Log Entry 1,784,652.33 ATD

The ship is filled with voice-activated computers that are embedded into the walls and the screens are holograms which appear wherever your bracelet is. I am in the domed observatory. This is the shifting room. I am here because Poseidon invited me to watch the final shift.

All bracelets are based on the crystalline composite technology. This means that you can make it look like anything you wish. It could be both decorative or utilitarian. After viewing some of the original information from the new planet, I altered my data bracelet. It now looks like a collection of shells and fire coral. If we are to have limited contact with Homo sapiens, I did not want my bracelet to be out of place.

All of my people receive a bracelet when they reach their bicentennial. It was kind of a cross between a coming-of-age and a necessity. The bracelet enabled you to access any and all computer data available. They also allow you to tap into the transformative programs. They change your body to be something else. It will enable you to blend in so that you can better study whatever subject you were focusing on at the time.

Scientific research is the main focus of our people. Ever since The Great Division, our people had chosen science and research as the great motivators for our civilization, but the dividers had chosen anger and domination to their detriment.

Much of the information our project is studying was lost during the Great Division. How did we evolve to what we are now? Not only that it will help us understand our history, but also this study can help answer where we will be in the future. Genetic manipulation is not enough. The mind also must grow. If we were to move on to the next plane of existence, we have to understand where we first came from.

I have spent much of my time studying the intricacies of the mind. How it thinks, how the pathways are determined, set, and changed. What fascinates me the most is the thought process that brings a person from one place to another. I've watched many lower life-forms on the homeworlds, studying them carefully. I've reached many conclusions, most of which I am mocked for. I follow my gut, a feeling, something deep inside that tells me this is the answer.

One of the reasons I want to study Homo sapiens and the process of evolution is to understand some questions that at this moment have no answers. Why are the powers not distributed equally among us? Why are some weaker than others? A great deal of my people have control of the forces, but a goodly portion does not. Very few of our population have what is called the shifting, which is the ability to move things with only the mind. I don't mean just moving objects from across the room. Those who master it can shift an entire planet's orbit from one part of a solar system to another, repositioning it, thereby creating a new world. Shifting is the only way to move a spaceship from one planet to the other without losing time.

This ability came to our people before the Great Division. We do not have recorded how we came to have this ability. But, it has always been rare. This is why so few projects are chosen. We can only fulfill as many projects as we have shifters available. No shifter, no space travel. It is the only way we survive.

Some shifters can shift an entire spaceship in one fell swoop, from one solar system to another, from one Galaxy to another, one side of the known universe to the other. They simply must picture it in their mind, or so I've been told.

CHAPTER 10

SYDNEY

I did get into Washington HS, and I was pleased about it. It was the only bright spot in an otherwise dull life. It was a good school, and I enjoyed my classes. It was funny how I wasn't supposed to talk to boys or be alone with a boy, but I went to a mostly boys' school. Yea, I didn't get that either, but I didn't actually care.

My freshman year was a big dull blur of being desperate to hide my problems. I didn't have a game plan. When you are in survival mode, you don't plan. You just stay alert and dodge when needed.

My brother made sure that none of the boys in my high school even wanted to talk to me. On my first day, a few boys came up to say 'Hi'. One even said he would help me find my class, but that was until I said my name. After that, he gave me a funny look and asked: "Are you Tobias's little sister?"

I responded "Yes." He didn't even say 'Goodbye'. He just turned around and walked away.

Later that day in my Geography class, a girl made an attempt to talk to me.

"Are you Tobias O'Dear's little sister?" I just nodded. "Your brother put the word out that anyone who talked to or touched you, would die."

Great, as if I didn't have enough problems meeting people. Thanks, T!

After about 3 days not only every boy in the school avoided me like the plague, but a lot of the girls steered clear too. Except for Trish. She was the girl who told me about T putting the word out.

"You want to be my locker partner?" the sound of her voice so close jolted me back to reality. I glanced around, shifting my head left and right.

"Yeah, I'm talking to you, Sydney. So, do you want to?" She repeated.

"Yes, I would love to. Thank you!" I couldn't believe that Trish treated me like I was normal and made me feel welcome.

I became great at seeing several moves ahead. I guess that was kind of like planning. Reacting becomes easier when you can see what's coming. I held on to the hope that I could get through. There was only one way to survive this, and that was to get out as soon as you can.

My plan was to finish school early and maybe move out. With this in mind, I skipped all the electives and went straight for the required classes. I packed as many junior classes as I could into my sophomore year. US History, Government, Civics, Economics, if there was room for a class that I needed to get out of there, I took it. My grades were okay. Only A's and B's.

I didn't have many real friends. I just didn't have anything in common with them. The other girls wore makeup and cute clothes, went to the movies, parties, shopping, hanging out with their friends and boyfriends. I couldn't do any of those things. I wasn't allowed to wear makeup, or anything sexy. For me, clothes were a camouflage, a tool to hide under. A way to disappear into the woodwork. It was as if I were a ninja.

My parents didn't like movies. Plus, I didn't have anyone to go with, so there was no point in even talking about it. As for boys, well, I had already learned that lesson. Over and over again, every other Sunday.

The only time that I felt happy was when I played the piano and got lost in the music or when I was reading a book. At least in a book, I could go anywhere and be anyone. With a book, I was free, and my parents couldn't beat me. I could feel what it was like to be young and a teenager. I could even be normal. I didn't have to always keep an eye out for danger. My parents didn't pay much attention to what I read. Thank God for that! I made book covers so that no matter what book I was reading, they didn't see the title.

My favorite book was 'The Count of Monte Cristo' by Alexandre Dumas. The main guy was Edmond Dantès, who was imprisoned for a crime he didn't commit. After being beaten for years, he breaks out and gets wealthy, takes a new identity and seeks revenge.

That is what my life felt like. I was in prison for a crime that every girl in my church committed every day. My only desire was to break out. As for what I was going to do when I got out… I couldn't think that far ahead.

My music tended to be sad and heartbreaking, melancholy. This might sound absurd, but the only thing that kept me from crying was music to make you cry. My father hated it but left me alone.

After a while, everything that was not normal about me became normal. I learned to control the super focus of my eyes. It became easy to filter out the loud noises from all the humanity I could hear. I found out that eye contact was a trigger for the visions, so avoiding eye contact became second nature.

On a Monday morning, someone mused or inquired about a lost item. I could see this in my mind. I knew exactly where to find it. It didn't matter if I had never been to their home. I didn't have to be personally acquainted with them. They could desire anything, and I would be able to see right where it was.

At first, it was cool. I could overhear every conversation for about two classrooms around. I overheard one of the popular girls telling her friend she couldn't find her lipstick. The flash I received was of her in her boyfriend's truck. It fell out of her purse with all the rocking. I couldn't help myself and I snickered.

I realized the real impact of my power one day when I heard the news. Three boys went missing. The site that invaded my mind filled me with horror. Tears spilled from my eyes, as my mind filled with information. They were gone. I could see the place where they had been dumped. Their small bodies were battered and broken. All three of them were dead, and the amount of abuse they had endured was more than I could handle. The bile rose in my throat. I barreled into the bathroom just in time to vomit.

Nightmares followed me for the next two weeks. I sat up late every night, to avoid the senses that were filling my mind in the moments I drifted off, only to jolt out of my horror soaking wet from sweat. Every time I fell asleep, I could feel my chest heaving and my throat closing with the pain from the pressing hands of the murderer around my neck. By the time they found them, I was weak from the lack of sleep.

I had to stop watching the news or listening to the radio. I could read papers or books, but I couldn't stomach the news or radio. When the news was on, I went to my room and turned on my tape deck or played the piano. Any noise was good, as long as I didn't hear it.

Trish was my only friend. She had gone to middle school with me, but we weren't close. Only three girls from my middle school went to Washington High, and Trish was one of them. She didn't ask a lot of questions about my clothes or family. She was a little self-absorbed. That suited me just fine because it meant no questions and most importantly, no uncomfortable avoidance. I didn't have to be clever around Trish. I could just be me.

Trish was gorgeous. All the boys wanted to talk to her, to buy her lunch and date her. She was one of those beautiful people with blond thick, shiny hair and big blue eyes. Her skin was peach and cream clear, thin and perfect. She modeled for several companies around the state. She could charm anyone. Things always seemed to go her way. She made sure of that.

She invited me to go to all kinds of parties, but I knew I wouldn't be allowed to go, so I always declined. She never asked why. She just smiled.

"Maybe next time Syd, right?" Why she even bothered with that reply, mystified me. I think she just didn't want me to feel left out.

I'm not sure why she wanted to be my friend or my locker mate, but she did. All the girls wanted to befriend her, but she only hung out with boring old me. She was the only girl in school that never talked about me to anyone.

One day, Trish pulled me into the bathroom and waited until everyone left.

"Take your hair out of the braid."

What was wrong with my hair?

"Why? Is it messy?"

"Aw Syd, you are never a mess. Look in the mirror!"

I turned my head this way and that. All the color drained from my face. There were bruises above my collar. She reached for my hair and started pulling the braid out. I looked at her face. She smiled nervously.

"Lucky catch, right? Don't want anyone asking too many questions, right?" Her eyes opened wide "Right?"

"Yes," I stood there while she rearranged my hair. When she finished, I actually looked a little cuter. Then she pulled out her makeup.

"No, I'm not allowed to use any of that. Thank you! I'll just keep my hair down." She smiled, "You should tell your dad you needed some to cover your bruises. "

Anxiety gripped me and made my tummy flop around. "I don't know what you mean. I...I've fallen. That's all"

She snorted, laughing out loud. However, it wasn't a mocking laugh.

"Right. You fall into his hands over and over, twice a month, Right? " She hugged me from the side so that it didn't hurt my back. She knew. She'd known all along.

"Don't worry! I won't tell on him, even though I should. The Bastard!"

Somehow, acknowledging the bruises hurt me more than the physical pain. I took a big breath before I managed to say, "Thank you!"

Her smile was infectious as it lit up the room. "Just wish I could get you to wear better clothes. It's hard when your best friend is a fashion retard."

"You know I'm not allowed to wear anything from this century" We both laughed, and she put the makeup on my neck.

When I got home, I explained to my mother about the bruises above my collar and about the cover-up. She told my father, of course...

"SYDNEY! COME HERE, GIRL!" He was wrenching me by my hair and pushed me into my bed. He started hitting me with the belt AGAIN and AGAIN and AGAIN, AGAIN. I got an extra beating for not asking first. Of course, why wouldn't I?

What the hell was wrong with him? I was just trying to keep everyone from finding out what he was doing to me. But even that was wrong somehow. I was only supposed to be obedient and quiet. I wasn't a person in his eyes. Just a thing that had to do as it was told. I was like a dog. He was trying to train me, to make me follow his orders without question or reason.

The pain was the only way he knew how to get his way. I'm not even sure what his method was. I wished he would talk to my mother about it. This way, maybe I could listen in and get a few answers, but he was tight-lipped.

I hated him. I wanted to get revenge just like Edmond Dantes. I wanted him to suffer the same way he made me suffer. He was always banging on about an eye for an eye. I wanted him to be beaten for years for no actual reason. After reading books about abusers, all I could come up with was that my father was a crazy sociopath and got a sick pleasure out of hurting me for any reason.

Sunday came and with it so did the pain, the screaming, crying, and the bruises that never had enough time to fully heal. I remember how I would listen to at Church how the priest talked about hell and about how the devil tortures you. Sinners burn in the fiery pit of hell or the lake of fire, but that sounded like a vacation compared to my life. If hell was worse than what I was living now, I couldn't wrap my brain around how.

It was like a trick was being played on me, a sick twisted joke. I felt dead inside, but it was the only way to survive. If I didn't feel it, I couldn't get hurt. All the voices, all the listening, all the findings, everything strange that was happening to me made me just numb.

Then there was the dream that came at night in my sleep. It was always the same but also different. I saw a little more every time. At the end of it, the wind always blows. I knew that I needed to do or hear something, but it always ends so abruptly. Just when I'm about to reach it, it's gone. It's frustrating.

CHAPTER 11

HERATHINA

Log entry 1,784,652.34 ATD

It took me a few minutes to follow the corridors to the Citadel. Where I would find Poseidon along with the rest of the project Council. What did surprise me was the image of Athena sitting in one of the Council's chairs. She raised her hand and beckoned me with an inviting smile.

"I'm so glad you're here because they didn't really want to take you. It took a lot of convincing." Athena said.

My eyes widening and my eyebrows raised. The only reason I knew that my mouth was open, was because the air moved across my tongue.

"Don't look so surprised. You are several thousand years younger than me. This is a great honor because you have not reached the age of responsibility. You are the youngest member of the project. You're also the only one here to study human emotion."

Athena was only 2000 years older than me. Still, the idea that she had to fight for me to be on this project was embarrassing. I shoved that thought aside. I was here, and I had to focus on the work ahead.

"You are part of the council, Athena. That is a truly great honor and I congratulate you for it." I made a pause before I continued. "What is to be your area of specialty?"

Her smile widened, and her stormy blue eyes took on a faraway look.

"War. I'm going to study war and human tactics of warfare. We have a minimal record of actual conflict, other than the Great Division. I'm to provide that information." She made a small pause just to take in some air. "Wherever Humanity wages War, I will be there."

A cold shiver ran down my spine. The idea of witnessing the butchering of one life-form or another based merely on a disagreement of ideas frightens me to my core. Athena has always been a different type of scientist than me. The gory details never bother her.

The rest of the council chamber was filled with other members; some I recognized, others I did not. Osiris and Isis sit alongside each other, along with Tyche, and it seemed that our Council was to have 12 members.

The Citadel was designed to hold tens of thousands. The arena was even bigger. It was designed to hold millions. However, this project only entailed 50,000 of us. Why we were given such a large ship, I'm not quite sure. As far as I understood, we weren't mandated to bring back any life samples. Plants, yes, but only ones with food or medicinal qualities. No wildlife and certainly not any sentient beings. So, who were they thinking was going to be filling all the rest of the rooms on this ship?

Again, questions were raging in my mind. This needed to stop. In two days, we would leave for Terra, and my entire universe would change. The image of the blue ball floating in the void penetrated my mind, exciting me in ways I cannot begin to describe.

I had no desire whatsoever to leave the ship for any of the celebrations, but attendance was expected by all members of the projects for as many festivals as possible. My people enjoyed witnessing the birth of Heroes. Everyone who attended a project would return to a celebration. That is how it was done. You are hailed as a hero, even if you discover nothing.

I was not sure if our culture was on the rise or the decline. Everywhere I look, I saw much stagnation. The fifty homeworlds had changed very little since my birth and my childhood. It seemed that the only people who changed and grew within our culture were the heroes who left and came back a Millennia later.

The rest were like rocks locked in one place, letting time flow over them, changing very little. Maybe this is why I was so desperate to join a project. I needed something to change. I know my kind desperately needed this to happen. They are all complacent, happy to wait for their mate to be born, to have children and spend all their existence in luxury, at ease of traveling from one planet to another.

A great deal of our population had not even joined the Sciences. They contributed nothing to our society. They simply existed. We had an eternity to live. But my people, instead of using it for the common good, they simply ate, drank, and were merry. For all, this was the idea of a perfect society, but I could see only its imperfections. I was so desperate to be away from them.

Many claimed that my over-emotional behavior made me unbalanced. Maybe they were right, but even so, I didn't have to agree with them. What I did know was that I wanted to live not just exist, that I wanted to explore and discover new things. I wanted to understand the minds of humans because they are so like our own, yet so very different. I could spend several lifetimes on Terra. I already knew it deep in my soul. So, yes, perhaps I was an idealist.

Maybe it was my youth that made me feel this way. I don't know. What I did know was that the Homo sapiens were a race of the young, and my bet was that their youthful vigor would provide an interesting experience.

CHAPTER 12

SYDNEY

A fight started in the hall. Why does everyone love to watch a fight? These are people that we know. We see them every day and have been doing so for at least the last decade. Two of the jocks started going at each other. The crowd pushed and shoved to create the circle that all fights must happen in.

I was not interested in staying to watch, so I skirted around the edges. This section of the halls was a choke point in the school. Not inside but not out either. I was working my way around the jostling crowd when I saw an opening to slip through. I darted into it, just as the back of a big guy stepped my way, and I careened face first into a large chest.

Adrian broke my fall by wrapping his arms around my shoulders. Dad had deeply bruised both of them. I wanted to beat the pain, but I couldn't control the tears that started to run down my face. I tried to pull away, but he didn't let go.

"Sydney, what's wrong? Why are you crying? Did I hurt you?"

I couldn't respond. My sweater had pulled away from the tank top that I had safety pinned it too. I know he saw some of the marks, but it's okay. He doesn't care, so no biggie.

I pulled the sweater back onto my shoulder and righted myself to walk away, but Adrian clamped a hand around my bicep and jerked my arm, pulling me into the band room. No one was in there, and he locked the door to make sure that no one would come in either. He let his bag down but didn't move from the door.

He crossed his arms and asked in a grave voice, "Where did you get those bruises?"

Don't say anything stupid.

I just stood there looking at the floor. I knew that I had to say something, but what could I say? I knew I shouldn't have worn this sweater, no matter how cool it was. I knew it could fall off my shoulder. That's how all the girls were wearing them, though. I just wanted to look cool for once.

I didn't want to talk about it. And why should I? It's just a bruise. So, I remained silent, hoping he would let it go. He didn't say anything else. I couldn't stand the situation anymore so I broke it.

"I fell."

But then a voice in my head rang:

< Not buying it >

"Sure. Show me now, or you aren't leaving until you do!"

What was it with pushy men? Why were they all around me and more importantly, what gave him the right to tell me what to do and interrogate me?

I was so just so tired. I thrust my chin out at him and what came out of my mouth sounded like it came from one of the books I like to read. I sounded like some woman who knew what she wanted and how to get it.

"You want to see? Okay. Here you go!" I didn't know anymore if I was furious with him or the situation, but I turned around, unpinned and yanked the whole sweater off. I lifted my tank top up so he could see my back and belly. I unbuttoned my pants and lowered them just enough so he understood it went down a lot further than my back. And then, I stood still, and like time just stopped.

The beating from the previous night was very fresh, so all the bruises had their full color. I actually knew that some of the ones on my shoulders had a little green to them. But most of them were purple, brown and blackish.

I don't know if he wanted to say something or not, but the sound that came out of him was more of a choke than a word. I closed my eyes and hoped that everything would go away.

I think I might be sick.

The vision slammed into my mind. My back was a quilt of bruising, with varying jewel tones. I could feel the bile climbing up the inside of his and therefore, my throat.

This is how I looked most of the times. A skeleton covered in bruises, but no scars.

I figured that was enough, so I tucked my tank top back in my pants, buttoned my jeans, pulled my sweater back on and repinned it in its place. I picked up my bag and turned around.

Adrian looked a little green, and I wasn't sure if he was going to puke or not.

"Now you've seen it. Can I please go?" I just wanted to go and never come back, but it didn't appear that he would leave me do that.

"Who did that to you?"

Feeling very cocky and angry, I put my hands on my hips and cocked them to the side. "You don't know? I thought everyone at church knew that my father was beating me."

His eyebrows rose up as both brows pinched together along with his lips. Astonishment and horror covered his face.

"I didn't know… w…why, is he beating you?"

"Oh, I thought everyone knew that too. Why don't you go ask my cousin James? You're still friends with him. I'm sure he'll tell you." I took a breath and continued, "Adrian, I don't have time for this. If anyone finds out I was talking to you or that I was alone with you..." I choked but managed to add in a lower voice "What happened last night, will happen tonight too. I've already had 2 this week, so please leave me alone, and go back to ignoring me like everyone else."

Tears threatened to fill my eyes, and my chest was on fire. I could feel the heat in my face as my throat was closing up. I wanted him to leave, but he didn't move. Instead, he stood there with his Adam's apple working up and down. When he managed to swallow, he asked, "How long has this been going on?"

"Almost three years. You would know that if you were my friend, but you aren't. So, go back to your nice life. Don't talk to me, don't worry about me, don't even think about me. It's what you've been doing til' now, so it will be easy. I'm sure your parents don't want you to associate with me in any way." It appeared that my words didn't have any effect on him, but I continued nevertheless.

"If my father thinks I talked to you, there will just be more of what you just saw. Only this time he'll use the belt. So please don't tell me you suddenly care, after not talking to me for three years."

"I do care." His voice was pleading and so were his eyes.

That was like a shot across my bow, and I was on a roll now. All the shit I had been carrying around with me for years came pouring out, but with a vengeance. All those people who looked at me with their accusing eyes. I just wanted to scratch them out, and Adrian seemed like the perfect person to take the brunt. He started all of this for me. It was his fault I was labeled a whore. I didn't care anymore if somebody heard me, so I started to scream.

"YOU CARE. REALLY?!! WHAT KIND OF CARE IS IT? IS IT THE CARE OF IGNORING ME FOR THREE YEARS KIND OF CARE OR THE PEOPLE WHO SEE ME AT CHURCH 3-4 TIMES A WEEK AND WON'T EVEN TALK TO ME CARE, OR MAYBE YOU ARE JUST LIKE MY FATHER..." I felt somehow relieved, so I stopped yelling. I let my voice drop really low, and I looked deep into his beautiful blue eyes.

"He always says he cares right before he beats me, so tell me, which one is it, cause I don't know what the word care means anymore. I just accept how everyone uses it to hurt me. I don't need someone else to CARE about me. I don't believe anyone does, and no one has for a long time." I pushed him to the side with my shoulder so I could get out, but he stopped me from opening the door. I gazed at him out with the corner of my eye.

"I really do care what happens to you, Sydney. "

"Really? Prove it! Why should you? No one else does."

This time I really shoved him. His hand fell away, and I ran out of the room. Once I was out, I kept running. I didn't even know where I was going but it felt good to run. I had the sensation that if I didn't stop, I could get away from all the shit in my life, leaving it all behind. But I did stop.

I was standing at the end of the track field where the trees and picnic tables were. That's when I realized I didn't have my bag with my books and my bus pass. I didn't want to go back and see him or anyone else, so I sat down on the ground. My chest was heaving with the strain of holding it all in for so long. I cried like I'd wanted to cry for years. I held myself and rocked back and forth, wishing I was dead. Actually, this was the first time I'd really wanted to die. For all these years I hadn't been thinking about it that much. My only focus was on finding a way to survive. But I had opened that door, and now I couldn't stop what was coming out, so I just kept sobbing and rocking.

Warm arms were around me, holding me and rocking with me. I froze because someone else was touching me. No one had touched me in years. Except on Sundays, and that was far from what a touch should be. I looked at the hands that were holding me. They were large, strong hands, but they were cradling me gently. The warmth of a body behind me filled me with comfort. I heard crying, but it wasn't mine. It was soft and quiet.

It was good to be held. I wanted to burrow into those arms. I felt safe and complete but also tense because people might see. Someone might tell. I had to get up. I had to move. I had to get away from those big hands that were holding me. I tried to pull away, but they didn't let go.

I was shaking and my teeth were chattering. It took me a lot of strength to open my mouth and articulate actual words. "Please, let me go! I can't be here like this."

The hands didn't move an inch, so panic rose in me "Please, please, please! Someone will see and tell him, and he will hit me again." I felt the breath on my neck, then in my ear. It was warm and moist. The lips were so close that when they moved, they brushed the edge of my ear. Adrian whispered lightly, "That's what care means". And with that, he opened his arms and let go of me.

I stood up and took one look at him. He had tears glistening on his face. I was afraid that I would see pity. I didn't want mercy, but there was nothing there other than a pained expression. I turned, grabbed my bag laying on the ground at

Adrian's side and ran again. First to the bathroom and then to class.

I don't know why, but I felt better after that. My books would say that I needed to release the tension, to face my fears, and confront my anger. What a pile of shit... I only felt better because he, Adrian, had held me. It was that simple. I didn't feel alone. T had tried to help me, but he also told on me. I had never shown anyone my back, but when I showed him, I had gotten a picture of what it looked like.

Why don't I have scars?

*****

A couple of weeks went by, and life had gone on like before. He didn't talk to me again. I figured he had spoken to James. Trish asked me about what was going on because I had been different. I smiled.

Deflect, deny, and change the conversation.

Whatever to keep the spotlight off of what I really felt or thought. I told her that I was training, and I couldn't wait because then I could earn money to move out. The best lie is the one that is as close to the facts as possible. It was easier to remember that way.

Later that day, I was heading to my major class. As I was passing the teachers' bathroom I was dragged in by my coat, and the door clicked shut after me and the lock sent home.

"How often does he beat you?"

GOD, why does he care? And why now all of a sudden?

"What difference does it make? It happens about every two weeks unless he thinks I messed up. Why?" I was cocking my hip to one side feeling the exasperation pouring from me.

"I talked to my aunt, the nurse. She gave me this ointment for the bruising and said it would make them go away faster."

He's attempting to help me, to be nice to me. T did try to help a little. Trish just kept her mouth shut. But this was kind, thoughtful even.

I had so many words that I wanted to tell him. I wanted him to know that I believe him when he said he cared, that he is the only one who in all these years offered me comfort, but I couldn't. So, I just simply said, "Thank you", and hope that he understands from the tone of my voice how much I appreciate his gesture.

"She said it cuts the pain too, so maybe you won't hurt so much when someone hugs you." He gave me a smile, but I laughed out loud like a crazy person.

Hug me?

I was shaking my head in denial before I responded "No one hugs me. You were the last person to hug me, and before that, I don't remember who did. But, thank you. In an ideal world, it would be nice to receive an unpainful hug."

< I would hug you >

It made me crazy whenever I heard this voice. It was like I was losing my mind.

< *Shut up!* >

When I finished hearing voices, I noticed that Adrian was standing close to me.

When had he moved so close?

His eyes were searching my face, and my body reacted to the proximity of him. He had a light smell of cologne; it was spicy and clean. My heart was hammering, and I couldn't control it or myself for that matter. I don't know how and when, but a moment later I was staring at his lips.

I was brought back from my daze when his entrancing lips started moving, "Do you want me to put some on you?"

"Yes."

God damn it, Sydney!

"I mean, no! I don't need it right now. I should save it until I need it. Thank you." I started talking really fast thinking that will bring me back to normalcy. When I finished, I noticed that his face looked confused.

"You need it now. Please, let me put it on your back."

I stood there thinking of it for a moment before deciding. In my head, there was a fight between the relief I could get from the ointment versus getting caught with Adrian in the bathroom. I concluded that, even though someone would find out about this, the worst thing that could happen was to be beaten with a belt, and I had lived through that before.

So, I pulled my shirt up and turned away from him so he could see my back and bra. There was a brief exhale of air as he surveyed the damage. His rough hands began to rub my bruised body.

"When do you need it?" He didn't stop massaging me, but his motions became gentler.

"On Sunday."

"Why Sunday, is that when he….?" His hand stilled, but he didn't take them off of me. They were still there, giving me comfort.

"Yes. Most people dread church. I dread Sunday evenings."

"Why did he begin beating you?" He started rubbing the ointment again, but I could tell he was tense.

I didn't want to reply. What would be the point of telling him? Besides honesty.

The scene from that night replayed over in my mind. I could hear my father screaming, "You talked to a boy alone!!"

As I listen to it in my head, the words tumble from my lips in a low voice. "Because I talked to a boy and was alone with him."

His hands stilled against me, but I move away. I took the ointment back from him and put it in my bag.

Adrian's face was pulled tight and pinched at the mouth with his jaw clenching. His brow furled as he watched how I pulled my shirt down inching toward the door to leave. I didn't turn to look him in the eyes. I was too ashamed to do so. I just kept my back to him, staring at the door. I didn't want to see what I'm sure was in his eyes, so I put my hand upon the lock.

"I'm sure by now, you talked to James. So, he told you I'm a whore, and I'm not good for anything. I don't learn, which is why my dad has to keep beating me." If I said it out loud, maybe I could figure out what the fuck it meant.

He didn't seem to care about what I just told him. He only had one question that came out cold and clipped.

"Who was the boy?"

I could actually hear his jaw snapping when he put the question to an end. But, would it make any difference if I told him? What would he think?

I could feel the room filling with electricity from the tension pouring off of him. It was so intense that it made the hair on my arm rise.

"You, three years ago." And with that, I opened the door and bolted out. I knew as long as I was in the hall with everyone else, he wouldn't make a scene. I just needed to get away from him. I don't know what he really wanted from me, but whatever it was, I couldn't have anything to do with it.

The voice mumbled something, yet I pushed it to the back of my mind. Thank you very much, but I don't have time for crazy right now.

The rest of the day was pretty uneventful. However, after school, Adrian brushed by me and put a note in my hand - 'Wrights Field restroom 5 minutes.'

I looked at Trish, and she said smiling, "Do it! I'll catch up to you."

So, I grabbed all my homework and headed for the front halls to leave. Trish came up beside me and pushed me out the side door that leads to Wrights Field. Then she pulled it shut so that it locked me out. She shrugged her shoulders and waved goodbye, mouthing, "Have fun for once!"

Aggravated didn't even begin to describe how I was feeling. I couldn't meet a boy alone. I wanted to live to 18, so I could get the hell out of here. What the fuck was I going to do? I really wanted to meet him, but I didn't want to get caught either. My traitorous feet found their way to the restrooms.

A whistle came softly from the doorway. He was next to the girls' door. I entered the bathroom and turned around to face him. I knew that I had to get this over with. And I needed to do it quickly.

He jumped in before I could get a word out. "Sydney, he beat you for talking to me at the ski lodge 3 years ago?" The disbelief in his voice was agonizing.

Okay just square your shoulders and face him. Do it and leave.

"Yes"

"Because we talked. That's it? He does that to you for talking to me?" He was outraged and shocked at the same time.

I was tilting my head to the side, trying to figure out of a way to explain my father's way of thinking.

"That time, yes. After that, he said it was because I was a woman, and he couldn't let me become a whore." I stopped because I knew how absurd all this was, but the look in his eyes demanded more, so I continued, "Then, it was because I am a whore. Then it was because I'm stupid and fat and ugly and I put makeup on my bruises." Now, it felt that somebody plugged me into an electricity source because I couldn't hold it in anymore. Words came out of my mouth without even thinking them "Also, I...I danced with a boy that wasn't my family at a wedding once. Dinner wasn't good enough. I didn't clean the house to his liking." Finally, I exhaled, raising my arms in frustration. "What difference does it make? He does it, and that's that."

All this time, I tried to look only at the floor to find the strength to make him believe my words, but now was the time to face him.

Okay lift your head and look him in the eyes. 1,2,3 go!

"Adrian, you have been kind to me, but I'm just not worth it. Everyone thinks I am a whore. You have a nice life with great parents, who love you. People at church look at you and see an excellent wholesome young man. You have a good reputation. You're smart and going places. I'm not, I don't, and I would ruin all of that for you. My father might beat me to death if he found out I talked to you or any other boy. If he knew I was here with you like this ...I...I... Just let it go, please. Leave me alone, I'm not worth it."

I could feel myself shrinking inside while I turned to move away. All that puffing up had leaked out, and now only the husk was left.

Voice crowded in <NO> I pushed the sound back and away.

He grabbed my hand to stop me. "You are beautiful and smart. You are definitely not fat. I might be the only person who knows that, but you're too thin. Talking to someone doesn't make you a whore. My parents told me not to talk to you. So, I didn't."

I snatched my hand back from him. "You should do what your parents tell you to do, and stay away from me." I wanted to add 'before you get me killed', but that didn't need to be said.

< Are you going to run off again? >

< *YES, I'm going to run off before he gets me killed. So, shut up!* >

I whirled around and pulled the door open to leave, but I stopped before I exited. I turned slightly to look over my shoulder. He seemed so wounded.

"Adrian, I would love to be friends with you again, but I have to do as my father wants. I have two years before I can do any of the things I want to do. If I can make it that far, maybe if you still remember me, we can be friends."

He coughed to clear his throat, "I'm not going to wait two years to be your friend."

I knew that he meant well, but it felt like it was one of my father punches, and a sound of despair flew from my mouth.

"I'll see you around, Sydney."

He pushed past me through the door and left. It took a moment for my motion to start, but I was running again. It was the only way I knew to survive. His words had burned me. I didn't think I had a heart left. When he said he wouldn't wait, he crushed it. The running helped to hide the squeezing pain in my chest. He knew he wouldn't see me around. We didn't travel in the same circles. There was no hope there. He was out of my league.

CHAPTER 13

HERATHINA

Log entry 1,784,652.35 ATD

"Would you like to join us? Our shifter is about to move Alethea." When Poseidon issues an invitation, you never say no. He is one of the greatest heroes of our people. He is so ancient that he was present for the Great Division. Poseidon has always shown me kindness. I suppose other people might assume that he was even playing favorites. He had always treated me with respect and kindness, but I didn't expect to be given such a choice mission. Or be invited to attend the council. Although, why he would choose me to join them in the shifting chamber, I can't imagine. I've never actually seen a station shift from one world to another.

"Thank you, Poseidon! I would be most honored to witness the shifting. May I ask who the shifter is for this project?"

"Mica, the grand Council chose Mica. He is a competent shifter; I believe he will serve this project well. He's not as strong as Ixis, but Ixis is still moving worlds. His heart still lies with the Thema-forming projects. He believes bringing life to the universe is the most important project. He has moved hundreds of worlds. For all we know, this could have been one of them." Poseidon chuckled under his breath.

I knew that Terra was not one of the Thema-formed worlds. "Ixis is an important shifter; I would have been surprised if he had been assigned to this project."

"It's true Ixis is our strongest shifter. I too would have been surprised had they assigned him to us. Mica will cut his teeth on this project. I'm sure he will move on to bigger and better things. We will not be disappointed."

If I would have been a shifter, I would be guaranteed respect in all corners of the universe. How exciting it must be to move an entire planet into a better orbit, thereby allowing life to exist. I can understand why Ixis would want to continue such work. It must be fulfilling.

Our shifter Mica is one of my brothers' closest friends. He is dedicated to the project. I didn't think that Mica would be capable of it. He is one of the weaker shifters. Mica is not much older than me. I've been told that as shifters grow, so do their abilities.

To say it was spectacular would not be doing it the justice it deserves. You always feel the pressure change. As if you're only partially in the real world. I didn't expect to see the stars shifting. One moment they were there dancing lights from the stars off in the distance and the next one they had all moved. The world grew larger and smaller all at once. Our green world shifted from the red star to a blue planet with a yellow star. Amazing!

There had been much talk among everyone about having a stronger shifter, then how it should be assigned to someone like Markham or Ixis. But in one jump, Mica had silenced all of that. The Council chose wisely, again. The background murmuring had pressed in questioning his ability to move us in one leap. A collective sigh ran through the ship.

A background buzzing filled my head, pushing the collective away. I turned my head to find the source only to view motion waves. Pressure filled my cranium. Emotions, like I had never known, crashed, and rebounded in my skull.

The floor came up to meet me. Poseidon's face filled my vision. His blues eyes search, brows pinch with concern. I stared through him with the anger, joy, lust, and pain that became my world.

Log entry 1,784,652.51 ATD

I awakened a few weeks later. However, I can feel the pressure in the background. The onslaught of emotions batters me constantly. I know it's the Homo sapiens. All their emotions weigh on me like a gravity well. Pushing and pulling me, with each pass of the planet to the moon. Their emotions ebb and flow like the wave of the moons' control.

Many of the members from the project are arguing. Their rage fills me, and I claw at it, pushing with my mind to keep my balance. Fighting has broken out in different areas of the ship. Being an empath, I have always felt everyone's emotions. My people are subdued to the extreme. The humans, however, run wild almost like a sickness.

But that's impossible because Themian's don't get sick. We haven't encountered anything capable of hurting us in a long time. I'm not even sure there is anything out there that can. I know that sounds arrogant. Of course, there has to be something out there that can hurt us, other than being crushed or falling from a great height.

These emotions are crippling for me. I'm an empath and it affects me differently. Every day and night, I battle with them. Why would it be affecting anyone else? They have never shown any sensitivity to emotions, so I don't understand why it's affecting the rest of the crew, but every living member is in an emotional labyrinth.

*****

"Until we have control of the ship, no one may visit the planet." The muscles in his jaw clenched as he snaps his mouth shut. Poseidon thinks we should wait here in orbit. See if he can get some of the outbreaks under control.

"I need loyal people to help retake the ship."

I can feel his stare as his blue eyes bore into me. An intense feeling of fierce righteousness fills his countenance. The pressure from his probing fills my mind. He is vigorous and forceful. He stabs at me using his mind like a blade. A struggle of wills takes over. My body turns of its own will to align with his. My eyes lock with his. I see him but am unseeing. It is war.

His will is stronger than mine, and he means to dominate me. The world is spinning around off to the sides, and my eyes are staring unseeing into his soul. If I don't push him out, he will take over and dominate me. I can't let him break me. I have to win. Intense pain spikes through my mind as he digs into my memories. Every part of his power is snaking into the dark recesses of me. I try to wrestle him back and my body trembles. Sweat has formed on my upper lip and hairline. He pushes his will in again. I raised my hands to the power of the onslaught rolls through me, and I push him back with my mind and the force of wind. My hair is rising as the chamber fills with kinetic energy. He is close, so I need to push harder. With that, his body slams into the bulkhead.

My attack is two-fold, and I dive into his mind. Visions of his life flash through me. My father, the war, the cleaning, sexual encounters. It speeds past me; I slow it down as I reach our time.

I see my body crumpled to the floor. "Herathina!" He grabs my shoulders shaking me. "She is being attacked." Many in the council are holding their heads. His mind is overrun with emotions and anger fills him.

He lashes out mentally to every mind on board. The force of his onslaught is epic. Many in the room turn to him and bow. The control he excerpts over the ship is incredible.

Gaea raises her hand. "Stop Poseidon! You cannot rule us all. Cease your attack! I will retreat, and you may have control of the ship. Mica, please shift me and mine to the planet." He/I release thousands of minds. Most of the Council disappears from the room.

I pull back to myself. Poseidon has his arms locked around me. "I will not defy you, but you cannot rule me." His lips curl into a sneer. "Give me your allegiance! Swear never to contact the High Council. Or dream walk to anyone about this." His breath fills my senses.

He needs me, I can feel it. "I swear to keep my own counsel and not betray you. But, you must release me to continue our research." I stumble as he thrusts me away.

He tilts his head back, raising his eyes to the dome. His lips lifted in a sneering smile of triumph. He turns to stare at me. His eyes are boring into mine yet again. This time there is no pressure. He quickly looks away, and I survived, for now.

I have never needed to protect my thoughts. My mental protection is not strong. I imagine the walls, building them in my mind as my mother instructed. He barks a laugh at me. "You are only strong enough to keep your mind. You can't keep me out of it."

Osiris and Isis have taken control over ring A and B. Apollo and Artemis have assumed control in C and D. Other council members have also taken compartments, and they are ruling them as fiefdoms, subjecting weaker, younger Themians to their will.

I should have known Isis would follow Osiris. The twin bond is strong. Even now, with the distance of a billion stars, I feel the pull of my brother. Our thoughts are only a breath away. I block him out. Poseidon is listening, watching. I must keep my word.

CHAPTER 14

SYDNEY

Summer came. T was living on his own, working full time, so he didn't have a chance to go to the river.

I went strawberry picking like I did every year. I was up at 4:00 am to catch the bus filled with migrant workers who didn't speak English. They leered at every woman they saw. This meant working in the sun and rain, wearing the crappiest clothes you own because strawberry picking stains everything, clothes, hands, anything you get juice on.

In the morning time, it was an hour and a half drive out to the farm. All those roads were smooth and even, but once on the farm, it was all dirt, making the bus pitch right and left as it ground its way over the ruts in the mud. By the time we'd reached the field, our insides were mush. We started picking, close to the buses and trucks.

We were paid by the flat, and it takes a ton of berries to fill a flat. When picking strawberries, your body becomes cramped as you're bent over for hours, and your hands ache from clutching as many berries as you can. But that's not all. Your thighs hurt from the bending and squatting, while your arms and shoulders ache from carrying the flats. The more you pick, the further you have to walk to turn them in, making the walk back to the berries longer with every flat.

The migrants worked in teams, and the families picked together. While the children and mothers never stop picking, the men carried the flats back and forth. They were grown men and could move 4 or 5 flats at a time, but I only had me. I couldn't carry more than one. I couldn't leave a half full flat in the field, or someone would come and steal it. I couldn't afford losing the money. I needed it.

Then, there were the sun burns. I wore a hat, but the back of my neck always got burned. Sweat rolled down my head and brows. I had a bandana that I wore around my head to hold the sweat out of my eyes. However, I suffered from heat more than others. I couldn't take my shirt off; everyone would have seen the bruises. I couldn't wear shorts for the same reason. So, I worked and sweated. I carried a bottle of water with me. The migrants tied long strings on theirs then slung them over an arm. I did that too.

My father never made my brothers go, so this year, just as always, I was alone. Plus, I still had all of my chores at home and church. I didn't get to sleep much because most of the time church was usually over at 10:30-11:00 PM. Why they made me stay, I couldn't understand. It wasn't like anyone ever talked to me or even had the intention of doing so.

Most of the girls at church would point at my stained hands and snicker. I was sure that not one of them understood what a hard day of work truly was.

My parents could have let me walk home or sit/sleep in the car. But no, I had to stand against a wall being ignored by everyone and waiting for my family to leave.

Every dollar I earned was for school clothes and shoes. So, I went every day. The strawberry bus came to pick up the day laborers, 6 days a week for 3 weeks. My father always asked for the money. He said it was for safekeeping.

I tried to talk my parents into letting me get a job, but that meant I would be out on my own unsupervised, so I received a big, 'No'. I had to watch the boys with no pay. However, I felt it was more like they were watching me. Matt was always making sure I didn't call anyone. My mother called three times a day to check up on us and always asked to speak to Matt. Then, she would tell me what to make for dinner.

Once a week, we went to the library for the summer book club and to the park every other day. I cooked and cleaned the house, practiced the piano, rinse, and repeat.

Also, I had paying babysitting jobs twice a week, but I wasn't allowed to keep that money either. Every time, I heard the same thing, "It's for your clothes kitty Sydney; you need to pay your own way as much as you can."

Why exactly was that?

There were always a lot of weddings in the summer at our church, and I played at most of them. At first, I thought they just liked to hear me play, so I enjoyed doing it. In July, my father handed me some music sheets and instructed me to practice. I had two weeks before the wedding, but it wasn't that hard. When the day of the wedding arrived, my mother came to my room with a plain black dress.

"You are to wear this, Sydney. Put your hair in a bun, and don't talk to anyone."

It was the doughtiest dress I'd ever seen. It was like a dress from Little House on the Prairie, a muumuu with a belt. I would look like the old maid librarian, not that it mattered. The 'don't talk to anyone' comment I took as a joke, because no one from the church had spoken to me in years.

The bride was radiant, and the groom was dashing. I performed the song for the first dance. The music flowed from my fingers and across the room, enveloping the couple. When I finished and rose to leave the area, a few people clapped. Most just went on with the night, and the DJ who started the music made a comment about waking everyone up after I had put them to sleep. I didn't care. I just went and sat in the corner of the room.

< I thought it was fabulous >

Great! My mind thinks I played well.

I didn't finish my thought because the father of the bride approached me.

"Thank you for helping us with the wedding! Your father said you wouldn't let us down, and he was right." He extended his hand. I thought that he wanted to shake mine, but it had cash in it.

Astonishment filled me. No one had ever tipped me before. A smile cracked my face. "Thank you very much! You don't have to tip me. I was happy to help your family on their special day."

His eyes widened as his jaw locked down. A look of confusion rippled over him. "Tip?" his voice filled with incredulity. "Your father said you wouldn't play unless we paid you." I didn't know what he was talking about, so I took a step back as he leaned over, and his eyes leveled with mine. His warm moist breath laced with a touch of alcohol that floated to my nose.

Just then, a vise-like hand landed on my shoulder and began to squeeze. Tears came to my eyes when his fingers dug into the soft parts and wedged between the bones causing them to spread apart. I bit my lower lip to keep any sound from escaping my mouth. The voice was dark and as cold as the Arctic.

"Thank you for your patronage, Bob! Sydney was happy to work for you. This is a beautiful wedding. I hope your daughter and her new husband are pleased." He snatched the money from my hand. He used his grip to turn me around and walked me out to the car. He spoke only after he shoved me inside.

"I told you not to talk to anyone. You just don't listen, do you? Why God gave me such a stupid child, I will never know." He raised his hand and I knew the blow was coming. My eyes squinted as my head turned down to deflect. The slap landed on my cheek with a sting and then stopped but not before adding, "We'll finish this later."

He finished it alright. Once on Saturday and once on Sunday. It was a good thing I didn't have school.

And of course, I didn't get that money either. Just as always, he took it all. There was about one hundred bucks there.

God, I hated him.

He kept me broke and under a tight watch. I was never allowed to do or go anywhere without the family. I was surprised that I could use the restroom alone. Sometimes I said that I was going to bed early just so I could be alone. Without them watching me.

Thankfully, school came around again. I couldn't wait to get out of the house and away from my loving family of jailers.

*****

Once again, I packed my schedule with as many classes as I could. I also signed up for a few crossover courses for college credit. It wasn't like I was ever going to go to college because that was what normal kids did. I was anything, but a normal kid. Yes, my family was poor, and I would need a scholarship, but even if I got one, my father would end that because probably only whores go to college.

A few of my classes were senior levels. I had to practically beg the school to let me take double English. Math was the only area I just didn't seem to get above average grades. Overall, at the end of the year, I was only going to have a half day of school the next one.

Trish had gotten even more beautiful over the summer. I guess that when you travel all over Europe, it changes you. She couldn't shut up about all the boys she met. She drank in every country. I asked her about the museums, but she didn't really remember. Art and culture were just not her forte. Her zest for life was infectious. You just couldn't hate her even if you tried.

She ran off to her major, and I went to mine. Everything was running smoothly until I got to the senior English class.

There, in the front row, was Adrian. He looked up and smiled at me. I must have had my mouth open because one of the other girls squeezed by and laughing said, "Looks like the junior girl is going to let flies land in her mouth."

I panicked, and I closed my lips. I picked a place to sit that was on the other side of the room from him, but he picked up his things, taking the chair right next to me. I stared straight ahead, not wanting to look at him. He leaned over and whispered, "You look well, Syd."

All summer the voice had been pretty quiet, but now it screamed in my head.

< YES > I rubbed my temples it was so loud.

< Shut up! You'll give me a headache. >

I was saved by the teacher who walked in and closed the door.

"This year, you are going to have an English partner. With this person, you will read all the books, sonnets and plays. There will be an in-class performance at the end of each semester and joint homework to turn in. I will be matching you randomly, so don't get your hopes up."

The only thing that kept going through my head was '*Let it be a girl! Please, let it be a girl! If there is a God, let it be a girl!*'

She looked around the room and started pairing us up. "Adrian, Sydney, you two" I didn't hear any of the other matches. All I heard was a ringing in my head from the

< YESYESYESYES >

< *Shut up, you stupid voice! You are hurting my head! Why are you so fucking happy? It's not like we can actually do the school work together. Now I have to tell my dad about this, and he's going to beat me for not trying hard enough to get a girl.* >

Fuck, fuck, fuck!!!!!

My hand shot up without me thinking of it too much, "Mrs. Thompson?"

She looked up at me "Yes, Sydney?"

I think I was shaking, but I was not sure. What I knew for sure was that my voice trailed off and the heat filled my face from the blush, staining my cheeks as I asked "Can I have a girl as my partner? My father..."

I didn't manage to finish because the class burst out into laughter. I actually heard a few of the comments such as "What does she think is going to happen while reading a book?", "Maybe reading is too much for her" or "Is your dad in the dark ages?"

Yes, he is.

"Quiet down class! Sydney, no, you will stick to the partner I've assigned you, and if your father has a problem with that, he can call me. Here is my number."

A few of my classmates were still laughing when Adrian leaned back in his chair and said, "You'll have to talk to me now" he stopped only to put a smug smile on his gorgeous face and continued, "Can't run away this time, Syd."

My heart was pounding. I stole a glance at him, and he winked with a big smile. All I could think was that he knew this was going to happen. I didn't know how, but he knew. I couldn't drop out of class. This was the only one that fit into my schedule.

Fuck!

"The first book we are going to read is 'Pride and Prejudice' by Jane Austen. Has anyone read this or heard of it at least?"

My hand shot up. I was the only one in the class, and of course, they all started laughing again, throwing comments such as "bookworm", "geek" or "that must be how she got into the senior class."

Mrs. Thompson didn't seem to care about the other kids' opinion regarding me. She smiled and asked me, "Sydney, what did you think about the book?"

I didn't need too much thinking to answer that. "Jane Austen has a way with romance, which is tragically sweet. All her books end with the lovers together, married and happy. In real life, it isn't all wrapped up with a bow. I think life is more like what happened to Charlotte, you settle for what you can get or for a little bit of happiness. "

"Interesting! Let's all read the book and see what everyone else thinks. Read chapters 1-5 by Friday, and be ready to talk about it."

Thankfully, the rest of the class was uneventful, but that doesn't mean that I was less tense.

After the English class, I was heading to lunch, when he pulled me into the teachers' bathroom, again.

I was nervous. "What do I have to say to get this to stop?" He didn't respond so I continued "Adrian, you don't understand. My father will make me drop that class if I don't get a new partner. Then I won't be able to graduate early." The thought of not graduating early was scarier than the actual beating and it took all of my strength not to cry.

He just smiled and said, "You can't avoid me now, Syd. You won't drop the class, and I won't stop being your partner. I'll tell my parents, and you tell yours. I'll get my dad to call yours, and let's let them work it out."

It sounded like it could work, but they didn't know my father. It didn't matter what the outcome would be. What was the worst that could happen? Beat me harder?

"Okay, but I don't think it will work." How those words left my mouth, I don't know.

He gave me a big hug, I cried out from the ferocity of it. When he realized he was hurting me, he let go and said, "Sorry!" Then, he leaned down and kissed my forehead. When his lips touched me, I jumped back like I was electrocuted.

"Don't do that!!" My heart was pounding.

He just kissed me

I knew that it was silly because it was just my forehead. T did that too. Adrian didn't like me in the same way I did. I was like a little sister to him.

< Not like a little sister. >

< *Great! Now you are trying to get me killed, again! Shut up for God's sake! I have 2 more years of this before I can even consider this possibility. Anyway, love is for other people, not me.* >

< You are loveable. >

< *Yea, sure! To whom? All the people that are supposed to love me, don't. Go away, voice!* >

I don't know how long the discussion in my head lasted but I realized that I was walking to the door to leave. I stopped because I was always the one running out the door and decided that for the first time to let him exit first. So, I turned and looked at him. Adrian walked over to me, leaned down, reached for my hand, put it to his lips, and kissed it. He then stepped back and gave me a little bow, just like he did in the ski lodge.

"You are more like Miss Elizabeth Bennet than Charlotte any day of the week," and with that, he left. I was a little flabbergasted. I didn't think he even knew who Elizabeth Bennet was.

When I got home, I went straight to my father with the teacher's number. It was a band-aid, better to rip it off. "Mrs. Arden assigned everyone a partner today. She gave me Adrian Shipman."

I didn't have time to give him the telephone number. I steeled myself as he jumped up, slapping me full in the face. My head snapped to the side, blood trickled from my nose and ringing filled my ears. My eye pulsed with the blood swelling, and hot tears rolled down my cheeks. The ringing was subsided, only to be replaced with his shouting.

"YOU ARE A GOD DAMNED WHORE! I SAID NO BOYS! AND WHAT DO YOU DO? PARTNER WITH ONE? I GUESS YOU HAVEN'T BEEN PAYING ATTENTION." This whole time he was holding me by my hair, shaking my head. He was bellowing in my face. His eyes bulged from his face, along with several blood vessels. Every word came with a little spittle. "WELL, I CAN CHANGE THAT! MAYBE MORE IS WHAT YOU NEED!"

My mother opened the side door. The first words out of her mouth were enough to make me want to scream and never stop.

"Please, stop shouting! They can hear you down the street."

Now you care.

He released my hair, shoving me down into the nearest chair. The phone started ringing.

"STOP CRYING, WHORE!" His bloodshot eyes shot me an evil glare as he picked up the phone.

"Yes, Tom. Sydney just told me about the class assignment…. You talked to her…. Well, maybe I should have her drop the class…… Yes, she would have to take it next year. I'll just get a different teacher…Oh, I didn't know she was the only one…That is true. At least he is a good boy…. That's an idea…. Let me talk to the teacher and my wife. I'll call you back later. Thank you for the call, Tom...Yes, you too."

He came so close to me, and I thought he would hit me again, but he didn't.

"Give me the teacher's number!"

I rose and held out the crumpled paper to him. He ripped it out of my hand, then pushed me back down into the chair.

Is this how men on death row feel?

They just sit in the chair waiting for that last jolt of electricity to flow through them as they cook to death. I waited for what I knew was going to come.

"Hello, Mrs. Thompson! This is Sydney's father, Edward O'Dear. Yes, she told me about the partnering. I want her with a girl. What do you mean…So you won't change her partner? Should I call the principal? ….. Well, then maybe, I should have her drop the class all together…Yes, she is a smart girl…I didn't know that she had read most of the material already…I don't want her to participate in any romantic stuff like Romeo and Juliet or other things like that. So, you don't think there will be that much contact. Can that happen at my home?.... If there is a problem, I will not shut up until I have your job. Do you understand?…As long as you and I understand each other. Yes, thank you!… You have a good evening too." He put the phone down.

I was still, in shock. He said I was smart. It was the first nice thing he'd said to me or about me in years. He spent most of the time telling me how stupid I was. That I wouldn't amount to anything. He glared over his shoulder at me and I watched his fingers work over the buttons on the avocado green phone.

"Hello, Tom! Yes, I spoke to her…No, she didn't….Sydney has read most of the books for class anyway so I guess she would just be helping your boy out like tutoring him…Well, any work that needs to be done outside school can be done at my house…yes or yours….he wants piano lessons too….. You should talk to Sydney's teacher…. Oh, well, I didn't know she was full up…She mentioned Sydney as a teacher?... Sydney is always talking about paying her fair share…. Okay, I'll tell her… Sundays after your church sounds fine….As long as one of you is there the whole time. I don't want them left alone at all….Well, let's give it a try ….Yeah, we can always call it off if it gets out of hand…Yes, thank you….Okay, I'll see you on Sunday. Bye!"

I was frozen. Had he just agreed to let me talk to a boy? Adrian, the same boy, who he beat me for talking to 3 years ago? Now I was going to teach him to play the piano!!!

Apparently, the word 'hypocrite' was not in my father's vocabulary. I snapped out of it because he was coming toward me. He leaned down, blowing his rancid breath in my face. He never smiled, his teeth just peeled back in a grimace. I tried to focus on his lips and his teeth. I already knew how he was twisting his mouth before taking a strike, so I wanted to be prepared.

"They are going to pay you $100.00 a month to teach their boy. You are only going to teach him piano and nothing else. Do you hear me? You will not teach him any of your whoring ways. Only talk about music and playing that thing."

He was raising his arm, so I flinched. His index finger jabbed in the direction of my piano. "As for the class, you are only to talk about the books and none of that romance trash. You will sit across from him, not next to him. All your money will go to pay for your upkeep at home and the lessons I have already paid for." He stopped for a second and then screamed "DO YOU UNDERSTAND?"

I raised a shaking hand. I didn't know if he was going to hit me again. "WHAT?"

I cringed back. "Um, I will need a little money to buy his books. Unless, of course, they already have them."

"I'll tell them to get them from your teacher. You don't need to fool around with that. Now, should we finish what we started?"

That was a joke, right?

My mother stood up "She needs to make dinner. Can we do it after that?"

My father whipped his head around and looked at her with disgust. "Fine, but dinner better be good, or else."

Or else, what?

I was going to get it even if that food tasted good or not.

*****

I tried to make a fabulous dinner. I laid the table out as if it was in a restaurant. Or at least what I thought a restaurant table looked like. I hadn't been to one in a long time. My father looked at it and grunted. I watched my father eat. I didn't. I couldn't. He didn't say anything when he finished. He just got up and left the room.

It was the first time I had been saved from a beating. I pulled out some frozen peas, put them on my face, and went to my room.

My mother followed me to my room and shut the door. "Your f-father is trusting you not to behave like a whore."

God, why now?

I had learned that my mother is spineless and scared of anyone smarter, bigger or more alive than her. I looked at her and said:

"Am I a whore mom? I don't even know what a whore would do. So how can I be one?"

All I received back was silence. She couldn't think for herself, so she didn't know what to say. I could see her mind running through the files of ingrained replies before she opened her mouth.

"That is not for me to say."

"But you have an opinion. Do you think I am one?"

I was aware that she just echoed my father's sentiments, but I wanted to hear her saying it.

"I don't know. Just don't be one when you are around that boy. Your f-father will not tolerate your disobedience." She always stuttered on the word father.

"Why do you let him hurt me?"

She didn't say a word back. She just turned her back on me. Either she was just as trapped as I was, or she didn't care. I didn't know which one it was. Either way, she was a waste of human flesh, and I hated her for being so spineless and pitiful. I never wanted to be like that.

"Go to bed! I'll see you in the morning." I knew she wouldn't answer me. She was a chicken shit. I wondered if he had beat her before she had us. She didn't think for herself or talk about anything but church and work. It was like she was a dead person walking around in an alive body. A zombie.

I washed my face and put the peas back on my eye. Just before bed, I put the ointment on my face. It soothed the ache but didn't cure the pain.

CHAPTER 15

SYDNEY

Looking in the mirror, my eye was puffy but not closed. It had a color that was going to be hard to explain. I walked into the kitchen and looked my mother full in the face.

"Now what do I do?"

She stopped fiddling with the toast, and without even raising her eyes to look at me she responded

"Tell them you got into a fight."

Matt countered, "You should see the other guy." Did he think this was a joke?

It isn't funny, you dumbass.

"Can't I just cover it up with makeup?" I asked.

She turned away so I couldn't see her face. "No, you can't. It's a sign of what you are," she replied.

I rolled my eyes and couldn't control myself.

"Why don't you just make me wear a red-letter A and call it good?"

Her response came as a flash of lightning. I didn't know she could move that fast, but apparently, she could. She slapped me in the same place my father had. The hit was not nearly as hard, yet it stung nonetheless. I was surprised that she even knew what that meant.

"I won't tell your father what you said. Now get ready for school!"

I wore my hair down to keep people from noticing. Most backed off when I said it was from a fight.

Trish didn't buy it but said nothing. She did offer me her makeup, but I turned her down. What was the point? It could only hide what was going on, but it didn't have the power to stop it. Nothing had that power.

My father wanted to break me and turn me into my mother, stupid and subservient, but I wasn't going to let that happen.

Keep your head down focus on class work. Those were my only thoughts every time I felt like cracking.

Everything was fine until English. I entered the classroom, and I sat in my usual spot. He wasn't there yet. The bruise was on the left side of my face, and he sat on my right. So, maybe, just maybe, he wouldn't notice. I just looked out the window. Perhaps he won't even be here today.

The way people were staring at me made me want to die. Freak was the word that came to mind. I heard him sit down, but I didn't turn to look at him. He leaned over and said, "So Teach, what did I tell you? I knew it would work out…"

I could feel he was smiling from the tone of his voice. I glanced at him only with the corner of my eye. I couldn't look at him because if I did, I couldn't stand there and lie to his face.

"Sydney?" He reached out and turned my face toward him. His words died, and his eyes grew from the sight of my face.

It took all of my will to school my face into a smile and formulate a sentence. "I got into a fight on the way home. You should see the other guy."

He attempted to touch my hand, but I snatched it away, reaching back to touch my neck. I pulled my hair back over my face. I held my head as high as I could without looking like a bitch and said as if nothing had happened,

"So, piano on Sunday after church, right? I told my teacher. She has the books you need. Feel free to go get them whenever you want. " I angled my body back towards the window.

< What an animal!! >

It is only getting worse.

Mrs. Thompson began her lecture only to falter when she saw me. "Sydney, see me after class please."

Great another do-gooder.

"Yes, mama," She went on with the lecture, but I saw her stealing looks at me. Adrian didn't attempt to speak to me again, but I felt his foot right next to mine several times.

Mrs. Thompson wasted no time, demanding to know what happened to me. "I got into a fight on the way home from school. You know, I ride the public bus."

From the look on her face, I was convinced that she wasn't buying it, but I didn't care anymore. I was tired of trying to hide what he did to me. My father was growing more brazen as time went on. She let me go, but I knew she would be watching.

Trish tried to get me to leave campus for lunch. I turned her down because I just wanted to be alone. She ran off to have lunch with one of the many boys who liked her.

I went to the end of Wrights Field to eat in peace. I sat down in the grass under the trees and stared out at the field.

This can't be all there is.

I wanted to see the world and be free. It was funny. I read books about everywhere on earth but here. I didn't read Oregon Trail books, books about the Great North West, or pioneers. I was willing to go anywhere but stay here. But where could I go, and what could I do when I got there?

Who am I kidding?

I was never going to get away from this town, or my father. I was trapped here. It was like Hotel California, you can check out, but you can never leave. My family was never going to let me have a life of my own. Turning eighteen is my only way out. Or I hoped, at least.

Adrian didn't try to talk to me for the rest of the week. I just kept putting on the ointment to help my face.

Sunday came. We went to church and then back home. This Sunday, my father started the "ritual" early rather than wait until bedtime. He gripped the back of my neck and marched me to my room before lunch.

"This is, so you understand that you are not to act like a whore during those piano lessons girl." His large hand lashed out, and the burning on the back of my shoulders began.

AGAIN! Stinging on a thigh. AGAIN! Whimpering. AGAIN! And sobbing. AGAIN!

The pain blurred into a waking dream state.

*****

Blinding Blue, Azure, Sapphire, midnight. It stretched to the horizon where it met the warm aquamarine of the ocean. Dividing the two is the island.

Wind whips hair into my face. The humidity of a tropical rain forest replaces the ocean. The entire mountain is covered with large-leaved climbing plants. The scent of flowers envelops me.

In the center is the shining White Palace. The building grows out of the side of the mountain. It dazzles my eyes, glistening in the sun. I raise my hand to shield me from the brilliance. I follow the underside of my hand down.

My gaze lands on the cloud of mist lingering at the base of the building. A torrent of water pours from it. The illusion that it's floating taunts me. I'm floating. It gives the vision a free-flowing feel.

Rings surrounded the mountain. The land is ridged with watery channels. Everything has a symmetry to it. It has balance.

The roar of the waves rocks me with its rhythm. The wind caresses my face and throws my hair around my head. I can make out the murmuring. It comes in rhythm with the waves. She is whispering to me, but it's intangible.

Say it one more time! My ears are straining to hear her.

I snap out of the vision only to find myself in the car. How did I get here?

*****

He never failed to make sure that I wouldn't be able to walk or sit, without difficulty for a few days. Pain was my reminder of the consequences of my actions, but he added just in case, "Remember only piano teaching. Nothing else, girl. You hear me?"

I turned to look him in the eye. He liked that. It made him think I was listening.

"Yes, father!"

Every step that I took to the front door was in rigid motions. I was counting, lifting each leg in turn with care. Twenty-six, there were twenty-six steps. It was a strain lifting my legs, flexing the muscles from one side to the other. Balance. I wanted to fall over, but I had to keep my balance. You never appreciate how many muscles you need to walk until you can feel every one of them throbbing with pain. A whimper escaped just before the top step.

The door opened before I got to it. Anne's fake smile died on her face, only to be replaced by shock. With her lips tightened and pinched together she said, "Come on in, Sydney! Adrian is waiting."

Somewhere between eleven and sixteen, I'd outgrown her. Now, she was tiny compared to me. I towered over her by four inches. I had never noticed what a delicate woman she was.

The crease between her eyebrows told me she wasn't too happy to see me. All of her moves faltered. She was unsure of what to do next. She hmphed as she made up her mind.

Turning, she led me into the house as if I had never been there before. All the furniture was in the same place. The room shouted at me to leave. Anne had always been warm and open, but this new Anne was cold and withdrawn. She treated me like a stranger, and that hurt. I thought maybe she would see me and realize she was wrong, or mistaken, or something. She had always been kind, til' she wasn't.

People really are simple creatures. They naturally follow the herd. All you have to do is tell them that something is true, and they believe it.

My movements were slow, robotic, deliberate. The pain on the back side of my body wasn't easy to mask. I didn't want them to see how much pain I was in. The last thing I wanted was pity.

The living room was untouched. Every piece of furniture was in the same place. Adrian sat stiffly on the couch.

The pain from the beating returned full force. "May I please, use your restroom." Anne nodded and led me to the basement door. I was baffled.

"Down the stairs to the left."

It must have been new. They didn't have a bathroom here the last time. But, that was five years ago. Many things had changed since I was last here. I went in and took an Ibuprofen. The reflection in the mirror revealed that my black eye was no different than before.

Why did I keep looking in the mirror? It was a joke. What I looked like didn't matter to anyone but me, and I wasn't allowed to do anything about it.

So why look, dummy?

I shifted my hair to hang over the bruised eye.

As I climbed the stairs, I noticed a door to a room. It was ajar, and it had a light on. All of Adrian's things that I remembered from upstairs were there. I pushed the door a little, and it revealed a clean room. Adrian had always been a tidy person. Again, I got a feeling that I didn't belong there.

Sitting in the far corner, was the rocking elephant. Seeing it, brought a small smile to my face. The overwhelming desire to jump on it for a short ride filled me. I backed out and continued to go upstairs. Adrian was already seated at the piano.

Anne still had that pinched look. "Sydney, where did you get that black eye?"

Taken aback, I was reluctant to answer. My eyes darted around the room, looking for answers to the question. It was not in my nature to lie to an adult. She already knew the answer, so I guess the lie wouldn't matter.

"I got into a fight at the bus stop by the Steel Bridge."

She looked at me funny but didn't ask what the fight was about. It was funny because no one had.

It was all just going through the motions. They asked a question to be polite, not caring what the answer actually was. Then, when they got it, they just moved on with their lives. They didn't really care how it happened or why. They all knew I was lying. The lack of authenticity in people was shocking.

One of the side effects of being ignored all the time was my ability to observe the human animal. Most humans were indeed animals. You could teach them the basics of social interaction. They didn't get the underlying message. If you didn't have anything of value to say you should refrain from speaking, mean what you say. It was all just a show.

I sat down by the piano wincing. The bench was hard without a cushion. Adrian followed all of my instructions. He was thirsty for knowledge. Sharing my love with someone was refreshing. My music had always been just that. It was mine. I had never had anyone to talk to about it. My teacher was all business and didn't stand on intimacies. We talked about music and style.

In the beginning, I had thought this was all a ploy, but he really had an aptitude for music. I gave him the assignment for the week. When we were done, I got up to leave, but he stopped me.

"Will you play for us? I want my mother to see how great you are." I didn't want to refuse, they were my clients. I knew if I lost the money from this job, my father would have made me pay one way or another, so I returned to my seat.

I rifled through my bag looking at the music before deciding on a song from Phantom of the Opera – "Wishing You Were Somehow Here Again."

I placed the book on the piano and let the notes flow from my fingers. The melody washed over my senses. I heard my own voice singing. I was transported to another place. Some place where anything was possible. Somewhere I didn't actually exist, but the music did, and my body made it exist. I leaned, tensing all my muscles before the thundering of a chord. My stomach tightened as my fingers lightly caressed the higher trilling of the melody. I wanted to fly with it, up and down, softly and deftly. It was like a mighty wind that just swept you along with its pressure rising and falling.

I could feel the cold snow from the graveyard on my face with every note as I pictured the play. My eyes burned as I ached with the music. Then the power of the music pounded, and I heard it soar along with my voice.

I wasn't just aching with the music. I became the music. I wanted the past to die. I was desperate to stop fighting the tears. I didn't wish for anyone to be here. I wished I wasn't here. I wished my world could go back, before all of the hell, to when I was small and loved. But just as all music ends with a soft finish, so did my hopes. The spell broke, and the sound reverberating from the piano faded from the room.

As I was lifting my foot off the sustain pedal, the levers inside the piano move, lowering the dampener onto the strings.

I sat for a moment, then gathered my music and myself. I mumbled a good night, bowing slightly. I didn't look at anyone. I just wanted to leave, so I picked up my bag and walked to the door. But then, I hesitated and glanced back at the room.

Adrian's blue eyes were wide with awe. Anne was frozen in a state of disbelief. They both clapped. It was the first time I had actually been applauded for a performance. There were a lot of recitals being held, but I was never allowed to perform in them.

I was in a state of some kind of shock. I don't know if I waited in silence for a few seconds or minutes, but I managed to say in a small voice.

"Thank you; I don't know how I am supposed to get home."

I don't think I finished the sentence, and Adrian was already on his feet.

"I'll drive you."

That's not going to work

"You can't. My father was very explicit"

Adrian just stood there smiling, and then turned to his mother

"Can I walk her home?"

The response didn't come from Anne, but from a deep voice from the dining room

"Yes. But don't take too long." Tom entered the room. His face was a study of composure.

As soon as I reached the bottom of the stairs, adrenaline coursed through my veins. I was practically jogging to get away from Adrian, but he caught up to me quickly. He grabbed my hand, but I yanked it back.

"I don't know what you want from me, Adrian, but whatever it is, I can't give it to you. My family has made sure that if I do anything, I will regret it." It sounded so melodramatic, but it was true.

There were eyes everywhere. They were watching me all the time. I felt like at any moment, my father could jump out of a bush and scream 'WHORE'. Or, maybe, in one of the cars driving by would be someone I know, and they would tell him. I was terrified by every person walking on the street.

I rushed in the direction of my house, but Adrian had no problem keeping up with his long legs which carried him along with ease. I didn't want to talk to him.

The road was close to a bluff, so I followed it until it reached the turn where we crossed the street. There, he reached for my arm, gripping it tightly. "Stop, stop, Sydney, stop!" He yanked me around, but I managed to shrink away from him. Tears sprang to my eyes along with sudden, unreasonable fear. I couldn't say a word, so I waited for him to speak or hit me. At that moment, I was unsure of what his intent was. But, there was only silence that filled the space around us. No words, no nothing. It was just like either of us was even breathing. I needed to leave; he had to let go of me.

"What? Adrian, do you see my face? That's what happens to me. My father didn't want me to partner with a boy. I didn't try hard enough to be with a girl. I'm a whore, and this was the lesson."

What was I supposed to do? I looked around, frightened like an animal. We were on a side street. We were still heading to my house but by the side roads. How had that happened?

"Adrian, I can't do this every time I am with you. I feel…" He stopped, dragging me with him. Then he pulled my body tight against his. His arms locked around me. My head was forced back as he bore down into my eyes. His eyes were so blue and clear. His stare was so direct and intense that I couldn't look away.

I was paralyzed until he demanded, "Are you happy with your life?"

With the sound of his voice, I woke up, and I started struggling against him to get away. But the more I struggled, the more I was rubbing my body against his, so I stopped and said: "Let go of me!"

His face was so close to mine, I felt his warm breath. "Answer the question!"

My body wanted him to kiss me, to touch me. I was ablaze. "No, I'm not happy with my life. It sucks!" He was a wall of muscle, immovable. I could have been naked standing there with heat rolling off of me against him. The pain from earlier wasn't there. I felt my chest heaving, pressing my breast against his chest. Desire rolled through me, hoping he would kiss me and hoping he would let me go. His lips were so close. If I just stretched an inch, they would be touching

What am I thinking?

I stared into his eyes, looking from one to the other, then to his full mouth. My tongue slid along my lips, wetting them. His eyes following its every move, shifting from desire to hunger. My breathing became ragged, and I could feel his heart pounding through his chest into mine.

His face changed while he was clamping down his jaw. Furrow formed between his eyes. And then he said something that I never thought I would ever hear.

"I am in love with you, and I am never going to let you go no matter what. That will never change." He stopped only to take in some air, and then continued, "You don't need to run from me. I will never hurt you." I leaned closer to him with every spoken word. As he let me go, I practically fell forward. I was breathing hard, and my whole body was like molten steel. My mouth was dry, and all I could do, was to stare at him.

"I…have to go home," stuttered out of my mouth. Without taking his eyes from me, keeping my gaze locked into his, he took my hand and kissed it. I felt the blue electricity again.

The moment he released me, I turned to do what I did best. I started running. When I got home, my father demanded to know why I was breathing so hard.

"I ran back."

He gave me a curt nod. "Bath and go to bed!"

CHAPTER 16

HERATHINA

Log entry 1,784,947.48 ATD

Nothing about Terra is what I expected it to be. Poseidon refuses to land the ship. We've spent several hundred years doing nothing but studying the planet from space. It is a big beautiful blue and green world floating in the void, swirling with white fluffy clouds. It's torturous sitting here watching other scientists take samples from the air, water, and soil. Poseidon allowed a landing party to transfer to the planet. They would be given a couple of hours to study and then return, but no interactions with Homo sapiens. Gaea and her followers never contacted us once.

Using our drone technology, I was able to watch the humans. I listened in on their conversations, learning syntax and speech patterns. I found that their way of speech came easily to me. I learned several dialects some of which carried similarities to our own. Even that grew stale. Eavesdropping on the Humans could only satisfy my thirst for knowledge for so long.

Sitting on the viewing deck, watching screens and controlling drones was not my idea of a great step forward in studying our Origins. The whole purpose of Alethea was to understand the development of the mind and evolution. Homo sapiens genome was so close to ours. It was almost as if we seeded this world. For all we knew this world could have been seeded by our own people before the Great Division.

We were never going to gain anything by sitting on this ship, floating in space and looking at air samples.

The proximity to the planet, along with my ability to pick up the emotions of the Homo sapiens, made every day a challenge. I feel what they feel. Anger, confusion, love. It was washing over me like a giant wave, bringing me up, then pushing me down. I found more and more, and I had to block myself off from everyone just so I didn't pick up these human emotions. In some days, it was too much, and it flowed through me. I could measure the difference in my shipmates. They felt what I was feeling.

On those days, many of my fellows became amorous towards myself or others. Sometimes you would see them openly in the corridors fondling one another. Other days it was not so docile. Rage and anger caused many battles to break out. Every so often, someone would be hurt to the point of death. They were submerged into the infinitum pool and revived, but we did lose a few.

I believed Poseidon might contact the High Council for instructions, but he never did.

"There's to be a Council meeting, and all are to attend. I think Poseidon will make the announcement, and we'll choose our landing place. I cannot wait. There are different conflicts around the planet that I would like to witness. If we land, I'm sure he will allow some of us to go off on our own," Athena said, but I was not as convinced as she was. Every time Poseidon announced one of these Council meetings, it was usually to give us an excuse as to why we shouldn't land now.

As one of the few dream-walkers on the ship, I was beginning to believe it might be my duty to inform the High

Council of Poseidon's inaction. My oath was the only thing holding me back.

Dreamwalking between non-mates is challenging and sometimes dangerous, and not everyone can accomplish it. I have a natural ability. It came to me easily as a child. I don't just dream walk I can give others visions and manipulate minds. When I first discovered this, it scared me. To have such power to alter someone's very thoughts was not something to play with.

My oath not to dreamwalk to the High Council was one thing. I didn't swear not to dreamwalk anyone ever again. I had to convince Poseidon to land with a dream-walk. The latter rather than the former was the wisest choice. I've no desire to embarrass my father's friend and our great hero. Poseidon's threat still rang in my mind.

I am getting stronger. I can keep him out more now. Every Themian grows stronger with age. I am finding that time is not part of my growth factor. I am not sure what is causing my growth. But my growth is exponential.

"We shall see, Athena. Perhaps the Ancient One is satisfied that the planet is safe for us now."

She smiled in her quiet, controlled way, linking her arm with mine as we strode to the Citadel together where she headed off to the council chamber.

Tens of thousands of members of the project had gathered. Most had taken seats on the benches that lined the walls. There was a loud murmuring reverberating around the giant room. The council filed in and took their seats, and a hush fell over the crowd. I could feel the mental leaning in of all participants in order to hear the answers to their multitude of questions. Only one question rose above the din, 'When do we land?'

After all council members were seated, Poseidon rose. In his loud and commanding voice, he boomed fourth "Tomorrow, we should take Alethea and descend through the cloud layer to land. There's a rectangular shaped land formation. It's adjacent to many continents. Most of the intelligent Homo sapiens have created settlements near there. We will land on the water and disguise ourselves using Obscure-a. Several groups will be allowed to leave the ship and begin exploring."

The chamber erupted with a roar. Many stood up and clapped their hands together. I heard crying! Crying! Themians don't cry. The joy and relief in the chamber filled me. I turned my head to survey the crowd. Themians don't feel.

Why are they crying out with …Happiness?

CHAPTER 17

SYDNEY

Monday dawned, and there were butterflies in my tummy. I hadn't looked forward to a Monday so much in my entire life. My classes couldn't finish fast enough to get me to English. I walked in, and he wasn't there. I sat and waited.

God, let him come!

He came and sat down. A giant smile was painted all across my face. I suddenly felt stupid and turned to the front of the class.

< Happy looks good on you >

< Shut up! How would you even know? It's not like you've ever seen me happy. I just want to pretend for a little while that this can be. And that he likes me. >

< Didn't say like you, he said LOVE. >

< Okay, he loves me. Now, shut it! >

He was smiling back. The class went on as usual with homework and a lecture.

Suddenly my life wasn't just a dull repeating wash cycle. Every day, I would rise filled with joy at the idea of seeing him. Teaching him on Sundays and walking home together. This happened unless it was raining because my dad came to get me on rainy days. I think I actually started to hate rain.

I had always been a rather quiet kid. Now, I had even less to say, but with him, I had a voice. We talked about books, art, music, the future. He wanted to become an architect or engineer. I had no idea what I wanted to become, or if I was allowed to become anything. I couldn't think beyond the moment. The moment when he touched me the first time, he touched my soul too, and he had become my world. I knew that it sounded cheesy, but I could almost feel what he was feeling, or at least I thought so.

November came with all the holidays, but I was not looking forward to the Christmas break. Two weeks at home alone with my family was like having a root canal without all the pain killers. My father would find some household job that sucked that needed to be done.

We did a spring cleaning of the kitchen in December. I watched as he pulled everything out of every shelf, drawer, and cupboard. He heaped it on every surface. The chaos covered every counter, table, chair, appliance. Everything had to be wiped out or scrubbed. Then you had to scrape or pull up all the old contact paper and put down new. Every dish had to be washed fresh and put back in order. Next, was the refrigerator and then, the freezer. My family had to be fed and cared for throughout the process. It took me almost a week to complete the kitchen. The fridge and freezer another two days.

I should have taken more time to finish. "Idle hands and idle minds make for the devil's work. I want you to clean the windows inside and out with screens. That should keep you out of trouble til' school starts again. Oh, and pack more wood in. I don't want to run out of firewood in the house." His words were filled with hate.

It was December and freezing outside, so of course, it was an excellent time to clean the screens and windows. He was the biggest asshole in the world. 'Oh, and just to be sure pack wood'. In all the books I read, packing wood was a man's work, or the work of servants. But I guess that was me. Actually, the servants got paid. I was a slave.

I didn't see Adrian. His family had gone on a holiday. I didn't even have the lessons to break up the monotony. Life settled back into the dull drums as if he had never spoken to me.

The voice tried to converse with me several times. I could feel it watching, listening like a creepy stalker.

Time seemed to be flying faster that year than it had before. Before I knew it, February had arrived. Everyone was talking about Valentine's Day and Junior Prom. I wouldn't be allowed to participate. Being happy was better than attending any dance.

When Valentine's Day dawned, it was fun to see all the boys trying to kiss the girls. English rolled around, and Adrian winked at me. I smiled like a fool. The bell rang, and as I got up to leave, he placed a note in my hand. I didn't want to read it there. I wanted to have some intimacy, so I kept it safe in my hand as I headed for my locker. Trish was lurking. She snatched the letter out of my hand. She read it, smiled and handed it back. It had happened so fast, I didn't even realize but now she was laughing.

"If you don't kiss that boy, I will!"

No, she wouldn't. He wasn't her type. Also, friends don't kiss a friend's squeeze.

I was almost certainly sure that I was blushing, but I played the stupid card, "Why would I kiss him?"

I want to kiss him.

"Because you are smiling, and you are happy, silly. I've never seen you this way. Syd, you deserve to be happy, you know? It's okay, you're allowed"

< You do, and you should get that kiss. >

< I can't kiss any boy. I have one year and four months to get through before I can do anything. Please shut up and leave me alone! >

"Trish, you know I can't do that, but I am happy." She winked at me in her knowing fashion, pinching her lips and making kissy noises.

I read the note

Dear O'Dear,

I just wanted to tell you how dazzling you look today. Meet me for lunch under our tree.

AS

I don't know how many times, I'd read the note, but when I looked up, I was surprised to see that I had walked out on to the Wrights Field. How is it that the human body automatically follows the heart even when the mind doesn't want it?

Now was as good a time as any. I stilled my mind and closed my eyes. I let the sounds of the school fill my mind, searching through each individual noise to find the out of place one. I had to double check. I didn't want to be caught. I didn't even know if this would work.

Being with Adrian caused me to throw caution to the wind. I had become careless. I didn't hear anyone close by, so for the moment it was safe. I took a deep breath, and I kept going.

Adrian stood up as I got closer. "Our picnic awaits you." His smile was breathtaking.

I looked at him and smiled back. Then, my eyes started to survey the scene. He had put down a red and white checkered blanket.

That's a little overdone.

The wicker basket had small finger sandwiches, mixed fruit with grapes, a few soft kinds of cheese, a loaf of sliced rustic crusty bread and glistening bottles of water.

My astonishment reined. I hadn't been on a picnic in so long. My family of loving jailers didn't do things like that.

"You did all this for me?" I asked a little overwhelmed.

His smile broadened, and he gently took my hand inviting me to sit. "Why wouldn't I? Actions speak louder than words, Sydney. So, let my actions speak for me." His eyes held a longing for acceptance. I couldn't turn away from it. "I was hoping that this would be special, just like you."

When my eyes met his, I could see myself. I looked timid and aloof. My smile flashed across my face. His eyes roamed over my body.

Woo back off there, hot dog.

But, his rush of desire and joy was infectious, heat filled my face. All the feelings running through me were a big jumble. He didn't just desire me, he ached for me. It mirrored a place deep inside of me. As if he felt the same way I did and flashed it back at me. The blue electricity bloomed. I had to pull back from it. That way lead to danger. He didn't know what I could do.

Words didn't come out of either of us. We sat, looked at each other and ate in silence. He took out his Walkman and put the headphones on me. The aria from an opera filled my ears. 'O Mio Babbino Caro' by Kiri Te Kanawa. It was the most beautiful song I had ever heard. I felt the tears form in my eyes as her voice soared. My throat tightened, staring at Adrian while he held my hand with his eyes boring into mine. The blue threatened to return with every note of the song. We sat in a bubble of music and magic, but then, the song ended.

"I know that I can't give you anything that you can take home, so I give you this song. Every time you hear it, I want you to think of me and this day."

< Kiss, kiss, kiss >

I don't know if it was the voice in my head or if it was an impulse of my heart, but I leaned over, closed my eyes, and slowly touched my lips to his. They were soft and warm. It was quick. He touched my face and leaned forward smiling. I would have probably stayed there hypnotized forever if the voice didn't ring in my head like a bull horn.

< YES >

< *Shut up!* >

"Thank you...I don't know what came over me. I didn't mean to... I..."

His hands were still on my face when I got up to leave. He caught my arm, stopping me in mid-motion.

"You remind me of Lucy Honeychurch. She ran away from her heart too"

I stopped and looked at him, "Who?"

"A Room with a View. It's a movie. I think you'd like it," he smirked

"Is there a book?" I smiled back.

"There is. It's by E. M. Forster."

< Do it again, beautiful girl. >

< *Shut up you!* >

I wanted to kiss him again so badly, but I couldn't. I was too afraid. That is why I insisted that we leave separately. I didn't want us to be seen together. I couldn't hear anyone, but I wasn't sure how reliable my scans really were. I felt terrible about it. Just thinking about Adrian made my stomach flip. Thinking of my father brought a petrifying fear. In the warring of the two feelings, fear always won. Adrian's love couldn't protect me behind the closed doors of my father's house.

*****

Spring break came and with it so did a week with my loving family of jailers. I wondered what chores my father would dig up this year.

I had a babysitting job every night that week. At least I would be able to escape them for a few hours every day. When it came time to be paid on Friday, the first night of spring break, they gave me double the usual pay. "I really appreciate you not going out on a date or running off to the beach. Staying to watch my kids couldn't have been high on your list of things to do over spring break."

"I'm not allowed to date, Mrs. Hansen." I tried not to look her in the eyes.

She winked at me. "Next time, you can use the phone to call that person you aren't dating."

I didn't know how to respond, so I just smiled and said, "Thank you".

I grabbed my purse, but instead of putting all the money in my wallet, I only put half in. The rest I put in my change purse. I don't know why I did it or why I didn't think of it before. A stash. I should have been doing that all along.

My parents didn't know how much I was paid. Everyone paid me a little differently. I always handed everything over. But I could give up the smallest amount, and they would never know.

That was my "eureka" moment. I had been taking personal finance that semester. We had just finished all the banking and life insurance stuff. Mr. Grayson was going over about owning your own business and running it along with bookkeeping. I had been thinking about this babysitting thing all wrong. It was a business, and I should be treating it like one.

When I got home, I wrote out all of the hours that I was supposed to work that week. There were like six nights. The average sitting time was 3-4 hours and I usually got about 20-25 per job. That meant that if I only gave my parents 20 and kept anything over that for myself, I could save money for my big move out.

Mrs. Hansen had given me 45, 20 went to mom, and I kept 25. That was a good start. I just didn't know where I was going to hide it.

I turned around in my room, but there weren't many choices. My eyes kept going back to my vanity. I found a cardboard box in the house about the right size for my vanity drawers. I waited until everyone had gone to bed and then, I pulled all the drawers out of my vanity. I turned them over and traced the size on to cardboard. I cut every one out neatly. I covered them in contact paper and put them at the bottom of the drawers, with the money underneath.

At first glance, the drawers looked normal. My mother lined everything in contact paper, so it wasn't out of order for it to be in my drawers. I added a piece of paper to the bottom of the cardboard creating a pocket to slide the money into it, just in case anyone lifted the liner. This way they wouldn't see anything. I just couldn't risk him finding my money and taking it from me.

That Sunday, for the first time, when my father came to keep me from being a whore, it didn't hurt as much. I was on my way out. This wasn't going to last too much longer. There was a light at the end of the tunnel. It was small, but it was there. I could make it. Saving money meant that I could leave this house the moment I turned eighteen.

I had fifty-eight weeks left until I turned eighteen and finished school. 58 divided by 2 equals 27. That was how many beatings I had to look forward to. Of course, if I didn't screw up along the way. It was a sick countdown to freedom, but it was one that I was happy to keep track of.

I walked to Adrian's house. I was sore, but it was a faint throbbing in the background. Anne opened the door. I smiled at her, but she didn't smile back. She took me inside, and I found Adrian at the piano.

He was always so reserved on Sundays. Not withdrawn, but sullen maybe. He seemed stiff too. I made a note in my mind to ask him about that.

Maybe he was embarrassed in front of his family. They wouldn't approve of me. It doesn't matter. They didn't know and probably never will. He said he loved me, but this was his last year of high-school. People change after they leave school.

I know T did. He never came to see me anymore. He moved out and didn't come home, not that I could blame him for that. I was not allowed to use the phone, so it's not like I could call him either.

I sat down and gave Adrian his lesson. When we were done, I got up to leave.

He stood up too. "I'll walk you home."

"No, let her walk herself." Anne had no love for me, not anymore. I didn't blame her either. If I had a son, I wouldn't want him to run around with a girl from a crazy family like mine.

I was just about to walk out the door when Tom came out, "No. Adrian will walk her. She should not be walking home alone in the dark, Anne!"

I could hear her dig into Tom, yelling about how unsuitable an associate I was. How he should drive me home himself. "I don't understand why Adrian even wants to learn the piano. I don't think he has the talent for it."

I'm glad Adrian doesn't have superhuman hearing. Listening to all the crap my father says about me is hard to take. I don't know if he could handle it.

"Anne, we have been over this. Music helps with spotting patterns and math. Adrian wants to become an engineer, and he needs that edge in order to succeed." The further away from the house, we got, the less I heard. After we were over a block away, I couldn't listen to it anymore.

"I finally figured out how to save money to get out of my parents' house!"

Instead of responding, he bumped his shoulder into me without removing his hands from his pocket. It threw me off balance but didn't knock me down. He first gave me a 'badass' look before talking.

"Really, how are you doing that?" he seemed amused, not surprised.

"I'm not turning all my babysitting money over to them. I've got it hidden."

"They take all your money?" disgust filled his voice.

I didn't turn to look at him. I didn't want to see it as well.

"So, all this time my parents have been paying your parents and not you?" he rounded on me. His mouth set in a grim line, and his eyes were blazing with indignation.

I was confused so I sputtered "Yes…I thought you knew that."

"They just want to keep you like…like a slave."

I thought about it too, but my automatic response was "I'm not a slave, slavery is illegal." I stopped in my tracks, cemented in place. Who was I kidding? Yes, I was a slave.

I was not allowed to get a job or my driver license or save any money. They took everything and told me it was to pay for my upkeep.

"It's true, you're right. I am their slave. I cook and clean only to be beaten whether I do a good job or not. They don't talk to me. They just give me orders."

The idea whirled around in my head. I have been trying to figure out how I was going to get away from them when I turned eighteen year's old. His hands were on my shoulders as he bore down at my face.

"I have some money. I can help you." He blurted it out.

"NO, I mean. I just don't want to get anyone involved. I just wish I could get a bank account so I can save my money there instead of hiding it in my bedroom."

I was talking really fast, and he was just calm.

"Why? Do they go into your room?"

To spy, why do you think?

"Yes, they do. All of them. They take whatever they want…" I continued with more confidence, "That's what I'll do tomorrow. I'll go to the bank, and see what I need to open an account. That's a fabulous idea. Thank you!" I kissed him on the cheek without thinking of what I was doing.

He put his arms around me and held on to me. I was looking into his eyes and at his lips at the same time. I didn't think it was possible to do so, but that was what I was doing. My heart was pounding through my chest. I was sure he could feel it.

My body had just gone from zero to on fire in like 1.2 seconds. I felt his hand drift down below my waist as he leaned in and kissed me back. But he didn't do it on the cheek. He pressed his lips into mine in a very demanding way. I didn't know what to do, but it appeared that my body did because my mouth opened inviting his tongue in. My body was pressed up against his body. He broke the kiss and moved down to my neck. As he did that, I felt a million volts of electric shock run throughout my being and a moan escaped my lips. His lips moved back to my mine. He was hungry and finally managed to eat. I was in a trance. His kiss was what kept me alive because I didn't need air anymore. I realized that my hand was on his face only when he let go of my lips and turned to kiss it. I opened my eyes just to look at him, and the words came out without my brain having anything to say about it.

"I love you!"

I don't know if he waited for me to finish the sentence before he crashed his lips back into mine. I pulled back and took a breath but didn't let go. He kept kissing my neck.

< More, please more. >

< Oh, God, yes! >

Logic kicked in.

"Adrian, I have to get home… oh God, I… wished you didn't…but..." I wanted him not to stop, and the voice in my head did too. He stopped and looked in my eyes, and then at my lips.

"I love you, Sydney! I don't want to let you go."

I smiled and got some control so I could let go of him "Don't worry, I'll see you tomorrow."

< You bet! I'll see you tomorrow? >

< Oh, God! What I am I going to do now that I told him I loved him. >

<Yes, you did. Did you mean it? >

< Yes, I did, but it's not like we can be together. Oh, there's no school tomorrow...fuck I can't see him. >

< Call him from your babysitting job!!!! >

< But what if he doesn't answer? >

< Nothing ventured, nothing gained, right? >

I didn't answer back. I ran the rest of the way home. It was the only way to explain why I was breathing hard and flushed. Father took one look at me.

"You're grimy and smell. Go bathe! Next time you go anywhere, I want you clean. You make me look bad when you're filthy."

What an ass. 'I make him look bad'?

Because I'm only here to make you look good? Go piss on someone else's parade.

The next day after my parents went to work, the boys went to a friend's house. There was a knock at the door. It was Adrian. I smiled to myself and opened the door.

"Adrian, you can't be here!" My head swung left and right checking for informers.

"Is anyone else, home?"

"No, but the boys could come back at any time!" Oh God! I did another quick hearing scan. It was clean for now.

< Come in, come in. They won't be back for hours. Trust me!! >

< *You say that now, but if they come back will you take my beating for me????? >*

< Yes, always. >

< *What if the boys come back??? >*

< Listen to me I know exactly where your brothers are, and they won't be back for three hours. Long enough to do whatever you want. I'll tell you if anything changes. >

< *I don't believe you! >*

As I argued with the voice from my head, Adrian just stood there. I only realized that when he asked me, "Can I come in?"

< Let him in. I'll prove it. The phone will ring in two minutes. It will be your mother wanting to know about dinner. >

< *Okay. If you are right, we will have a long talk after.* >

< Yes. >

"Come on in, but you can't stay long," he ducked his head and entered.

The phone did ring. I put my finger to my lips as I picked it up. "Hello! Oh, hi mom… oh no I hadn't picked anything yet…. okay that sounds good I'll do that... okay bye." I hung the phone up.

< I told you!!!! Now you have three hours to have fun. >

< *Thank you.* >

Adrian and I talked and laughed for about two hours. It wasn't until he was ready to leave that he kissed me.

This time it was slow and tender and not devouring as it was the other night. My arms went around him, and he pulled my body closer. I felt him pressing against me. He teased my mouth open and tasted me. I didn't know when it happened, but his hand was holding one of my breasts. I didn't oppose his touch. I leaned into his hand while my whole body was humming. I moaned as he was kissing my neck. He opened my shirt a couple of buttons and kissed a trail to my collarbone.

Oh my God!

I was wet, hot and aching. He pulled back, but I pulled him back to my lips. He began to extract himself again. I moved my mouth to his neck. I wanted to taste and nibble him.

He groaned, "Sydney, I love you!" He locked his mouth again into mine. We moved together in our love dance. Our hands were exploring, squeezing, and pressing. He released me, then gave me a quick kiss on the lips while stepping back. He was still touching my face. I didn't want him to stop, but I knew he had to leave, and he had to do it soon. I needed to calm down, and so did he. I could see how much he wanted me. His eyes beamed with blue desire.

"Can I use the restroom? I need a moment." He sounded strained and impatient.

"Yes. It's down the hall, first door on the left."

< Are you out there? >

< Yes, beautiful girl. >

< *How long do we have left?* >

< Forty minutes. >

< *God, I want him! But not like this, I want it to be special.* >

< Don't worry. It will be special. >

< *Okay, I can wait for that.* >

Adrian came back and patted my face again. "I love you, Sydney! Call me from your babysitting job if you can. I'll make sure I get the phone."

He leaned down, and I closed my eyes, leaning into him. I saw blue. He laid his lips lightly on mine. It was over too quickly.

"You should go before we can't stop."

"You'll call me?" He asked

"Yes." I muttered.

He left, and I went to my room. For the first time in my life, I was horny. I wanted to have sex with Adrian. I wanted desperately to make love to him, but I settled for a cold shower. I was as good as I was going to get for at least a year.

< Are you so sure? It could happen. >

< *As long as I live with my family? I'm lucky that happened, and my father doesn't know. So, how did you know about the phone call and the time of the boys' return?* >

< I can hear people's thoughts. >

< *Holy shit! No way I'm talking to myself and I have delusions of grandeur.* >

< No delusions. You are special and different. >

< *Well, can you help me get out of this house, or save enough money to get out?* >

< Yes, sort of. If you want a bank account, you need the signature of someone over eighteen. >

< *I turn seventeen in two weeks on the 22nd. I'm sure my father will give me his special present. Can you help me with that?* >

< Maybe. I can try, I'll keep you posted. >

It was time to cook for my loving family of jailers.

*****

I did call Adrian every night from one of my babysitting jobs. I managed to save one hundred dollars. Also, one of my jobs wanted me to come regularly on Saturday nights from 6:00 PM – 12:00 AM for a month. My father approved it for me as long as I got a ride home.

She said she would pay me eighty dollars every Saturday. I told dad fifty. That meant thirty extra a week for me. It didn't sound like much, but even if I could save enough to get a car, I could live in that. Anything was better than living here.

A couple of girls from school found out that I could sew and asked me to alter their prom dresses, and I made two hundred more dollars for the getaway fund. By the end of April, I had almost five hundred dollars saved.

I didn't have to ask Adrian to sign for the checking account. My Grandmother on my mom's side came to visit and asked what I wanted for my birthday. When I told her, she smiled and took me right to the bank. Got me all signed up for a savings account, kissed me and said, "It will all be over soon, dear."

I felt better with my money out of the house.

My grandmother called me a couple of days later and told me to look into my account when I got a chance for her gift. I did, and she had deposited two thousand dollars into the account. I got a card that said 'For your future. A girl should always have enough money to do what she wants.'

Adrian and I stole a few moments here and there at school and after lessons on Sundays but nothing more. I just couldn't risk getting caught even with an all-knowing voice in my head.

CHAPTER 18

SYDNEY

Finally, I looked around, and we were four weeks away from summer break and the strawberry picking season again. I was all ready to go and toil in the dirt when my father announced that I wouldn't be going that year. There was an elderly woman from the church who needed help moving, and I was going to help her. Without pay, I might add. I know that it sounds like all I could think about was money, but it was the only way I was ever going to get away from my father. So, yea, I thought about it a lot.

A week before school got out, Adrian walked me home from our lessons. He looked like he had something to say, but he needed strength to do it. Then it all came pouring out.

"Sydney, my parents gave me a graduation present…. I always told them I would do missionary work for the church, and they are sending me to Costa Rica and parts of Nicaragua. I leave in a week."

I was stunned, so the only words that came to my mind were, "How long will you be gone?"

"Usually it's for a year, but I got a scholarship to PSU. So, I would be back by school time. Look, I promised to do this four years ago, so I can't go back on my word." It all came out in a rush from him. I could see he was terrified about what I would say.

"No, you shouldn't go back on your word, you should go. It's not like I would see you over the summer anyway. You can write to me if you want to."

"I will return on September 5th, and maybe after I get back, we could…will you m..m…marry, me?"

My head snapped up, and I couldn't believe my ears. "What did you just say?" I squinted up at him through my eyebrows.

< Marry. He asked you to marry him. >

"Marry me! Make me the luckiest man alive. I'll take you away from all this and love you. We can be happy. We can make a real family. I love you. I think you are perfect."

Yes, yes! I wanted that so much I didn't know how or even if it was possible to work out, but I wanted it with all my heart. "Yes, yes, yes, I'll marry you!"

< Yesssss. >

He grabbed me and kissed me. I don't know for how long. All I knew was that I didn't want it to end. He finally pulled away.

"I know that you have to go home, but I didn't want you to think that I hadn't done this right." He got on one knee and pulled out a ring sliding it on my finger.

It was a large square diamond. "Where did you get this? It is so beautiful." It shot stars at me in a rainbow of colors.

"It was my grandmother's; she gave it to me for you. Will you wait for me?"

"Yes, of course, I will. Until the ends of the Earth, I'll wait for you." I threw myself at him wrapping my arms around his neck and planting my lips over his.

"Now listen, I am going to write to you under the name Alice Silver, AS. When I get back home, we will go to the Justice of the Peace and get married. Okay?"

"Yes, yes! I'll find a way to hide my ring until then." He kissed me again.

Adrian had thought of everything. He planned it out, then executed it. I didn't know if it was possible to die of happiness, but that was exactly how I felt.

The summer suddenly didn't look so bad. Next day, I told Trish and showed her the ring. She was about to fall over.

"Sydney this is a five-carat princess cut diamond. Probably worth a ton of money. He gave it to you? Wow, he must really love you. I wish I had a guy who loved me like that." She held my hand up, turning it this way and that. Her eyes shined with wonder.

"I don't care what the ring is worth. He's the real prize; I'm the happiest girl alive. I could just float away. Three months, and I will be married to the most wonderful man on Earth."

*****

That week went by fast, and I didn't get to talk to Adrian again before he left. But, I did get my first letter in the mail. I told my parents that she was a friend from school and was on her way to missionary work in Central America. They seemed pleased that my friend was a missionary.

The first day of summer dawned, and I was given the address to the elder lady's home. Matt drove me. He had his driver's license, I could never have one, but he could.

My father, the sexist prick.

I got out of the car and looked at the house. It was huge…it would take all summer to pack this up. The house sat on a quadruple lot. In the city that was unheard of. It was surrounded by gardens. I couldn't imagine why anyone would want to sell this lovely home.

< Don't worry. I don't think you will do much packing. >

< Right. Cause you are the all-knowing voice in my head. That is going to save me, right? >

< No, I can't save you. Only you can save you. >

< Well, I don't need you to save me. I have Adrian, and we are going to save each other. >

< Don't make me jealous of Adrian. >

< *Your emotions are your problems, not mine. Touché*! >

I walked up to the long walkway to the large front door. Matt waited at the curb, watching my every step. The woman who opened the door was a perfect lady in every way. She had a charming smile, perfect hair, clothes, makeup, and manners. I smiled back at her and wished that I had dressed better.

"Good morning, you must be Sydney. Come in and sit down, we have so much to talk about."

We do?

"Good morning, thank you! I'm sorry, but my father didn't tell me your name. What do you want me to call you?"

"Grace, my name is Grace Shipman."

Oh my God! It is Adrian's grandmother.

< You aren't here to move stuff, beautiful girl. >

It was very hard to acknowledge what had just happened, so it took me a few minutes before answering, "It is very nice to meet you."

"I have met you before, but you were very small." I felt the ring, in my bra, the rock cutting into my tender flesh.

< She doesn't know anything. >

< Okay, thank you! >

I couldn't say anything, so she just continued to talk.

"My grandson usually does little jobs for me, but he is away right now." I smiled and nodded my head.

It turned out that she really didn't want to move but chat. Every now and again, she would have me move things, but it was just from one room to another. One day she asked me to drive her to the store. When I told her I couldn't drive, she was shocked.

"Well, I need someone who can drive!"

"My brother can drive if we need him to."

"No. The only boy I let drive me is my grandson. I'll talk to your father."

I figured he would say no. She was wasting her time, but I didn't tell her that.

< He'll say yes, beautiful girl. >

< I am engaged, so you can't talk to me like that anymore. I'm not your beautiful girl. >

< It's not like he will know. >

< I don't care. I know, and I don't like it. I am going to be someone's wife; it's not right.>

I figured she would find someone else to help her, but she didn't. My father told me that I was to go with her and get my permit. The next day she began to teach me to drive.

She owned a 1951 Mercedes Benz. It was a stick shift. To start it, you had to turn the key and hold it till the solenoid glowed. Only then, could you turn it over. I didn't think I was perfect. The clutch was very touchy, and I killed the car over and over again. We jerked back and forth every time I popped the clutch to shift gears. She made me work on it every day, in the morning. In the afternoon we collaborated in the garden.

A month went by, and she asked me to drive her to her son's house. Adrian's dad, Tom, was home.

The house had a sold sign in the yard. We went inside, and there were boxes everywhere. I told her I could wait outside, but she asked me to sit in the living room. She went into Tom's office. Being able to overhear everything sucks sometimes.

She asked when the house was sold and why.

"It was sold two days ago."

My mouth went dry.

"Why did you sell it? You never even told me you were thinking of selling. Where will you live now?"

"Because Anne wants to get Adrian away from some girl." Fear took hold of my body. If they know about me, they'll tell my father.

Calm down, he didn't say my name. You're reading too much into it.

I took deep breaths, in and out, but the clenching in my belly would not loosen up.

"We're going to put everything into storage and join Adrian in Costa Rica. He's signed up for a year, and Anne wants him to complete it. Maybe it will be enough time to get him over the infatuation with this girl. He can go to college a year later."

I didn't know what to say. My mouth had gone dry, and my eyes were burning. I couldn't breathe anymore, so I got up to leave the room.

"You have no right to control his life like that. Do you know that girl out there in your living room?"

"Yes!"

"Did you know that her parents won't let her get a job, or go anywhere alone or even a driver's license? I pay for her time but to her father, not her. He said she can't be trusted with money. I bet she doesn't even have a bank account. Do you think she is prepared for the real world? She is a lovely beautiful girl whose family is crippling her. She doesn't even talk that much. She dresses like an old bag lady. She will never amount to anything, they won't let her. Don't do that to Adrian, please! He's eighteen, so let him make a few of his own mistakes."

"He gave some girl the ring. We don't know who, he wouldn't tell us."

I froze. They were talking about me, but they didn't know it. Oh, thank God. I wanted to leave. I got up to walk outside but the door squeaked as I opened it. I heard a sound but ran to the car.

I got in the driver's seat and sat there. My eyes were burning while I waited. When I saw Grace coming, I wiped my face and tried to look normal. She got into the car and asked me to take her home.

"I think we should be done for the day."

As I was walking out the door, she asked, "How much did you hear?"

"I didn't hear anything. I don't eavesdrop." I moved to continue out the door ... "I didn't mean to hurt your feelings, I know you heard me." I could have turned around to face her, but I didn't want her to see how much her words had hurt me.

"It is okay Grace, I've had worse said about me. At least what you said was true." I left, and I didn't turn back. I walked to the bus stop and took it home. I was hoping the voice would have something to say, but it was quiet. So, I just went home and cried. They wanted to keep him away from me. A year, that's how long they're going to stay away.

I was lonely, but Adrian kept sending his letters. He said he would be back, reassuring me that we would be together. Nothing would stop him from coming home to me.

The summer went by quickly, and I got my schedule for school in the mail.

On the second of September, I went to bed early.

*****

The dream began

Azure, the unbelievable blue of a tropical sky. It reached out to meet the aquamarine blue of the warm ocean. Waves were rising and falling, merging together, forming more massive waves. All of them divided by a perfect island. Birds calling to one another, Parrots were flying from one tree to the next. The mountain was lush and full of life.

A shining white palace jutting from the side of the mountain with the waterfall out of its base. Mist wet my face. I licked my lips to taste the jungle water. It had a clear earthy flavor.

The wind began to pick up. I tensed. I had to be ready for when she was going to speak. I had to hear her this time. I cupped my hands around my ears, hoping to direct the sound better. The roar of the mumbling rose, blasting my hair back from my face, but her voice never came.

Pain.

I was in the water, and my heart was pounding. I couldn't move my legs. I was terrified. The water was bone-chilling cold and everywhere. I couldn't see any land. I was desperately holding on to some wood that was helping me stay afloat. My arms had cuts all over them, but they weren't my arms…they looked hairy and large like a man's arms. I was in excruciating pain, everywhere. I felt broken and lost. I woke up screaming in pain.

My mother was there. She slapped me. "Shut up! You want to wake up the whole house? You, stupid girl!" I was turning my head left and right, searching for my location. My heart was still pounding, and I was enveloped with the feeling of terror. I kept looking around. I tried to grab my mother and hold her, but she pushed me off.

The vision cleared, and I shook my head in an attempt to regain my composure.

"I'm… Um… sorry. I had a nightmare….I'm sorry, I'll be quiet." She just gave me a disgusted look and left. The voice was screaming in my mind, my head was pounding. The terror was still there.

<   PPPPAAAAIIIIIINNNNNN!!!!!! HHHHHEEEELLLLPPP MMMEEE. >

< Voice are you okay? What is wrong? >

But for the first time, the voice never replied.

Over and over it wailed. I couldn't sleep. I just laid there rocking, holding my head and feeling every kind of pain and horror. When the sun came up, I went to school, but the screaming never stopped. I couldn't concentrate on any of the instructions. I threw up in the bathroom just before lunch. I took several pain pills, but nothing dulled the deep throbbing in my body.

The day dragged on and on. There would be no salvation in sleep, either. It was just a mix of drowning and deep bone grinding pain with the screaming in my mind.

The next few days were just more of the same. Both the screaming in my mind and the aching pain in my body from the waist down were present. I was chilled to the bone. My skin felt tight and hurt. I woke up Friday morning to discover sunburns and blisters all over my arms. My lips chapped to the point of cracking and bleeding.

Sunday came. I told my mother I wasn't feeling well

"Can I please stay home?"

She sneered at me, "No."

So, I sat in that church listening to the moaning and wailing in my mind looking straight ahead, wishing that it was over. I felt every heartbeat thumping through my body. My eyes were scratchy and dry from lack of sleep.

At the end there were announcements, but I wasn't actually listening

"Lastly, I have some very sad news. There was an earthquake, followed by a tsunami in Nicaragua and Costa Rica on September 2nd. As many of you may know, the Shipman family had gone there for missionary work. They were all killed in the tsunami. There will be a memorial held for them this Saturday at 2 PM for anyone who would like to attend."

CHAPTER 19

HERATHINA

Log entry - trying to decide if I still want to use Themian time stamps.

The humans were the most fascinating creatures I have ever encountered. Every one of them was a unique specimen. The differences between males and females were small and vast, amazing. They were entirely different in physiology and yet the same. They emotionally needed different things for happiness. Yet somehow, they managed to find someone the opposite of themselves and mate nonetheless. They reproduced at a rapid pace. However, due to the level of science available to them, many died.

The diseases they succumb to are easily cured. The High Council's directive was light interaction. Saving a life with primordium would taint the project.

I tried to keep my emotions in check around them. It was difficult with all the bleed over. There were a few that could touch me, mentally. It was a light brushing of the minds. The feeling was that of an infant in the womb. It was amazing. I have no doubt that at some point in the future they will achieve our level. I only hope we can survive to meet them.

Log entry

A delegation of humans has arrived. They disembarked from land in one of their primitive boats. It looked more like a war party to me. Their leader was a small male with dark skin. Most of the group are males, but there were three women with them. One female led the others.

Two of the females have blond hair and one red. They are all light-skinned. They look like they're Northerners. The redheaded woman appears to be of a higher status than the two blondes. Ropes were surrounding their wrists, connecting them. They were leashed as if they were animals.

"Herathina you seem to be the most talented with the Homo sapiens language. Please translate. What it is they're trying to impart to us?"

The leader stepped forward, waved his hands about and said a few words, most of which I couldn't understand because it was garbled. Then, he leaned over and waved one of the blondes forward. She was quite striking with her hair long and thick with wavy curls. It framed her face and fell down her back to her waist. She had a willowy figure. She was full everywhere it mattered. Her head hung as he waved his arms around. He spoke to her in one of the dialects of the people of the mid-region of the planet.

"My master wishes to give myself and my sister as a token of peace between our people." A murmur filled The Citadel. I side glanced over at Poseidon as I translated. His face was wrapped with concentration. He seemed like a man who'd been struck, frozen. He never even acknowledged my words.

The collective murmuring ran through our crowd. It was buffeting my mind, filling with anger against humans. It came from my people, unfathomable. I had never felt such vehemence. My own kind is usually so much more subdued. However, this was clearly an emotion coming from them. Themians are never like this.

Several women stood up and screamed in outrage. Poseidon raised his hands, stood up from the dais and spoke. "We shall accept these women into our city. They should be free amongst us, for it is an abomination to take slaves."

Abomination, my eye! He'd been subjugating half the Themians on the ship for several thousand years, and now suddenly it's an abomination.

Poseidon has lost his mind. He glanced down at me sharply as if he'd heard something. Fear gripped me. Poseidon's eyes narrowed. I pushed my mental shields to the maximum.

The wizened little man placed his fingers under her chin forcing the woman's head up. Her hair fell away from her face, and a collective sigh passed around the room. She was divine, absolutely striking. There was no other way to describe her.

She had lovely turquoise eyes that were the color of the warm sea. Her eyes were slightly tilted at the sides. She had dark lashes surrounding them. Her cheekbones were high and smooth and her lips full and sensuous. The rags hanging off of their bodies were held on by leather thongs. The old man pulled them from both of the woman's shoulders at the same time. Their covering fell to the ground. Perfection was the best description. Long shapely legs , full breast, and hips. They couldn't have been any better even fresh from the infinitum pool. In a word, enchanting.

My eyes quickly glanced back at Poseidon. He was entranced like a man struck down by lightning. I knew this could spell nothing but trouble. These women had to be removed from Alethea. They had no place here; this was not for humans. Why has Poseidon landed us and removed the Obscure-a, making us so visible to everyone?

This was not what the High Council had in mind.

Poseidon's mind boomed inside of mine, "Your opinion has no place here, Herathina. You're only allowed to live by my good will. I suggest you tread lightly."

Not wishing to react to Poseidon's vehemence toward me, I bowed my head in acquiescence. The act was neither agreeing nor was it disagreeing. From the look on his face, I wasn't sure how I was going to break his will. I knew there was no way he would see any reason.

Log entry

I've decided to dreamwalk my brother. There's nothing I can do to convince anyone here, and I've sworn not to speak to the High Council, so it really only leaves me one option, my family. Perhaps they'll help me. I could use them as allies. Maybe my brother could dream-walk to the High Council. I am hopeful.

*****

Almost as soon as I arrived, I realized the folly of my venture. This could only be an innocent visit. He only wanted to talk about himself. I have my mind locked up so tight I didn't even let him in. He never noticed. Have we drifted so far apart? His wife was pregnant with their children, so his mind was filled with fatherhood and family. I couldn't blame him. If I were to become a parent, I too would not be able to think of anything else. With every word from his lips, I felt the fake smile on my face. My heart burned for his understanding and love. I knew he loved me. I wished I could hear him tell me he will free me, save me, help me in some way. I wished for the return to childhood when we did everything together.

I felt joy for him. As I should. I shall soon be an Aunt. But it was bitter in my mouth. He didn't stop for one moment to see me.

~ 237 ~

I am failing. I feel alone and frightened. I could have let him in, but I didn't want to complicate his life or spoil his joy. He would contact Mica, and Poseidon would know.

Poseidon threatens me daily with death. If he finds out that I have dreamwalked Helios, his rage will be great. He may cause the crust of this world to quake. I fear for humans more than for myself.

I can't rely on anyone else to save me. I will have to find a way to save myself.

The human women are still here on Alethea. They've been given quarters near Poseidon's.

The Enchantress, the elder of the two, is Cleito. She has gradually started to learn our language. I can see her mind working; she's the smart one. The other one is an average human. There is nothing special about her. But the enchantress, she's a problem solver. She is worming her way into Poseidon's good graces.

There are whisperings of night traveling. I'm not exactly sure what that means. Deep in my soul, I know, however, that I will not like the answer when I will find it.

Log entry

Poseidon has turned the whole of Alethea into not just a ship, but a village. He's allowing humans to build structures. Soil is building up on the outside of the hull. The reef around the ship is healthy and active. Many varieties of fish now call it home. I see a mammal, called a dolphin, swimming around the ships that sail by our earthbound vessel. They jump and spin in the air. Their clicks and whistles fascinate me almost as much as humans.

I have adjusted my bracelet to allow me to become a sea creature.

The bracelet only partially turned me. I was half Themian. The other half of me became fish like. I had a tail and scales. It was exciting and frightening. Several of my fellow shipmates have asked for the same change to their bracelets. They left in a group to explore the underworld.

Mere is the name we use for fish. Poseidon calls them Mer-people.

CHAPTER 20

SYDNEY

My throat closed. I tried to swallow, but nothing happened. There was a giant ball there. My heart felt like it was ripping out of my body. My eyes were burning, and I was shaking. Everyone got up to sing. I got up and crept to the bathroom, reaching the toilet just in time to throw up. I couldn't stop. I leaned my head on the side of the cool bowl, waiting for my body to calm down. When it finally ceased, I stood up and looked in the mirror. He was gone....

HE'S GONE...HE'S GONNNNNNNE.

The voice started blasting in subwoofer stereo. Every vowel pulsed with my heart.

I heard the same thing over and over again, but I couldn't talk to the voice in my head. I went to my father and asked if I could walk home. He half looked me over and agreed. When I was a block away, I started crying, then tripped and fell. Pulling myself up, I began to run. I was running as fast as I could.

He's gone why, why? Why him?

I was in shock. I just went into autopilot, making lunch, then cleaning the house. I just couldn't stop cleaning. I didn't talk to anyone or look at them. I felt dead inside and wanted to die myself. Nothing mattered anymore.

If I kept moving. This way I wouldn't feel it, and if I don't feel it, it didn't happen. Right? Every time I started to feel it, the panic would rise, along with the scream I wanted to release. I had to push it back.

My eyes were hot and burning, but I couldn't stop now. I had to keep going.

When bedtime came, my father visited me for our session. I didn't stop him. There was no fight left in me. I just laid down letting him hit me over and over and over. I didn't cry. I didn't even feel it. I was hoping he would kill me. My only thought was to die. If he killed me, then it would be over. As he was beating me, I was praying for God to take me, set me free from this miserable existence that I had been given.

Adrian was gone, and I was alone. He was gone. I just kept saying it over and over. All the while, the voice was screaming 'NOT DEAD'. I didn't even hear my father leaving the room. I just laid there in a catatonic state. I don't know when I fell asleep, but the dream came again.

*****

Water everywhere. I can't move my legs, and my arms are burned from the sun. There are blisters all over my arms. I can feel my face; it is burnt too, and my lips are chapped. The thirst is intense and so is the hunger –Wave. The aching. Oh God! The pain in my legs it's constant. There is no land around anywhere and the waves are coming rolling over me. Every wave burns me with salt water in my face, eyes and all the sores on my body. I'm gasping for air, only catching my breath just before the next wave hits me – Wave. My body is getting weaker with every wave. I know I need fresh water, but as I

~ 242 ~

think about how I am going to get any, another wave comes tumbling, rolling. I kick as hard as I can to catch my breath, but one of my legs won't work. I'm scared that I'm bleeding and sharks will come. The panic is rising again. I can't let that take over. If only I had some water. What if I am too weak and let go of the wood that's holding me up? Wave – it feels like hours, the horror keeps playing over and over again.

*****

I woke up crying and alone, except for the voice which wouldn't shut up. My body was so stiff from sleeping kneeling on the floor with my head on the bed. My knees made cracking noises as I tried to stand. My skin felt burned and slimy. I climbed into the shower, and the water was burning my skin; it felt like salt was in every wound. I couldn't scrub it off fast enough. I looked at my arms, there are splinters in them. I didn't remember touching anything made of wood, but my brain was in such a fog, I could have done anything and not realized it.

I was just running through the motions as I was getting ready for school. I didn't talk to anyone, but no one noticed because I hadn't really talked to them in years. There was nothing that I could say that they would listen to. I was on autopilot, just running on the preprogrammed day. I was a robot.

When I got to school, Trish stopped me to tell me something, but I didn't even hear her. I knew that she was shaking me, but I couldn't reach the surface of reality enough to interact with her.

Think. What am I supposed to say?

I didn't know what she was saying, but I replied, "That's nice, Trish."

The side of my face was burning. She hit me.

"SYDNEY, SYDNEY, CAN YOU HEAR ME????" I think she was screaming from the way her mouth moved, but I wasn't sure.

I looked at her the words coming out, but I don't remember thinking about them.

"He's dead."

My eyes were burning again. My chest felt like it was being ripped open and someone was standing on it. I was shaking, and tears rolled down my face. She pulled me to her car and put me in it. I had no idea where we were going, and I didn't care, but then I saw her house.

She pulled me out and took me to her room. I was a brainless lump that stayed where you put it. She made me sit me down on her bed and brought me a glass with something golden in it, telling me to drink it.

<It burns.>

I coughed. It made me start to feel funny. She wiped my face several times.

"What was that?"

"Bourbon. My mom likes it. Talk to me, Sydney. What happened?'

It began to pour out. The longer I talked, the louder I got. I felt hysterical like I was going crazy. Then, the wailing wasn't just in my head. I was wailing too. I didn't give a fuck about anything. My whole body was shaking. My teeth were chattering, my words were stunted. I was stuttering.

"I want to die. If I'm dead, I can be with him. Right?"

"I don't think it works that way, sweetie." She was crying too. "Sydney I'm sorry! I'm so, so sorry!" She held me while I cried. I don't know how long we sat like that.

< DON'T DIE, NOT DEAD. >

The voice was screaming again. I looked at the time. It had been hours. I had to go. I didn't want to be late and get another beating. Then, I sat back down. What did it matter? I suddenly was so mad. I fucking hated them, all of them. I wanted to die. They were ruining my life. I wanted to make them pay for everything that had happened to me.

"I hate them!"

"Who?"

"My family. I hate them all. They ruined my life. If they hadn't stopped me from being with him, he might not have gone, or I would have been with him. We would already be married." I stopped only to feel the anger rising so the next time I opened my mouth to talk I was screaming. "FOR BEATING ME AND IGNORING ME FOR YEARS. I AM NOT A WHORE. I HATE EVERY FUCKING ONE OF THEM. I WANT TO DIE!" The crying had started again, and I couldn't stop it.

Trish held me tight. "Honey listen, don't go back to that house, and stay with me."

"I can't. They own me. I'm their slave. Adrian said so, and he was right. They take my money. I cook and clean, and then they beat me. They are all in on it. Even my brothers tell on me. Even though they know what will happen to me, they tell anyway. I am broken. If I leave, they will have the police get me and take me home. My father told me he owns me. I'm sure he'll find me a husband in a couple of years who will beat me too. It will just go on and on and on." Hysteria was rising in my voice.

"Is that what you want?"

"No," I laid down wiping my nose. I was so tired.

"The next time that fucker lays a hand on you, tell him you are going to call the police and get him arrested for assault."

"I don't think that would help."

She pulled out a camera and started taking pictures and took my shirt off. She undressed me all, leaving only my panties on and took pictures, shaking her head as she did.

"Sydney, I could get him arrested with this alone."

"They would take my brothers away too. I would go to a group home. The boys might go into foster care. We would probably all get raped. No one cares about kids in the system. I can't do that to them."

"Yet, they all stand by for what happens to you. Do you think those boys wouldn't tell on you to save their own hides? They would. They look at you the same way your father does, whore, slave, good for nothing. When you are truly over it, let me know."

< Listen to her, PAIN, PAIN, NOT DEAD, NOT DEAD. >

The pounding never ended. As I rose from the bed, I declared, "I need to go home." She snorted, shook her head and delivered me to my *loving jailers*.

I didn't really pay attention to what was going on in my life. I was on rinse and repeat. School, chores, every other Sunday beating, rinse and repeat. I had lost a lot of weight. Remembering to eat was a chore. When I did, it didn't always stay down. I became a shadow of a person. I embraced the beating. Those were the only times when I could feel anything. Emptiness and vacancy enveloped me.

The voice stopped screaming in my mind, but I don't know when. I was relieved. One day, I wanted to talk to *it*, and *it* just wasn't there. I was alone in every way. I didn't know when this happened, but I had been alone for months. No Adrian, no voice, no feelings, nothing. Just the air going in and out of my chest. The solitude of my existence was comforting in a way.

I looked up one day, and it was March. My birthday was coming. I would be eighteen and alone. He was gone and never to return.

The only thing that filled the void was music. I kept the Walkman blasting everywhere I went unless my father was there. I turned it off around him just so I could gauge what was going on. I had found a band that helped keep the pain at bay - Depeche Mode. I kept their music playing over and over and over. My favorite was Blasphemous Rumors. It talked about God laughing.

I asked Trish if she believed in God. She did.

"I don't." I replied. She was shocked.

I didn't. God had never done anything to help me, and he didn't give a fuck about me. How could he say he loves you, and then let you be beaten for years for nothing? Then kill the one person I loved who loved me back. That wasn't love. He was just a mean cocksucker.

"People always say, 'Pray to God, and he will help you'. That is bullshit. Or 'God never gives you more than you can bear.' Double bullshit. That is just the best way that power hungry people have found to control the masses." I spouted.

"Syd, I don't know if God is real. I understand where you are coming from. If I were you, I wouldn't believe either. For all the church going that your family does, you would think they would be better." She remarked

HAHA!

That was one of the funniest things I had ever heard.

"You do know that church people are the worst people in the world. Right? They lie, cheat, steal. They are the biggest hypocrites I have ever seen. And I quote 'judge not, less you be judged' that is all they do and have done to me. My mother ran around telling everyone I was a whore, gossiping about me. They all listened and repeated it, then judged that it must be true. I haven't done anything to be a whore, but I am marked as one by all of them. The people who were supposed to protect me, treated me worse than a stranger. The church is where like-minded mental cases go to feel better about being crazy." I scoffed.

She laughed so hard she started crying. I actually laughed a little too. It was my first laugh after Adrian.

"Yea, there's no God. Just a bunch of deluded people who need something to hope for, to go on." I remarked.

Fuck that!

I didn't care anymore.

CHAPTER 21

SYDNEY

My birthday arrived along with a courier carrying a letter from a lawyer and car service that said 'Mr. Charley Langtree Attorney at Law.' It was announcing an appointment that day, at 1:30 PM, to discuss an important matter having to do with my future. I was welcome to bring a friend if I so chose.

Very fancy.

I didn't know what they wanted, but I got in the car and went downtown anyway. I was ushered into a conference room and offered coffee, tea, or water, but I declined all of it. I sat looking out the window down onto 5th Street and waited.

Mr. Langtree came in and sat down to study me. Then he laid three big folders on the table and began.

"Are you Sydney Rhiannon O'Dear?" his deep voice vibrated the air with the inquiry.

I crossed my arms and snapped a "Yes."

"Do you have an ID, to prove it?" he inquired.

Pulling out my purse, I rummage around freeing my Driver's License. I place it in his extended hand. As I did this, his eyes were fixated on my hand.

He turned his attention back to my person. "Do you have the ring Adrian Shipman gave you one week before he left?"

I gasped and sputtered. "What do you need to see that ring for?"

Mr. Langtree quickly responds. "I need it to verify that you are the fiancée of Adrian Mitchell Shipman."

I laid both hands on the table flat out in front of him, and then I slowly reached inside my shirt. My fingers found the chain hanging around my neck. I pulled until the clasp appeared and released the end, allowing the ring to fall into my palm. I slipped down my finger to rest by my knuckles, then I offered my hand for viewing. His warm fingers clasp mine as he turned my hand this way and that to inspect the ring. He released my palm and he opened one of the folders and began reading.

"I, Adrian Mitchell Shipman, being of sound mind and body do hereby leave all my worldly good and estates to my beautiful and loving fiancée, Sydney Rhiannon O'Dear." Mr. Langtree paused, allowing me to take it all in.

What could he possibly leave me?

"Miss O'Dear, he also took out a life insurance policy before he left, listing your name as the beneficiary, in the amount of $500,000.00." He closed the file, and he opened the next. "I, Thomas Sheldon Shipman, being of sound mind…everything to my loving wife Anne Shipman and son Adrian Shipman." He then turned a few more pages. "He, too had a life insurance policy in the amount of $500,000.00, listing Adrian solely as the beneficiary."

The pressure in my chest grew.

He opened the last folder. It was more of the same only, Anne's.

I cut in, ending the long train of legal mumbo jumbo. "What do his parents have to do with me, and why are you just now telling me this?"

Clearing his throat, Mr. Langtree continues. "Miss O'Dear if you will just bear with me, I can explain. Adrian was his parents' sole beneficiary, i.e., making you his sole beneficiary of all three estates. All three life insurance policies had double indemnity clauses for natural disasters totaling a net worth of 3 million dollars altogether. The rest is about $800,000.00, being as they sold their house before they left. It's in cash. There are also some stocks and bonds, then the household goods in storage." He opened his mouth to continue.

I broke in and demanded, "What about Grace Shipman? Didn't they leave anything to her?"

Mr. Langtree sighs before replying. "No, Miss. I don't think they expected her to outlive them."

My mind raced with all the information that had been dumped in my lap.

I began, "What am I supposed to do with this, and why didn't you contact me sooner?" Irritation laced my retort. I hate having to repeat myself.

Mr. Langtree supplies. "Adrian left explicit instructions about how to handle his estate for you. He also left a letter for you to read." He laid an envelope on the table and pushed it toward me. "When you're ready, just tell the girl at the desk, and I will come back." Pushing his chair back from the table, he exited the room allowing the door to close with a little snick.

< READ, READ, READ BEAUTIFUL GIRL. >

My head rang with the volume of the voice's intensity.

I took the letter into my shaking hands. Every move I made to open it, ripped my heart out.

Dear O'Dear,

If you are reading this, then I didn't make it home, and today is your eighteenth birthday. I am very sorry that I'm not there to marry you and live the rest of my life with you. I had hoped to have a family and spend all my time showing you what care really meant and give that knowledge to our children. I love you and always will. You are the most exquisite girl in the world. You're intelligent, and I'm sure you need to eat something. I took care of everything. All you have to do is go and live for both of us. Find an exceptional man to marry and have a real family filled with all the love you can muster.

Don't let anyone abuse you ever again. Go to school if you want and get a degree or two or three or just travel to all those places that you read about. Buy a grand piano, then make the neighbors crazy night and day. Whatever you do, think of me every now and then and our lunch under our tree. The only gift I can give you now is your freedom. Take it and never look back.

I will be with you always.

Mr. Langtree should have secured a restraining order against your father. Also, there is an apartment for you. You will be driven to your parents' house with movers. Get everything you want. Don't worry about a piano; there will be one at the apartment for you. Everything is paid for until the end of June. After that, you can decide where to go. Trust Mr. Langtree. He has helped my family for many years. My car is now yours, and the title has been taken care of so it's in your name. Your phone number is unlisted, and your apartment is well away from your parents' house. You can go shopping without any problems. When you get to your new home call Trish and have a party with her to celebrate the beginning of your new life.

Love Always,

Adrian

P.S. This is what it means to care.

The weight of Adrian's loss slams down over me. I bowed with force and laid my head on the table. The heat behind my eyes releases the hot tears stored there. He really loved me. It felt like I'd lost him all over again, only this time I could cry about it. Even dead he took care of me. The wave of loss hit me so hard I couldn't breathe. I stared out the window looking for the answers that weren't there. Finally, as the light faded from the unseen window, I got up and opened the door.

The girl at the front desk jumped up and dashed in another door, which in turn Mr. Langtree returned through. "Do you understand what is happening?" He inquires.

"Sort of. The restraining order is to keep my father away from me, and I can move in right away?" I reply.

"Yes. There are a bunch of papers that need to be signed. Also, the sheriff will have to be there to serve your father the papers. We will need to have another meeting to finalize a few things, but I'll have my paralegal call you for that. There is food at the apartment. My paralegal went shopping for you, so don't fuss. She wanted to make sure there was coffee."

I glanced at the girl who followed Mr. Langtree from the office.

Langtree continues. "Adrian talked to her for a while about you, when he was here." He ended with a kind smile.

I signed everything he put in front of me, then thanked him. Mr. Langtree walked me to the door which was flanked by two men and an officer beyond in the foyer. The officer inquired, "Is this the young lady we need to look after?"

Langtree answers. "Yes, she just needs to get her things, and make sure no one follows her home." Mr. Langtree was very commanding but kind.

"Well, let's get a move on. We are burning daylight!"

At the house, I stayed in the truck while the officer served my father. It was followed by a lot of shouting, but I filtered them out with unexplored thoughts of the future. After a few minutes, the door opened, and the officer leaned in the door. "It's safe."

I got out and started to walk toward the house. I looked over and saw my father in a police cruiser. He carried a look of pure hatred.

My mother lingered just inside the door of the house. With bulging eyes and thin pressed lips, she released her anger. "You really are a whore! How could you do this to your father after everything he has done for you?" she demanded.

Freezing in place, I turned to stare her down. "You will never see me again. Don't even try to contact me. I only hope that one day you will grow a spine." I calmly replied.

She gasped then snapped her mouth shut.

There wasn't much in my room that I wanted. There was my dresser, some books, a blanket, a sewing machine, and some music sheets. I gazed around only to encounter clothes I didn't want, or the bed he beat me on. I stared at it for a long time to set in my mind what it looked like just in case I ever start feeling bad. Nothing could be as bad as living here.

Leaving the cold house, I embraced the warmth of the sunshine and my newfound freedom. Off to the side, were both my younger brothers.

"Goodbye." I offered the boys.

Matt lunged for me, wrapping both his arms around my waist, squeezing it. Edward didn't flinch. In my heart, an inevitable reality settled over me. This was the last time I would ever see them.

The apartment wasn't far from the school. I could walk if I wanted to. It was a garden apartment on the ground floor. Outside, the back French glass doors was a walled garden. The rooms were covered in a fine layer of dust. Adrian must have set it up before he left. The only item lacking dust was the piano.

The refrigerator was filled with food, and in the middle of all the delights, sat a bottle of Champagne with a water-stained note, *For new chapters.* He had thought of everything. The planning was apparent at every turn. There were candles and touches speaking quietly of Adrian's love. It was impossible to keep my tears from falling.

I was wondering the entombed rooms, trailing my fingers from one place to the next only to land on the mantle. Sitting in, as the centerpiece to draw your attention from all other places to this one, was a picture of Adrian and me, sitting at Adrian's piano. We were staring into each other's blue eyes. The light glinting from Adrian's revealed that indefinable quality of blue. The lump in my throat wedged itself tight, blocking my air flow. I looked again at the picture and saw how the shy smiles shaping our lips hit at our love. Our hands laid on the bench so close together as only to suggest a touch. My burning desire to touch Adrian returned with a vengeance, heating the molten lava tears pouring down my cheeks.

I didn't remember anyone taking this picture or any pictures. Every picture I had of Adrian was old, from when we were little.

I started to cry, releasing years' worth of tears I'd held in my chest. They were choking me as if they were freed from a physical prison that I had locked them in. I didn't realize when I started screaming at the waste of life and love, but I was, and I didn't stop until my eyes could barely see. It subsided into a hiccup here and there.

I grabbed the only phone in the apartment, and I dialed Trish's number with swollen eyes and blurry vision.

"Trish, can you come over?" I sputtered.

She gasped. "To your house? Are you sure it's okay with your dad?" Discomfort colored her reply.

I returned her inquiry with a dry reply. "I don't live there anymore. I'll explain when you get here." I supplied her with my new address, and I hung up. Then, I went to the bathroom to wash my face and get ready for my first guest.

Most of the evening was spent crying while I poured out my horror life story.

"Adrian left a bottle. Will you drink it with me? Otherwise, it will just sit there." I asked.

Trish burst into a blinding smile. "If you have alcohol, I can find a way to drink it." We drank and we cried.

.

CHAPTER 22

SYDNEY

I had never really contemplated life beyond getting out of the house or marrying Adrian. When Trish asked me what I was going to do after school, I didn't know. I always felt trapped, so just getting out of the trap seemed enough. Now there were suddenly so many options. I was overwhelmed.

*****

Blue, Azure, Teal, a sky so vast when it meets the ocean, and you can't see the defining line. Aquamarine the waves jump up at me spraying me with their salty tang. There, in the center dividing the air from the jewel toned sea, lies the island with the mountain at its center.

The shining palace rushes in, to replace my thoughts, making my eyes water with the brilliance of the blinding white marble. The way the palace is part of the mountain and in balance with the flattened side, throws my perspective off.

Before I can overthink it, it's over and gone, leaving only the echoing voice of a faceless woman and her indiscernible words.

*****

"We should hit the beach to catch some rays," Trish suggested. I demurred to stay in town, but it got me thinking.

It hit me and made me realize that the beach is where I wanted to be. I wanted to feel the sun on my face every day. I wanted to swim in the ocean and not freeze. Trish has been accepted to UC Berkeley, in California. Who knew that under all those beauty queen looks and shallow flirting was a big brain?

I didn't fancy Californians or their taxes, so that was out for me. After searching the lower forty-eight states, I settled in South Florida.

Why not?

It had no state tax, warm sandy beaches, lots of good schools. The best part was that I had no connections there, so I could really start over. That was what sealed it for me. I didn't know anyone, and they wouldn't know me. I could start from scratch.

The last few months of school flew by. I learned to put on makeup and do my hair and even shave my legs. I started dressing like a girl and I bought a sexy bikini. That was the only time the voice had spoken since my birthday. It said 'yum'. I went to prom with Harry. Trish and I were both his date. Afterwards they went on to a hotel room, and I went home alone.

I flung myself into my bed and embraced sleep.

*****

Warm and balmy breezes brush my cheek as palm trees dot the edge of the beach and rustle with the breeze. The water is a clear turquoise all the way to the white sandy bottom. Brightly colored fish dart around me in the water. A myriad of coral, in a rainbow of colors, proclaimed the area tropical. There were a few other people there, but I couldn't really make them out. I enter the water with a dive. It was still a man's body. Why was I dreaming about being a man? The body didn't seem strange, though. The chest was broad and rippling with muscles. The arms and legs are corded with strength every bit of it tan. The hair that lightly covered the arms and legs is blonde. His hands are large and strong. He dives down to the bottom and reached out to touch some fish, but they're too fast for him. He grabs an oyster instead, breaking it away from its seat, then pushes off the bottom and breaks the surface. The chuckling timbre of the voice is familiar. As the water settles from the dive, I focus on the image that appears in the reflection of the water. His voice rings "not dead."

Adrian.

*****

I woke up sobbing, my heart was pounding, and my whole body was coved in sweat. Tears poured from my eyes.

It can't be him. He is dead.

It was just wishful thinking. I wanted him to be on the beach alive, with me, but he was never going to be there. It was just going to be me.

Sleep eluded me. No matter how much I wanted to return to the dream I couldn't. I was tossing and turning until the light of dawn broke through, so I gave up and made coffee.

It was June second and it was one year since I last spoke to Adrian, held him, kissed him, said I would marry him. He was gone. My chest tightened. There was a weight sitting on it. No matter how many breaths I took, I couldn't catch it. Sitting down, I stared at the wall hoping that it wasn't a dream, fantasizing that the dream was our honeymoon, wishing that the tan body was next to me and not gone.

There hadn't been a body. They never found him, and no one ever saw him. I didn't have ashes or a gravestone to cry at. There was nothing. Just an empty space that would always be vacant. I could never find closure.

I dressed for graduation. I was thrilled to have my days to myself doing as I pleased for the first time in my life.

As I walked across the stage, I looked into the crowd and saw my parents standing there. What could they want? My father was far enough away that he wasn't violating the TRO. How did they even get tickets? They never wanted to see me on stage doing anything before, so why now?

I hate that Johnny come lately shit.

Trish informed Harry about the situation. He headed them off so I could slip away. I went to the seniors' after party. It was the only time I really felt like I was one of the normal kids.

Before I left to go home, Harry handed me a letter from my father. I put it in a box because I didn't want to read it, but I couldn't throw it away either.

I began packing all my things, had my car looked over and tuned up for the long drive to Florida. By June 20th I had everything done for my move. It just left one thing, Grace. I had to talk to Grace. I couldn't just go and not say anything. She had the right to know everything, and I didn't want to take any family heirlooms away from her.

I got dressed in a pastel flowered skirt and a white flowing blouse with low heels. I put on a little makeup and braided my hair and drove to Grace's house. I was not sure what to say. I had my ring on, and I was armed with Adrian's letter, a copy of our picture and a handkerchief. It took me a minute to work up the courage to knock on the door.

She pulled it open and smiled, but she had aged a great deal in the last year. Her hair was entirely gray now and her eyes had dulled. She had always had a sparkle about her. Now, the youthful hop in her step was gone.

"Sydney, I was wondering when I would see you again."

"Hi, Grace...I – came over to say goodbye. Um, awe–may I come in?" I asked. As she pushed the tremendous wooden door open and held it for me to pass, the knot in my throat grew to the size of a baseball.

"Sure, sure. Come right in!" She ushered me over to the couch. All this time, I kept my hand hidden. She scraped together some coffee and a few cookies. When she sat down next to me, that was when the real toll her loss became apparent. Grace sat down slowly with a plop at the end, as if she couldn't stop the descent.

I didn't know what to say, so I just held up my hand and started crying. She looked at me in disbelief. Her eyebrows knotted together, and the truth spread across her face. Astonishment was the only word to describe her reply.

"You are the girl?" she squeaked.

"Yes, Adrian and I were going–" I choked on the words, "He asked me just before he left." She hugged me and said she was so sorry.

I told her all about how we fell in love and gave her a picture of us. I let her read his letters to me.

"I want to thank you, Sydney." She murmured while holding me.

I was puzzled.

"I was afraid Adrian had died not knowing what love is. But, he did, and I am pleased it was you. You are an exceptional girl." She hugged me or held my hand for the rest of the time I spent with her. We cried for a long time.

I had brought all the family photo albums. I'd taken out the ones I wanted but gave the rest to her. She was frail. Having half your family die at one time would try anyone. I asked her if there was anything that she wanted from her family's things. She did ask for a few items, and I said I would bring them over.

I wanted to memorialize Adrian and his parents. I didn't have a grave to visit or an urn. It wasn't like I could spread his ashes anywhere. I'd decided I was going to buy three bricks in Pioneer Square and have Adrian and his parents' names put on them. Grace thought it was perfect. Tom and Anne's bodies had not been shipped back to the US. Grace said it was too costly. She had them buried at the mission with the rest of the victims along with a placard for the lost. I didn't know that. I hadn't gone to the memorial. None of my family did. If I had gone, the tears would come and never stop. They threatened to reach the surface even now.

"What are your plans for the future?" She asked, making small talk to fill the time. She doesn't know what to say anymore.

Ask the necessary questions until the guest leaves, that's how it works. It felt funny being there.

I'm me. I'm not hiding behind all those clothes or the mask. I can be me, but I don't know how to do that.

So, I followed her lead keeping to the small talk. "I'm going to Florida. You can contact me through Mr. Langtree until I have a phone and address."

I couldn't ask her if she was going to be okay because it would have seemed hollow. How was she ever going to be okay? Her child and grandchild were dead. She still had her daughter Emily and her kids. She said she would keep in touch.

A few days later, I dropped her items off. "If you need anything, call me. You are part of my family too. Just promise me that you won't go on a cruise or live in a flood zone or anything like that. Okay?" She said and pulled me into a warm desperate hug. The close contact felt strangely comforting.

I gave her my word, though it all seemed a bit over dramatic.

The moving truck came and picked everything up. It would take three weeks for my things to make it to Florida, and I was going to drive myself in seven days. It would give me about two weeks to find an apartment and get the lay of the land. I had planned everything from how far I would drive each day to my hotels and where to get gas. It was all marked on my map.

The big day came. I loaded the car the night before. Trish and Harry came to see me off along with a few other girls from school. Tobias showed up. I hadn't spoken to him since I left mom and dad's house.

Damn it, Trish!

He gave me a big hug and told me to call him every night on the way. There was so much I wanted to say to him, but there wasn't time. I only told him about the lawyer. I kissed everyone goodbye and left.

To tell you the truth, with all my planning, I was still scared to death. There were 3,486 miles to West Palm Beach. I had never driven out of the state, let alone across a continent. I didn't like the California freeways. I'd heard they were very bad, and the drivers were terrible, so I chose to drive down through the backside of Oregon through Las Vegas, Nevada until I reached Flagstaff, Arizona. From there, I would catch I-40 to Amarillo, Texas, to Dallas, then Mississippi, and

Alabama. After that, it was smooth sailing into Florida, I-95 to South Florida.

If everything went well, I would be there in seven days.

I made a few stops along the way, at the Grand Canyon, the Painted Desert, and New Orleans. The drive gave me a lot of time to think. One of the things that Mr. Langtree had said before I left was that I was going to need to do something with all that cash that I had. Plus, there were the stocks and bonds to think about. I didn't know that much about money, but I was going to have to learn and fast. Maybe I should go to the local community college for a couple of years and get my AA, but I wasn't sure that I wanted to do that either. I had so many options that I didn't know what to do. I didn't need to work, but I didn't want to be lazy either. I could buy a house, but I didn't know where I really wanted to be. I didn't know who I was without Adrian to love me and my father to beat me. That was the real problem.

The further South I went, the more palm trees and large green leaved plants. Then an armadillo, ran on its stubby legs across the highway. It barely made it. There were tons of lizards too. I had never seen so many, but they were everywhere. They called them geckos. They were all different colors, but most were brown and tan and had curled tails.

As I was heading south maybe to Fort Lauderdale, black bugs flew everywhere. They were stuck together. It was like one of those swarms you read about in the bible. I couldn't believe the heat rolling off the ground and the car.

When I stopped for gas and food, the waitress with her funny accent said, "they're love bugs, and they won't harm you." The further South I went, the hotter it got. I was so thankful I'd made sure the A/C was working in the car before I left.

The ground seemed to turn into sand everywhere I went, and the grass had big fat blades that were kind of sharp. They called it St Augustine grass, but I just called it crabgrass. The trees turned into thick vines wrapped around one another rather than an actual tree - banyan trees. They were huge and covered in rope like trendles hanging down from the branches. I expected Tarzan to swing by at any moment.

The further South I went, the less and less of a southern accent I ran into and more of a New York. A few sounded like they were from Boston. The roads in Florida were straight. You could see to the other end of the state with how straight they were.

When I reached Vero Beach, I left the highway and got on A1A. It followed the intercoastal waterway on the barrier islands. I went to South Beach Park and walked out to the beach with my bare feet for my first glimpse of the Atlantic Ocean.

The sand was so white, it dazzled my eyes. It was almost blinding, and it was scorching hot. I had to put my shoes back on to keep it from burning my toes. Once I reached the wet sand, I took my shoes off and set them down. I walked right into the water. It was warm, yet cool, perfect. I didn't stop until I was about to float away. I was in love. I never wanted to leave the beach again. Wherever I chose to live it had to be right by the water or in walking distance. Decision made.

The hotel I chose was the Hilton on Singer Island. It had a pool, and the beach was right there. When I pulled in, there was valet service, and they parked my car.

Fancy.

There was even a beachside food and drink service. I laid down on the bed in my room and gazed out the window. I longed for Adrian and fell asleep with the door to the balcony open to feel the breeze on my face.

The dream slammed into my mind.

*****

I was on the beach, but it wasn't in Florida. The water was warm and clear. So clear that I could see the fish swimming along with all the coral. I was floating, and the bottom was a long way down. I looked at my feet, but they weren't mine. They were large with a touch of blonde hair. I was a man. I looked at my hands. They were large and strong, with blood vessels cording over the top of the hand. The forearms were thick and corded, biceps and triceps thick with muscles.

Wherever I was swimming, I was naked and alone. I exited the water and dried myself then walked into the cottage on the beach. I stopped and looked in the mirror. It was his face. He was tan, and his hair had bleached out, but it was him. It was Adrian.

Every muscle on his body was ripped. I had never seen him naked. The hair on his chest was a golden blonde and ran down his flat belly right into his groin. I looked back into the mirror. He put his hand on the mirror, looked into my eyes, and said, "Sydney."

*****

I woke up. My heart was pounding, and I was sweating. My body was pulsing with desire, hungry for him. I was crying and hiccupping, and my nose was running. My throat had gone dry and scratchy for a little while.

< Sydney, are you okay? >

< *No, I keep dreaming about him, and I can't get him off my mind. How am I supposed to go on with my life? I can't forget him, and I don't want to. It has been a year, and I still wake up crying.*>

< You may always do that. Did you love him that much? >

< *Yes, he was my life, and I will never forget him.*>

< Why don't you find someone else? >

< *I can't. I look around, and when I look, all I can think is 'not Adrian', 'too short, not Adrian', 'too loud, not Adrian'. I know I shouldn't compare every man I meet to him, but I can't help it.* >

< You need a hobby, a way to meet people and make friends. >

< *I have hobbies, but they are all solo hobbies. I need a place to live in. Can you help me with that?* >

< Go next door to the condo. They will rent to you. Goodnight Beautiful Girl! >

< Thank you! Good night voice.>

CHAPTER 23

HERATHINA

Log entry 1,786,225.66 ATD

My relationship with Poseidon is deteriorating fast. His obsession with the human woman is out of control. He managed to impregnate her. I worry about the outcome of their coupling.

He built a causeway to Alethea, allowing the humans encamped on the plains access to the ship.

They believe he is a God and have built a temple for him. I am not sure our ship can ever enter the spatial void again. Poseidon altered the entrance to the Citadel. There are no doors to seal it from the outside. The temple is built into the side of the ship. You must pass through his temple to reach him and the Citadel. Statues have sprung up all over the ship's hull. Many are dedicated to Poseidon himself, others to various project members. I saw one of myself on the far side.

The humans lay flowers at the bases and light candles. I have seen many kneeling and praying to us. The people hold rites and sacrifices to us by killing animals and spreading the blood all around the base of an altar. They cut the throats of beautiful white doves, squeezing every last drop from the carcass then burning it with sweet incense. I find it disquieting that anyone would worship us or show obedience.

Many lay on the ground at my feet as I pass by. I plead with them to stand for I am not above them. But my pleas fall on deaf ears. They're blinded by their devotion.

Poseidon is sending teams out to inspect the humans' level of civilization. I can't imagine why he wants to know their level of civilization. We're here to study them, not enslave them or control them.

Every time I think about him with that woman, I become sick to my stomach. It's like manipulating a child. They are not evolved at the same level we are. The High Council's directive was not unambiguous. We are here to observe and learn, not to interfere or interact heavily. Light interaction. That's precisely what the directive said. I can't imagine how he's going to try and justify this.

When they said light interaction, I'm pretty sure they did not include sex. I'm absolutely positive they did not include procreation. He's polluted their gene pool. Why is it that I am the only person who sees this? He won't listen to reason. Perhaps my nagging about it is exacerbating the situation. Every time I bring up the High Council's directive, I can feel the anger that's boiling below the surface.

I've been contemplating contacting the High Council directly. Perhaps if I dreamwalk one of the members, I'll get some satisfaction or traction or something. But I can't, I swore. I can't break my word.

CHAPTER 24

SYDNEY

I couldn't go back to sleep, so I got up and got coffee from the café in the lobby. Then, I walked out to the beach. I sat and watched the waves roll one over the other. The sun rose in its golden orange glow. It made me feel cleansed of the dream. I went and got dressed. I wanted to rest for a few days after my long drive, but my voice had said next door had a place to rent. So, off I went to the Beachside Condos' office. I talked to the receptionist, and they did have one. A two-bedroom, two-bath for $1200.00 a month. The best part was the view. That big ocean filled the glass of the slider. I flashed back to my dream. Adrian had been in an ocean. Every time I saw the aquamarine of the water, it pulled to me. I needed to be near it.

"I'll take it." I stated.

The lady at the desk smiled and said, "Great! Let's go do some paperwork."

I leased it for a year and paid in full. Lisa, the manager, was floored.

She sputtered, "Until the check clears, I can't hand over the keys."

"It's okay. I'm staying next door at the Hilton. You can reach me there. Room 210." Her shoulders fell in relief. Lisa was older, a little outspoken, but nice.

"Where do you go to get a good meal around here? Oh, and outfit an apartment?" I asked.

"Now you're speaking my language. Go to PGA Boulevard. Just stay on it, and you will find anything you want. For dinner, I would go to Cosimo's. They have great food and an Italian market." I thanked her and left.

Cosimo's was packed. There wasn't a table to be had.

"Would you like to sit at the bar? We can seat you right away. The wait for a table is thirty-five minutes."

I wasn't old enough to drink, but she hadn't asked for my ID.

"Yes, that would be lovely. Thank you!" I felt silly. I'd never sat at a bar before. Watching the bartender play his trade was like watching a dance. Every drink was different and full of colors. I left through the market with a full belly and a bag of food.

I moved into the apartment two days later. Apparently, Lisa called the bank to confirm the fund was available and went from there. I didn't have anything to sleep on, so I bought a new mattress and had it delivered the next day. All that was left to make it a home was coffee and food until the truck arrived. I went to the mall down the street and bought a French press for coffee and hit the grocery store, and I was good to go.

July was over half done. My things would be here next week. So, I just decided to pretend it was a vacation. There was a little strip mall down the road from me. They had a store that made bikinis. I ordered a neon yellow one. I didn't have a tan, so I laid out every day for thirty minutes. I walked along the beach every morning.

The morning that the truck arrived I was at the pool, and Lisa came to get me.

"Hey, Sydney! The movers are here with your things. They are hunky too. You should keep that swimsuit on and show them where to put everything." She smiled and winked at me.

I think she was talking about sex. I tried to laugh it off. "Thank you, Lisa, I'll try to."

Upstairs, they were already waiting at my door. There were two large, well-built men. One of them had brown hair, hazel eyes, and the other had black hair and blue eyes. They were nice to look at, but I just wasn't interested. I still wanted Adrian.

They brought up my things. I had them set up Adrian's/my bed in the master bedroom. I set the second room up as a workroom/office with my sewing machine and all my crafts. With Adrian's desk and my computer. When they finished with all my things, one of the guys, Patrick, gave me his number. "If you need anything. I live west of here. I would love to see you or just help out."

I was flattered, but I didn't want to see anyone, so I just smiled a "thank you." I still didn't know what I wanted to do with the rest of my life. What I did know was that I wasn't ready for anyone else in it.

< You don't have to plan for forever. Just for what you need now.>

< Thank you! I'll make a list. I need to figure out what I'm going to do with all that money. Am I going to go to school? Where do you make friends? What do I want to do with myself? >

< Focus on the money. It is going to need attention first. >

< Well, whenever I want to learn something, I go to the library. All my stocks are through Merrill Lynch. I'll call my broker and see what he has to say. >

I had a plan. Sort of. It felt right.

The next morning, I went to the office, to Lisa. She knew her way around along with great ideas about meeting people and making friends. Lisa gave me the local rundown of where to go and what there was to do.

Cosimo's was quickly becoming my go-to for food and entertainment. I wasn't bothered by anyone at the bar. The food was always good, and it was close to home.

I started watching MSNBC all the time for financial information, and I got a subscription to the New York Times. I also heard the anchorwoman talking about Barron's magazine. I called around. A newsstand on Palm Beach sold it. It was published every Saturday. So, I went on Saturday morning to get one and get some coffee.

I sat down at the café next to the newsstand to read. When I heard a thick New York accent say, "What broker do you work for?" I looked up at the man asking.

"Excuse me. I don't know what you're talking about." I was met by hazel eyes and black well-groomed hair.

"Brokerage house. What is the one you work for? You're studying for your 7, right?" He turned the chair across from me around and sat on it. It was a move you always saw in movies by blowhards.

I didn't intend to make small talk with anyone, but I answered nevertheless. "No, I'm not studying for a 7. I don't work for a Brokerage."

He smiled, and it caused the skin on his crooked nose to tighten over the break.

"It's not a 7. It's the series 7 and 63 GSRE exams. Okay, you're not in the biz. So, what is a pretty little girl like you doing reading a Barron's?"

I was taken aback. He was kind of rude. Good looking but rude.

< Don't trust that guy! >

< *Thank you! I can tell a snake when I meet one.* >

"Sorry. My name is Zack, and I'm a flipper." He looked at me, but when he realized I had no idea of what he was talking about, he smiled and continued, "That means I flip stocks."

He stopped again. He probably wanted to hear me say something about his job, but I didn't. I wasn't interested. He didn't let go.

"What's your name, and what are you into?" His New York accent was funny.

For the first time in his monologue, I actually was about to answer, but he stood up and continued talking.

"How do ya like your coffee? Oh, do ye want a bagel or something?" His hand waved around in big arcs.

"I'll have a latte with five sugars, and yes I would like a bagel with cream cheese. Thank you!" I could see he was stifling a smile.

"You want Lox on it?"

"I don't know what Lox is." I replied.

He laughed at me and shook his head, "Smoked salmon. It's smoked salmon."

"Yes, please!"

He turned and walked away shaking his head. He was trying to imitate me talking under his breath in as high a voice as he could muster 'yes, please, I don't know what it is'. It was a little silly, so I laughed as I watched his 6'4" frame swagger inside.

He came back, balancing everything and sat down. I took a drink of my coffee, and he took a big bite of his bagel. We read in companionable silence for a few minutes. He set his paper down, and he raised one leg, resting his ankle on the other knee. He put one hand on the raised knee while running his other over his hair.

"Where are you from? You aren't from the East Coast!"

"Oregon" His eyebrows went up a fraction of an inch. "Oh, that makes more sense. So, what makes ye want to read Barron's?"

Boy, he is nosy.

"I want to learn about Economics and Finance."

"Why don't you just go to college and get a degree like all the other schmucks out there?"

I had been asking myself the same thing for days. "I don't really know what I want to do with the rest of my life, but I don't want to spend four more years in school hoping to figure it out."

He smiled and nodded his head. "Yea, me either. What brought you to Florida?"

The way he said Florida made me laugh. He was rude but in an honest, straight forward way. However, I didn't want to answer, so I changed the subject.

"So, you flip stocks. Did you take the series 7?" I asked taking the spot light off me.

"Ya, I took it and passed it, but I didn't like workin' for a broker, so I went out on my own."

"How can I take the series 7?" I asked to keep him focused on finance and not my life.

"You can't unless you get hired by a broker. But you don't need to do that to trade. All you have to do is have an account with a broker, and you can trade."

"I have an account, so I can trade, but I don't know how to tell what would be good or bad."

He lowered his leg and threw his head back and laughed at me.

"Well, knowing when to make a good trade, that's the hard part. I've seen good brokers fuck themselves out of everything cause they thought they were making a good trade. Look, little girl, it's a tough business, and you don't look like you could take it."

His smile had faded as he leaned forward with both elbows on his knees, but I just brushed his dismissal aside and kept going.

"Well, I want to learn. Can you teach me?"

"I don't have time for little girls that play with daddy's money." He remarked then waved his hand at me in a condescending fashion.

My mouth hung open. I think he just called me a silver spoon. Rage filled me.

"I am not playing with daddy's money. Just because I'm on Palm Beach doesn't mean I've had everything handed to me. You… you're an asshole!" I sputted.

I got up to leave, leaving everything on the table.

"I'll go buy my own coffee." I hissed with narrowed eyes.

He grabbed my hand and changed the tone of his voice.

"Look, I'm sorry pretty girl! I don't even know your name. The thing is that you have a big rock on your hand, and I got the wrong idea. If you can stand up to me, then I'll take a chance on you. If you want to leave, you can, or you can finish your breakfast, and I'll give you my number and an office address, and you can come to sit in at work with me."

I took a deep breath and sat back down. He gave me his card and said. "The market opens at 9:00 AM, but be there at 8:00."

"Thank you! And my name is Sydney." He got up and wandered over to the hot rod parked at the curb. It was red. It had to be red. He was just one of those guys.

I finished eating and ran off to the bookstore. I bought a bunch of books on finance, trading, and economics. I was so excited for Monday morning, I didn't sleep for the rest of the weekend.

*****

I was up and at it on Monday morning. I parked in the nearest parking building. It was a block away from Zack's office. I grabbed a coffee, and I was at the office about twenty minutes early. Zack came rolling in about five minutes before 8 o'clock. He laughed and shook his head at me.

"How long you been waiting, Syd?" he grabbed my coffee, taking a big gulp.

"About fifteen minutes," I wanted to protest, but he had what I wanted, information, so I didn't.

"Well, you're eager. That's good. I like hungry people. Listen, I have to have you sign a non-disclosure agreement. Okay? It's not a big deal. Do you know what that is?"

< It just means that you are not allowed to talk to anyone about what goes on here. >

< *Thank you!*>

"Yes, I do," I responded as I was lifting my chin.

"Good. Once you sign, we'll talk. Okay?"

"Okay!"

He took me inside. It was a bare-bones office. No attempt had been made to decorate. The only thing on the walls were push pins. Every office had a desk, some had two. There were cords everywhere. Every desk had two or three phones. I had never seen an office like it. There was trash everywhere, around the desks and the can, but not really in it. Every room reeked of teenage boy. There was a couple of college style refrigerators with pop and water inside.

After I finished signing all the paperwork he put in front of me, he booted up all his computers. There were three at his desk alone. Most of the desks had two each with at least 3-4 monitors. His desk had six screens, plus there was a big TV in his office set up like one of the monitors. He turned on MSNBC. One screen had the NYSE ticker running across it. Another was a Search page I had never seen before, and another page was listed as NASDAQ. One was his email, and one had a screen with four graphs on it that I had never seen before. My eyes must have been as large as a plate because he laughed at me.

"So, Syd, here ye are. I'll tell you what I really do. I'm an IPO whore, Initial Public Offerings. I flip them. Kind of like a hedge fund but with only one investor. My investor is Richard Giancarlo, and he is very wealthy. I run this small place for him. Now, while you're here, you will hear and see a lot of shit that I don't want anyone to know about. So that thing you signed," he pointed at the papers and continued, "That says 'keep your fucking mouth shut'. I don't even want you to talk about who works here, nothing. Got it?"

I nodded my head.

< You should leave. It doesn't sound legal. >

< No way. Whatever he's doing, he is making a lot of money. Look at his watch and shoes. Bruno Estibon's are fifteen hundred dollars and that watch is a Breitling®. They start at five grand.>

"So how much is in your book?"

I didn't know what that meant, so I didn't answer anything.

"Money, Syd. How much money do you have to trade with?"

I didn't like to talk about money. It made me uncomfortable. The only reason I had any was because of Adrian, so I deflected.

"How much do you need?"

I think that made him mad because his accent started to get really thick. "Are you jerking me off? I am trading with thirty million dollars. How much do you have little girl?"

I responded as calmly as I could, "I have 3.8 million to my name."

He looked stunned, and I could see the wheels turning in his mind. He turned away, looked at one of his screens, sat there a minute and swiveled his chair back around.

"How old are you? And how'd you got so much? What did someone die?"

I felt my mouth go dry, and my eyes started to burn. I couldn't answer that. I couldn't even look him in the eyes. Looking away, I went to grab my purse to leave, but he stopped me.

"Aww, Syd, I'm sorry! I didn't mean to hurt your feelings. Look, you don't have to tell me. Okay? If that is everything you have, fine. Don't trade it all. What do you have with a broker?"

I turned to him and answered, "Eight hundred thousand. I already have some stocks. They pay a dividend, so I want to keep them. But I would like to grow what I have a little."

"Okay, you said you're with Merrill, right?" I nodded.

"Okay. I want you to call Muriel Siebert and open an account there. Then, I want you to open one at Lehman and see if you can get one with Goldman. Put a half mill in each. You got that? I'm going to set you up with a desk here in my office, and you can trade your own book, so here's the catch. You don't make a trade unless I say so. If I tell you to make a trade, I get 10%. Whatever you trade on your own choice is all yours. There's a monthly office fee. You don't tell anyone here that you're trading your own got it?"

"Yes."

"The first month or so you're only going to sit, watch me and learn. Also, the guys here curse a lot and yell. You'll have to forget about that. That's just how it is. Got it?"

"Yes."

I had managed to dodge the age question. He was going to train me. It was everything I was looking for. He handed me a stack of binders and told me to start reading them. He called them rebuttal books and the study materials for the series 7. I was stoked. Now I was really getting somewhere. As I was contemplating what was happening to me, he started talking again.

"You need to know the rules if you want to break or bend them. ABC's Syd, Always Be Closing."

The day ran by fast. The other guys arrived, and after the introductions, they went to work. I heard Zack whisper something to them, but other than that, the day was a success. It went on like this for a few weeks. I had finished reading all of the books Zack had given me and started to get in the conversations from the office.

ABC, Always Be Closing, it made me laugh. Every broker lives and dies by the ABC's. The rebuttal books laid it out like this, pitch your deal and shut the fuck up. As Zack put it 'He who speaks first loses.' The books gave you all the bullshit they were going to shovel at you and a reply to it. My job was to rebut the rebuttal. Whatever deal they were selling, I would flip it around to the one I wanted. Then ask for the sale, or in my case, the trade. Rise and repeat until they gave you the trade or hung up on you. It was an industry standard. I opened all the accounts that Zack asked me to, even the Goldman account. I was the only one in the office with one. Zack was impressed. He asked me how I got Goldman to open the account. I smiled and said I would tell him sometime. He laughed and shook his head, but it was really the rebuttal books.

"Florida Girls."

August came and went and then September second came…. I didn't go to work. I was now older than Adrian would ever be. He had been dead a year. The voice started screaming.

< NOT DEAD, NOT DEAD >

The mantra played until I was sobbing and hiccupping. I curled up in a ball and I don't know when I heard the knocking on my door. I wiped my face, it was Zack. I didn't know how he got up here, there was a passcode.

"Sydney, what is wrong with you, why weren't you…." His word died on his lips as he gazed at me. I suddenly felt the image of my face slammed into my mind. I looked terrible.

"Hi Zack, umm… I'm sorry I didn't call. It's a bad day."

"Syd, you're not doing drugs are you? I don't want no part of that." He said.

"No I…I umm… a friend of mine died a year ago and a… I didn't think it would hit me this hard, but I just couldn't face it."

He looked around. He seemed very uncomfortable.

"Well, I'm sorry about your friend. Look, do you want me to stay? We could talk about it if you want."

I could tell he was just being nice.

"I know you are just nice, so you don't have to stay, but thank you for coming to check on me."

He gave me a hug, kissed me on the forehead and left.

< Maybe I was wrong about him. >

< *Really, you don't talk to me for weeks on end, and now you show up today to torture me? Then suddenly you're ok? What the fuck voice? You have been torturing me on and off for a year, always screaming in my mind. You need to stop! Voice? Voice?* >

He was gone. I didn't want him to be gone, but at least it was quiet in my mind.

Friday came. I went to Cosimo's for dinner and sat at the bar. It had become my habit. Next to me at the end of the bar was an old man. He introduced himself as Salvatore. He was nice. We chatted for most of my meal. He asked if I was going to come back again. I smiled and said,

"I'll be back for dinner next Friday."

CHAPTER 25

SYDNEY

December came. I had been doing more and more of my own trades and I was making about five thousand a week. That was enough to pay all my bills and not touch the capital.

Zack rolled his chair over to my desk, leaned over and put his elbows on his knees and looked up at me. I could see he was going to ask for something.

"What's up, Zack?"

"Well, Syd there is a big IPO coming out in a little over a week. Veritas BioTech is going to be big. Goldman has it, and you're the only one in the office that has an account. I want you to ask for it. Get as many shares as you can. I'll go fifty/fifty with you on it."

"So, you want me to trade my money on it? You will promise to pay me back for your share? Win or lose?"

"Yes."

"Okay, I'll do it, but I get to sell my shares when I say and not when you say. Got it?"

"Yeah, sure, Syd."

"Alright, we have a deal. If you fuck me, Zack. I'll find you in your sleep and I will dig your heart out with a rusty spoon."

I had learned a lot in the few months that I had been hanging around Zack. The guys were like a bunch of Sophomore College boys, always cursing. I learned more about the dirty male mind here than I ever could have by watching porn or reading Hustler forums. They loved to say the filthiest things and watch my face. It was like being surrounded by naughty little boys.

"Yea, I love it," he yelled out the office door, "Sydney's got a backbone, and she's going to get the shares for us." I picked up the phone, and dialed my broker.

"Hello, James, how are you?"

"Hey, Sydney, how's our favorite Florida Girl?"

"James, you have an allocation for Veritas BioTech VBT?"

"I can get you 70,000 shares" I put my hand over the phone and looked at Zack. He held up five fingers for fifty thousand. I gave him an okay.

"Okay, James, I'll take it. What's the catch?"

"I have a bet with a few guys here that you are scorching hot. We scrapped all our allocations together and we'll give them to you, but we want to see you in a bikini."

I was shocked. Zack got on his knees with his hands clasped and began to beg on the floor. So, did the rest of the guys. It was nice to see that they knew how to ask. I smiled.

"What's the open?" I needed to know the price per-share for my allocation.

"65." James replied.

"Okay, I'll move the 4.55 million day after tomorrow. But I want you to open an account for my friend today."

"Sure, but you have to webcam this first."

"No, I want his account with an allocation first. His name is Zackary Cosimo."

I heard James breathing.

"Okay. Have him call my back-office girl now."

"Okay. I'll call you back in 20 minutes, and I'll webcam you, then." I hung the phone up.

The room erupted in yelling and screaming, laughing. Zack picked me up and kissed me full on the mouth and then the guys all hugged me. Zack picked up the phone and took care of the details. I went to my car and got my bikini out with a towel. When I got back to the office, Zack gave me a thumbs up. I went to the bathroom and changed wrapping my towel around me. When I came out, Zack looked at me and smiled.

"I have never gotten that large an allocation. Tits and ass, boys. I'm telling you. Syd, she will make more money than we do any day of the week."

I was ready to start the webcam, but Zack walked over and told me to take my braid out.

"Why? I look fine."

"Because you want him to want more and trust me, he is going to want it."

I didn't blush when he kissed me, but I blushed when he said that. I pulled the braid out and shook my hair, and then I picked up the phone.

"James, I'm ready. Tell me where to go."

I loaded the program up and continued.

"Just remember, James that I know you are married, so no funny business. Also, don't you go back on me."

He laughed and said he wouldn't. I saw the office appear in the capture screen and I was in it. I waved at him. I didn't see him.

"Hey there, Sydney. Okay, let's see the bikini." I smiled and lowered the towel to my waist, then stopped. His office made a sound like awe.

"James, how many brokers are in your office?"

"10."

I pulled my towel back and said.

"Okay. I want 1,000 shares from each of them for the next IPO of my choosing. Then, I'll show the rest." There was murmuring and then James replied, "Sydney, we'll do it."

I let the towel drop to the floor. I heard from both sides 'hot', but Zack took the cake for the exclamations

"Sydney, you're fucking smoking hot!"

I waited for a few minutes standing there in my bikini. It felt good.

"Thank you! Now, if you gentlemen don't mind it is cold in here, and I would like to get dressed." I bent over and grabbed the towel. The room just froze, I didn't feel good anymore. I felt like a piece of meat. Zack saw that and stood up.

"Okay, guys! Party's over. Everyone, have a nice day."

I said bye to James and left the room to change. I heard them talking as I walked away, and as I came into the room, it got quiet again. Two of the guys just stared at me.

I needed to break the silence, "I hope this isn't going to affect our ability to work together."

Zack laughed out loud. "Syd, I may never look at you the same because you're fucking hot. But you're like a little sister to me, so I'll keep these pikers in line for ya."

"Thank you, Zack! So, now I'm not the only one with an account at Goldman."

"No, but you worked the fuck out of them. I'll bet they can and will give you shares for whatever you ask for from now on. Let's see how the trade goes. Okay? Good work!"

As it turned out later, I actually did get many trades from them. I left about 30 minutes later. The market had closed. I didn't have any trades open, so I went home.

A week later the market opened, and the open price on VBT was 68, so we were up 3 points already. Zack had 5,000 shares in his account. I had 70,000 in mine, 25,000 for Zack and his backer, 45,000 for me. When the stock reached 95, Zack told me to sell his 25k, and I called it in.

< Don't sell until it hits 125. >

< *Is it really going to hit 125?*>

< Yes, it will go higher. But you want to get out while the getting is good.>

< Okay, I'll call it for 125. >

As I sat and the number began to rise. It reached 110 and Zack started to get antsy. When it got to 115, he looked at me.

"Syd, I think you should get out."

"Zack, you're still in for 5,000 shares. When are you going to sell?" I raised an eyebrow as I looked at him. It was my best Spock maneuver.

"I'm going to ride your call." He says.

That was new because Zack never followed anyone. 120. I was surprised that he was following me. I had only been in this game for six months. As the ticker rolled across the computer screen and the TV, it was like watching grass grow. Finally, at 2:38 pm, the stock hit 125. I called James and said one thing.

"SELL!"

"How much?"

"All of it!"

The moment I had picked up the phone, Zack had too and called James only to be put on hold. When he got through, he also sold every share he had. He ended up selling at 123. I was out at 125 just like I wanted. The spread was 60. So, 45 thousand times 60 equal to 2.7 million minus tax. I had almost doubled my net worth in one trade. Zack was yelling at the top of his lungs.

"Sydney the rainmaker!!! I fuckin love ye Syd!! Ye know that!!" Zack picked me up and kissed me full on the mouth and hugged me so hard I had to tell him to stop because I couldn't breathe. He set me down and whooped.

"Tonight, Sydney buys the first round of drinks. Where should we get dinner, Syd?"

I didn't know where to go, so I said "Cosimo's".

Zack didn't say anything else. He just smiled and made a call.

I had been eating dinner at Cosimo's for eight months, so everyone knew me. It was nice to walk into a place where everybody smiled at you and said 'Hi'.

Zack had called ahead for a table, and we had a nice one near the window. I went over to the bar and kissed Salvatore on the cheek and then went to our table and sat down. Zack asked what I wanted to drink, and I asked for a glass of red wine. In his highest voice, he said "I'll have a glass of red wine, thank you". It was funny when he did it, but I didn't want him to mock me. So, I kicked him.

"Ouch! Hey Syd, why you kick me? I'm just making fun of ya." He pouted.

"You're as bad as one of my brothers. You know that, Zack?" I retorted

"Sure I am, but I'm much better looking," he gave me a badass smile.

The waiter came over and said 'Hi' to Zack. I think he'd been here before. I saw Zack whispering something to him, then he left. The waiter returned with a bottle of wine. He set the bottle down in front of me. Everyone else ordered a cocktail from the bar then we ordered our food. The food was fabulous, and it was nice to have people to eat with.

< You need to slow down. you're drinking too much. You won't be able to drive home. >

< *Shut up voice! I feel fine, and I'm having a good time. You know? Fun? Something I wasn't allowed to have my whole life?*>

The voice didn't reply back.

Zack stood up and held up his glass. "To, Sydney, our little rainmaker! That was one of the best trades I have ever witnessed. May you make many more!"

They all toasted me, and tears stung my eyes. I'd been accepted into their little world. Men didn't think that trading was a job for a woman unless you proved that you could do it. They wouldn't respect you unless you did it better than they did. You had to get one over on them. Well, I had just gotten one over on them, big time. I was feeling fuzzy. I got up to go to the bathroom, but I wasn't walking very well.

I had finished the bottle of wine by myself. Zack looked at me a little funny. I sat down with a plop. I reached for my glass to finish it off but knocked it over instead. Then I giggled. I didn't even see Zack get up. He grabbed my purse and took my keys. He threw them to Mark "Looks like you're driving Sydney's car home, Mark and I'll take her home because she can't drive."

"I can so drive home! It's only down the road."

Zack chuckled and shook his head. "Na Syd. You can't drive. You've had too much fun. I'll take you home. Don't worry, I'll be good." He grabbed my arm and stood me up, steering me to the door. I sputtered about the bill.

"I got it. Don't worry about it, little girl." He put me in his car and belted me in. "If you puke in my car, I'll kill ya."

By the time we got to my place, I was singing at the top of my lungs anything on the radio. I stumbled a few times and almost fell. Zack was laughing at me.

He had got me in the condo. I turned on the music and started to dance a little bit, but Zack turned it off. "Syd it's like midnight. I don't think your neighbors would like you playing loud music very much. I think ya should go to bed."

I kept dancing even though there was no more music on. I slurred my words and managed to ask, "Zack, why did you teach me to trade?" I wanted to know.

I think he was a little annoyed, but he answered, "I felt sorry for ya. You're young, and you seemed like you needed a friend." He exhaled and looked at me. "Anyway, I didn't think you would be any good at it. I thought I could stop you from throwing all your money away."

He went to the kitchen and returned with a glass of water, "Now, you need to drink some water and take an aspirin and go to bed."

"Why an aspirin? What does that do?"

"It'll keep you from getting a hangover."

"Oh! I didn't know that." I was laughing without any reason, and I was spinning in the middle of the room. "Probably because I've never been drunk before."

"Really?" He came to stop me and put me on a chair. "You should stop doing that. It won't help. You never drank this much before, why not?"

My body chose that moment to hiccup, and I giggled. "Because they don't serve 18-year-olds, silly," he was more shocked than mad.

"Sydney, your only 18? FUCK! Were you 18 when I met you?"

"Yea. My birthday's in March, and then I'll be 19. Did you know that I didn't even get a party for it? I moved out." He picked me up, took me to my room and set me on my bed. He took my shoes off and made sure I had some water, then told me to sleep. I did.

*****

The dream that came was mixed up and muddled. It had flashes of Adrian floating in the water, broken and bleeding. Then, I heard the announcement at church. I heard myself crying. I saw my father beating me, and I heard the voice screaming in my mind. I could feel my body thrashing, but I couldn't stop it. My father was slapping me over and over. He was dead, and I was alone. For a second, Adrian appeared holding me, telling me it was okay. He cared that I was safe, and I felt safe in his arms, but then I woke up.

*****

When I peeked my eyes open, they felt crusty. My mouth felt like a piece of carpet that had been danced on by a thousand people, but my head was okay. I grabbed for the water on my nightstand, but as I moved, I felt the weight of an arm on me. I froze.

Oh my God! What did I do?

I knew Zack drove me home, and I remembered telling him how old I was, but that was it. He was on top of the covers and fully clothed. The hand was touching my breast. I looked at it and, recognized the hand. It was Zack's. I reached down to my belly and checked to make sure I still had my panties on.

Thank God! Still there.

~ 317 ~

So why was he in my bed? I tried to slide out from under his hand, but it squeezed my breast. That was too much for me, so I sat straight up.

I looked over at him, and he opened his eyes and smiled. "Welcome back, little girl. Feeling better?"

My eyes must have been as big as a saucer. "Zack" I squeaked "Why are you in my bed, did we… I didn't… did I? I mean, what did I do?" I was so upset and scrunching my face.

"Hey, Syd, it was all platonic. I brought you home, put you to bed and went to sleep on your couch. You started crying, so I came to check on ya."

Relief washed over me, so he continued.

"You kept saying 'He's dead, he died. I miss him. Adrian can't be dead.' Who's Adrian, anyway?"

I turned away as the lump in my throat started to form, and the tears were filling my eyes. I looked out the window so he couldn't see my face and cleared my throat.

"Adrian was my fiancé. He is the one that died and left me the money." I just sat there feeling deflated and alone.

"Aw, I'm sorry, Syd! You must have loved him, and he appears to have been a good guy that took care of ya."

"Yes, I still do. I always will." I sighed.

"Well, I couldn't sleep with ya crying. So, I held you until you stopped. By then, I fell asleep too. That's why I'm in your bed."

Finally, I turned and looked at him. I was surprised. I didn't think he was a softy like that.

"Thank you, Zack!"

He smiled and looked a little sheepish. "Don't worry about it. Just don't tell the guys because they'll think I fucked ya."

I started to sputter. "I will not tell anyone you slept in my bed, but thank you for taking care of me."

He got up and went into the living room. I went into the bathroom. I looked a wreck. My hair was going everywhere, the make-up smudged like two black eyes, and my breath was so indescribably awful. It took me twenty minutes to clean up and look normal. When I was done, I noticed that Zack was gone. But he'd left a note:

Mark will bring your car later. Good job yesterday. See you on Monday. Z

CHAPTER 26

HERATHINA

Log Entry - 1,786,235.66 ATD

I observed Poseidon in the Citadel and the emotion coming from him. He is domineering. He craves power and her. Everything about it is primal, beneath us. Themians are not like this. Our emotions do not rule us. My entire life, from the moment we arrived here, I have been the only voice of reason. How am I supposed to explain any of this to the High Council when the time comes? Will I be held accountable for not saying more?

I know the emotions inside, and I feel his beneath the surface. Every day it's more of a chore for him to keep them in check. The time will come when we will need to go head-to-head again. I'm not sure if I'll be strong enough to withstand the onslaught. Maybe he will dominate me this time. There were stories from The Great Division, of Themian dominating Themian when people were taking over and controlling other people's minds and lives.

Until I came to this planet, I thought most of those stories were just stories, things parents tell their children to make them behave, similar to the humans' boogie man. However, having experienced Poseidon's attempted domination, I have no doubt every one of them is true. He was there when the Great Division happened, so he knows exactly what happened. Maybe that's how he learned.

"Herathina, you look as though you swallowed something sour that doesn't settle well in your stomach."

"Not at all Poseidon. I'm simply introspective, contemplating humanity and the human psyche."

His eyes twitched as the muscles from his jaw worked over the bone, clenching and unclenching. "I can feel the disapproval pouring off you. Your very presence questions my authority here. I will not have it. You will submit Herathina. You swore the oath."

"Have I not, in every way, kept my word? I have kept my counsel. I've not dreamwalked anyone except my family. You keep me here as a physical and mental prisoner. I bowed to your demands. What more would you have of me?"

"Your allegiance! I demand your allegiance."

I take a deep breath to control myself so I can give the answers using logic and science. I needed to remember that these human emotions are affecting him like a disease. It's not the Poseidon I know.

"I cannot give you my blind allegiance. Would you really have it? I do not wish to follow anyone blindly. You know my family. You know I was raised to question everything. We're scientists and our one mandate is to learn and understand. That is all I'm doing. I'm attempting to learn, to understand and ascertain our place in this universe. Our existence. Would you have me betray that oath too?"

His dark countenance doesn't waver from my face. Both brows are drawn together, creating a thick ridge between them. His body is coiled, ready to strike at me. His hands are gripping the rests on his throne. Because this is what it is - a throne. He has made himself the ruler of us all.

I internally fight with myself every day to maintain control. I can't falter. It would be easy to give in to Poseidon, perform all that he asks and not care what happens to this planet we have taken over, infected. Love for my family and the Themian way stops me. My mother's words ring in my mind. "A good scientist doesn't let their emotions cloud the work. Stay apart. The subject will reveal the answers that you seek." Patience, that's what she was talking about. We have an eternity to learn the outcome of any test, project or experiment.

I have to wait. Poseidon will be his own downfall. If I can wait long enough.

Cleito, the Enchantress, enters the citadel. She has a bracelet. He's given her free run of Alethea. She's been here hundreds of years but not aged a day. I know he is giving her the primordial waters. As she floats into the room, his eyes eat her alive. He's like a starving man who wishes to devour his last meal. With his every move, all thought or reason flees. Reaching up, he scratches his chin in contemplation.

"Herathina, I know your one desire is to study the Homo sapiens, to understand them. I will give you your chance. Be in The Citadel tomorrow when Sol reaches its zenith. We shall discuss your future on Alethea." His words ring in my head as its rage fills my belly. I know that whatever happens the next day, there is no getting away.

*****

"Since you desire to study the Homo sapiens, we will indulge it." He stops, and then commands, "Mica, send her where I do not have to look upon her face. Or feel her constant disdain and disapproval." Poseidon's face pulls back into a triumphant smile. The emotions swirling around him teeter on madness.

The ship dissolved, and the pressure changed around me. Suddenly, I'm standing in the center of a village with a craggy mountain top in the distance. Sheep are grazing around me. The people were cowed with fear and kneel down with their heads to the ground. A large man exits his hut and immediately kneels down in obeisance. His words are garbled. I have difficulty trying to decipher them. Turning on the bracelet, words begin to form.

"Oh, Goddess of the mountain, please find mercy in your soul. We will do whatever you ask. Do not lay waste to our village." He put his head down to the ground with his hands and arms spread wide in front of him. His grimy neck is fully exposed, gazing in shock around me. The words I keep hearing murmured are 'Goddess from the mountain'.

Log entry 1,786,254.16 ATD

Poseidon's sending out groups to gauge the level of civilization for Humanity was a ploy. He used it so he could justify sending me away. I have no way back to the ship. Nor do I have the necessary survival skills. I'm not even sure which way to go. My bracelet has been locked out of the system. I can't use the locator to find Alethea. I'm trapped here, for now.

CHAPTER 27

SYDNEY

"Hey, Salvatore! How are you this fine evening?" I was smiling at him as I kissed him on the cheek and sat down at the bar. He was a sweet man, and I liked talking to him.

"Awe Bella! Pretty good Syd-a-ney. How are you?" He was smiling back at me with a twinkle in his eyes. He always seemed to have a little joke that I didn't know about.

"Oh, you know. Another day, another dollar. What should I have for dinner? Does the chief have anything that looks good tonight?" I asked glancing at the specials board behind the bar.

He laughed out loud. "Yes, you should try the Veal Scaloppini, it looks delicious tonight. With a glass of vino and me as your companion. It will be the best meal in South Florida."

I laughed too. I couldn't help myself. He always made me laugh. Salvatore was like being with your fun Grandfather. He talked in his Italian accent, drinking a little glass of wine/vino. He didn't eat/mangia. He chatted with me and made me eat. Sometimes I would talk about my life, but mostly I listened to him talk. He told stories. I didn't consider all to be true, but they were funny. He teased me a lot about being too skinny. He was one of my few friends, and I loved him. He always made sure that I could drive before I left and kissed me on the forehead.

"Alright. Veal it is. Did you have a good week?" I inquired and winked back at him.

"It's alright. Syd-a-ney you have been coming here for almost four years. Why you don't have a boyfriend? Or come in with a few girlfriends? It is not good to always be alone." He chided.

I took a deep breath. I had to think about my reply. I didn't want to tell him everything, and I couldn't lie. "I don't have any friends. Anyway, if I came in with friends I couldn't sit at the bar and talk to you, or I would have to share you with them." I pouted.

"But you are alone, Bella, always alone." He looked down his nose at me and into his wine glass.

I was alone, and I was lonely, but I didn't know how to change that.

"I'm not good at meeting people. Anyway, I have you and my friend, Lisa." I deflected.

"It is not good. Why don't you meet some nice a boy and get married and have babies? Then bring them to see me." He patted my hand with bright inquiring eyes.

I shook my head and tried to forge an answer, "I can't meet someone, I just... I–", but he cut me off. "I can see that you had someone before. Where is he? Why is he not here to love you?"

I felt the lump in my throat and the tears in my eyes. I turned away from him. I didn't want him to see that I was going to cry.

I stared at the shelf of bottles behind the bar and the mirror behind them. My face a mask to hide the pain of the truth. "He died. That is why I am alone, and I can't forget him." I said in a low voice, almost a whisper.

His eye became heavy and sad. He touched my face. "Donna Bella, you see him everywhere you go, don't you?"

"Yes, I have all his furniture." I stopped for a second. "His family died too, and I got everything." I replied and lowered my eyes to the floor. This isn't the Friday dinner I had hoped for.

"I know what you must do. Bella, you must get rid of as much as you can. Give it away or sell it, it doesn't matter, but it must go. You are not living your life, you are living theirs. I am not saying you shouldn't keep some things but not everything. Get new curtains, keep only what you love. The rest should go. Then buy some new things, only what you want. You will be happier, and so will I." he finished with a kind smile.

My dinner came. I ate it and thought about what he had said. I was still thinking about it when I got home.

I turned on the lights as I walked through the condo. Salvatore was right. Everywhere I looked were his family's things. It wasn't my house, it was theirs.

I started taking down pictures, and I stacked them by the door. Then, I took all the curtains down in every room but mine. I put those on the pictures. I went into the kitchen and I took all the towels and put them in a pile. I moved the couch toward the door and next to the pile, along with the coffee table and the end tables. I didn't like any of the lamps, so they went too. I did like the dining table and chairs, so they stayed. There were a bunch of decorative items that I didn't like either.

I went into my room. That was the worst. There was Adrian's bedroom set. I wanted it, but I didn't want to sleep on it anymore. I moved the nightstands out of the room and changed my clothes for bed.

< Are you really going to get rid of everything?> The voice came through shocked and shaken.

< *Not everything but yes, a lot. I can't look at it anymore. I miss him, but I have to move on. He wanted me to be happy. I'm not happy this way.*>

< You should be happy; I want you to be happy. >

< *Thank you for understanding. What should I do with it?* >

< Give it to a charity, to help others. Abused women and children? >

< That is a great idea. Thank you. >

I went to bed feeling better than I had in years. I felt lighter.

*****

The dream slammed into me: He was holding my hand. Adrian's smile was as big as the sky. I smiled back at him. His lips were moving, but I couldn't hear him. I was in a bubble. He was wearing shorts and no shirt, and he was gorgeous. His muscles were tanned and gleamed with sweat. His chest was flexing with every move. His stomach was flat and rippling with muscles. He ran his hand through his hair and slicking it back. I couldn't take my eyes off his corded arms. His biceps were huge. When he put his arm down, he reached out and wrapped it around me, pulling me close.

I felt his breath on my face, and his lips touched mine warm and soft. His tongue invaded my mouth, and I was melting against his body, hungry for every touch that he gave me. His hands moved down my backside, splaying out and pressing me into his body. His mouth was teasing its way down my neck, nibbling as he went.

Then all of a sudden, everything was real. I could feel him and hear him. God, I didn't have any clothes on. I felt his hands gripping my ass, and I couldn't control myself.

I moaned "I love you! Make love to me, and don't leave me again."

"I will never leave you, my love. I said it would be special."

He led me to a cottage on the beach. It was picture perfect. Neat and tidy, just like Adrian liked it.

He kissed me again, his tongue tasting me and teaching me at the same time. I felt my skin burning with desire and lust. I was pudding in his arms, and I loved the feeling.

"I love you, Sydney" was the last thing I heard before the dream ended.

*****

Oh, God!

I sat up in bed. I was shaking and covered in sweat. My body had wanted him so bad. All I wanted was to feel him kissing me. I wanted him to be inside me and be just one.

After a while, I managed to relax enough to go back to sleep.

I woke up late and was in a rush to get ready for the day. I went into the bathroom only to find blood on my thighs. I wasn't due to start my period for another week, but I didn't give it too much thought. I took a shower and changed the sheets on the bed.

The dream was still vivid in my mind. I didn't know that a dream could feel so real.

I looked around the house and felt the loss sweep over me. He would never be here, no matter how many dreams I had, or how much I wanted him to be.

I called a charity for women and children, and they said they were coming on Monday to pick everything up. I went through everything. I even got rid of bath towels, sheets, and pillows. It was freeing.

When it was finally gone, the condo looked bare, but more like it was mine. I had taken Adrian's bed apart and put it into my storage closet in the condo basement, along with the elephant rocking horse, and the rest of Adrian's things that I didn't want to get rid of but couldn't look at every day. My bed was on the floor, but I didn't care.

I got in my car and went to the mall where I bought big fluffy towels, some beautiful curtains, and beautiful bedding. I went and got a couch and a chaise lounge. I bought some artwork, and I was having everything delivered on Thursday. I went home and hung up my white gauzy curtains and put away my towels. It was mine. All mine.

Friday, I entered Cosimo's with a bounce in my step until I spied someone was already sitting next to Salvatore. From the back, he had broad shoulders and golden-brown wavy hair. His suit was tailored to perfection stretching across his shoulders. My eyes followed his every move. Tearing my eyes away from the man flesh next to Salvatore, I leaned into Salvatore for a quick peck on the cheek.

"Good evening, Salvatore! It's great to see you."

"Aww, Syd-a-ney Bella. I am happy you are here." Salvatore said and winked at me.

I slid away to the next empty seat, but Salvatore didn't agree with my decision.

"Syd-a-ney, where are you going? Gabriel move over and let Syd-a-ney sit down."

"Oh, Salvatore, no. He doesn't need to move. I'll be fine over here. It's no big deal. I don't want to take his seat." I replied.

Gabriel was a feast for the eyes, mouth-wateringly gorgeous. His eyes were green with flecks of brown. He smiled at me with perfect teeth and full lips that looked like they wanted to kiss me everywhere. I must have been staring because his eyes started to twinkle with a knowing naughtiness. My mouth was dry. I opened and closed it a few times attempting to wet my lips. I refocused on Salvatore, but Gabriel chose that exact moment to move over.

"There, now we can have our dinner and chat like always." Salvatore clapped his hands for the bartender.

I didn't know what to do except sit down, so it did.

"Salvatore, I did it. I took your advice, and I got rid of almost everything. I feel better now. You were right. I wish you had said something sooner." I know my joy shone permeating my demeanor.

"Syd-a-ney, I am happy for you. So how does it look?" he inquired and pointed at his wine glass. The bartender topped the cup off and moved away.

"Bare. I did go and get a new couch and curtains, and it's all mine. I love it" I said and fingered the menu in front of me.

Salvatore stood up. A look of confusion plastered across my face. He said,

"Syd-a-ney I have to go talk to that man over there. Why don't you talk to Gabriel for a while, and I'll be back later okay?" He kissed my forehead.

"But I don't know Gabriel, I …um," I looked at him pleadingly, and he smiled.

"Gabriel will be good," he gave him a stern stare and added, "Won't you?".

"Yes, P… Salvatore, I'll be very respectful." Gabriel replied.

I repositioned myself facing the bar as Gabriel openly stared at me.

"Sydney, what are you drinking tonight?"

I was nervous and cleared my throat. "Um… red wine. There is a very nice Sangiovese on the list, which I order a lot." I don't know why I was so jittery, but I felt like at any moment I might dash out the door.

"Sangiovese, it is. Tony, get us a bottle of the Flora Springs Sangiovese, two glasses, and what are the specials for the night?" Gabriel asked.

Tony said something to him in Italian. He replied, and I heard vino, vongole, pasta, Insalata Caprese. The rest I didn't understand. Tony walked away, and Gabriel turned and looked at me.

"What do you like to eat? They have a Caprese Salad, clams in white wine, any pasta that you want." I was flattered he was trying to order for me but asking me what I like first.

I think he had been pumping Tony for information. I had never been on a date or out to eat with a man or even been hit on. At least, as far as I know, I hadn't been. So, I didn't know what I should do.

"I like the caprese, I'm not a fan of clams though and I don't want pasta tonight. But meat or fish sounds good. Why don't you choose, and I'll tell you how it was? I have never had a bad meal here." His smile got big, and I noticed he put his arm on the back of my chair.

"I will get you the best meal you have ever had that I didn't cook." He winked at me, and I chuckled.

"Are you a better cook?" I asked while cocking an eyebrow.

He turned his head from side to side and said, "Maybe, I'll cook for you one day, and you can decide." He replied with a husky laugh.

I smiled. He was funny. I don't know how, but I answered, "Okay, I'll let you cook for me, and we shall see."

"It is a date then. Excellent!"

I caught myself laughing out loud. "I have to get to know you better before that, but yes."

He hung his head holding his heart like I'd shot him. "I shall never recover from being shot down. So, I shall wait and ask the beautiful woman again later for her number."

He was funny. I found I was smiling through most of the dinner. He was from New York but had gone to college in Italy.

"So, what brings you to South Florida?" I asked.

"I am here to visit family and take care of some business."

"Oh, why aren't you eating with your family? You don't have to keep me company. I mean, I eat alone all the time at the bar." He looked at me funny.

"How long have you been coming here?" Gabriel inquired.

"About four years, every Friday. I sit at the bar next to Salvatore, and I eat dinner, and we talk. He is my friend." I found myself searching the room for him.

Gabriel raised an eyebrow. "Four years. I have never seen you here before, and I have been coming here for years. You've been eating dinner with P— Salvatore for four years? Does his wife know?" He was laughing at me

"I guess so, but we are just friends, I would love to meet her. She's a lucky lady. "

"Really, you think so?" he chuckled.

I was surprised. "Yes. He is kind and smart, funny. He listens to me like the Grandfather I wish I had."

Gabriel released a big belly laugh.

I didn't know what was so funny. But I found I was laughing too. Gabriel was making me laugh, and I liked it. He ordered another bottle of wine, and I was feeling a little light-headed. Salvatore came back when I was drinking my espresso. I went to pay for the bill, but Gabriel grabbed it before I did, then wagged his finger at me.

"A man never lets his beautiful dinner companion pay for anything." He gave me the most seductive smile before he continued, "I have enjoyed your company so much. I would like to see you again. May I have the pleasure of your company for another dinner and your phone number so I may call you." He had taken my hand in his and kissed it.

His hands were large. My hand felt like drowning in it. He took my breath away. I was blushing and looking around.

Salvatore returned my stare with a tight smile, then whispered, "You should say yes to both."

"Yes," I replied.

Gabriel kissed my hand again. I wrote my number down and got up to leave. He stood up too.

"I will walk you to your car." Gabriel offered his arm.

"Oh, you don't have to do that. I'll be okay. The parking lot is well lit, and everyone here knows me."

It didn't matter what I said because he simply took my hand and put it in the crook of his arm as we walked toward the door.

It seemed right to be walking with him. He didn't walk too fast, so I was able to keep up. He was taller than me. I felt like a little porcelain doll. I saw a reflection of the two of us walking through the glass door of the restaurant. I barely came up to his shoulder. He was well-built and strong.

He asked which car was mine, and I pointed to the beat-up Honda. He walked me to the door. He held the door for me. I set my purse inside. When I stood back up, he leaned in and kissed me on the cheek. I must have turned beet red. His eyes were twinkling in the dim parking lot lights. I stared at the ground because I couldn't look at him.

"Good night Gabriel! Thank you for dinner."

He took my hand in his. "The pleasure was all mine. I can't remember the last time I had such an enjoyable meal or such a beautiful woman to share it with. I'm going to call you tomorrow. Is that alright?"

"Um... yes." My heart fluttered. I climbed into the car so he didn't see that I was blushing.

Before he closed the door, he told me to call him Gabe and handed me a napkin with his number on it. "Call me if you need anything or just want to talk. I would love to hear from you."

"Thank you, Gabe. Good night!"

I drove home and put the number on the fridge and squealed.

< You like him? >

< *Yes. He was charming and amusing and didn't seem to be a rapist or want to hit me. Anyway, Adrian said I should be happy. I want to be with someone I can love. I don't know if this is the guy. But the way I'm going now, I'm never going to meet anyone if I don't try.* >

< That is true. He is a good guy. He will treat you right. >

< *Thanks!* >

Voice often lets emotions through, and this time, it was fear.

CHAPTER 28

SYDNEY

Zack had decided to move his office to South Beach, and I was relieved when he told me. Zack had moved the office every year. It got old to move everything at least once a year, so I moved to my condo to work on my own. Zack said that I could call whenever I wanted and stay with him and go out clubbing. I spent most of the week moving things, moving services and closing accounts. Plus, I had to get a cleaner for the old office. I didn't have time to call Gabe, and when he called, I couldn't talk to him. I felt terrible, but I was scared.

When Friday came, I was relieved to see only Salvatore at the bar. He smiled and waved.

"Syd-a-ney, how are you tonight?"

"I'm pretty good. I moved offices all week. I'm working out of my condo now, glad it has turned out this way. I think Zack was ready to move on, and I was too. We are still friends, so it's good."

Salvatore was nodding his head in approval.

"Time marches on, and things change. I can't eat with you tonight Syd-a-ney. My wife is not feeling well, so I have to go home, but I wanted to come and tell you."

I felt terrible that he had stayed for me. "Salvatore next time don't come in for me, just call me. I'll bring you both dinner or something. Okay?" I gave him my card with my home number on the back.

"Syd-a-ney, you are a good girl. Thank you!" He kissed me on the forehead and left.

Tony brought me my wine. I was looking over the menu when the tingling of a warm breath rolled across my neck. I sat up straight, and every hair on my neck stood up as my heart sped up. I looked in the mirror. His mouth was next to my ear. He had an arm on either side of my chair. The heat was coming off of his body. It was his eyes; they were boring into mine in the mirror. He looked like he was hungry but not for food.

He whispered low. "I think you are avoiding me."

I snickered. I turned my head as his lips grazed my ear, and I sucked in a breath, but I didn't say a word.

"Can I buy you dinner, Donna Bella Sydney?"

I was still looking in the mirror at his eyes. They resembled jade pools tonight.

"Yes, you have caught up with me. What else can I do?"

A low throaty chuckle escaped him. His smile could melt butter in Siberia. I knew I was in a lot of trouble if this went on too long.

I spent the evening laughing and wishing it wouldn't end, but it did. He walked me out to my car and kissed my cheek good night, and I went home. Every day was a struggle to keep my mind in the game. Zack called me a few times, but I couldn't focus on what he was saying. He asked me what was up, and I told him I wasn't feeling very well.

Gabe started calling me twice a week to talk. We loved to talk about opera, classical music, swimming, sailing and all kinds of literature. He constantly peppered me with questions about me. I had never been the center of attention before. It was a little disconcerting. He always ended our call by saying 'Good night, Bella'.

After two months, I was hoping that he would ask me out on a real date or kiss me. He was so gorgeous. When he entered Cosimo's, women would stare at him. Once I got up and went to the bathroom in the middle of dinner, and when I returned, a woman was sitting next to him and leaning over. She was practically rubbing her breast on his arm. I returned to my seat, to his relieved remark of 'Oh good, your back'. She huffed and moved away. He feigned that I had saved him from a fate worse than death.

I wanted to spend almost every day with him. I was finding more and more reasons to call him or excuses to leave work early on Friday to get dinner. I even started going to the mall to shop for clothes to wear to dinner. I wanted to look the best that I could.

Upon entering Cosimo's, I headed to the bar as usual. Gabriel was there with an exquisite tall, buxom woman. She had raven black long flowing locks and was whispering in his ear. His arm draped the back of her chair, intimately. I froze. Not knowing what to do, I changed course into the market.

I'll just go out the front door there, without Gabe even noticing me.

The burning in my chest was unbearable. He had been having a good time. I couldn't sit there and act like I didn't care that she was all over him. Heading to my car, I focused on the ground holding back tears. I hated that I was feeling this way.

Without hearing him coming, he blocked my way. "Sydney, where are you going? Are you okay?"

I just looked away. I didn't want him to see I was upset. "Um… I don't feel well, so I'm just going to go home and go to bed." I passed around him and kept moving. I didn't want to glance up at him or anyone else.

Right then, I heard Salvatore calling from across the way. "Syd-a-ney, are you okay? Where are you going?" It sounded like an echo.

"Salvatore, I don't feel well. I'm going home. I thought I would be okay, but I think I just need to leave. I'll see you next week, okay?"

I had reached my car, but in my attempt to unlock it, I dropped my keys. I was now shaking slightly. Gabe picked them up.

"Sydney what is wrong? I was waiting for you and you just... walked out."

I heard the laugh that came out of me, and I scoffed at him, "Sure. Waiting for me."

I covered my mouth with my hand. I swallowed back my tears, taking a deep breath.

I had said that out loud. What was wrong with me? Get control of yourself, Syd!

"Look Gabe, what you do with your time is your business, and who you do it with, isn't mine. I'm just some girl that you ate dinner with at the bar a few times. I don't feel well, and I want to go home."

His demeanor resonated hurt. "The girl at the bar. That's the problem? She's my cousin."

Yea right, your cousin.

Salvatore said something in Italian to Gabriel, and he replied.

"Syd-a-ney, what is wrong?"

"Papa, she saw me sitting at the bar with Maria, and I told her she was my cousin." He held his shoulders up and waved his hands around a bit and turned to me. "Look Sydney, ask Zack if you don't believe me. He will tell you she's his sister. He'll be here in a few minutes."

Now I was incensed. He was lying to me. What kind of an idiot did he think I was?

"You're a liar. Zack is an only child, and why would he be coming here? Why did you call Salvatore Papa?" The thoughts in my mind were spinning so I stopped for a second. "Wait, how do you know Zack? How do you know that I know Zack?"

I didn't get it, but I wasn't leaving until I figured it all out. How did he know about Zack? I never mentioned him to Gabriel. Salvatore knew my partner's name was Zack, but that was it, and I didn't think he would talk about my business.

Gabe replied, "Zack Cosimo, Gabriel Cosimo." He then looked at Salvatore and continued "Salvatore Cosimo is the owner of the restaurant, and he's my grandfather. Zack is my cousin."

It felt like I'd been slapped in the face. The look on my face must have been shocked. I was starting to feel a little light-headed. Why didn't they tell me…how could Zack not say anything? At that moment Zack walked over with his great timing.

"Hey, Syd, how's it going? Hey Gabe, Papa."

Now I was furious, he knew and had known all along.

"Fuck you, Zack! You knew the whole time and never told me that Salvatore was your Grandfather and owns this place? And you," I rounded on Gabe, "you didn't bother to tell me either." I turned at Salvatore. "I thought you were my friend. God all of you lied. You lied. Why? Why did you lie? God! Just get away from me! All of you."

Zack walked forward to touch my shoulder. "Hey Syd! It's not like that. I just asked Papa to keep an eye out for ya cause ya said ya came here, and I didn't want ya's to get taken advantage of by some shyster. I was lookin' out for ye. You're my friend." He remarked and smiled to try and shake it off.

I shrugged his hand off. I didn't want any of them to touch me. I was moving back and felt the car press into my back. I was starting to feel panicky, and my heart was racing. They were moving closer. I couldn't leave without my keys. Gabriel had them, and I needed to put on a strong face and get out of here. I stood up straight, lifted my chin and looked Zack in the eye.

"Thank you for looking out for me Zack, but the Cosimos' pity watch is over. I am a big girl. I can and have taken care of myself for a long time. I don't need you to have your grandfather babysit me, or you to set me up with your cousin so that I can get a date and he can get his rocks off. Thanks, but no thanks!"

Zack whipped around on Gabriel. "Son of a bitch! Did you fuck her? Gabe, why are you here, why aren't you in Roma? What did you do to her?"

Gabe paled then locked his jaw down. "Nice, Zack! Go ahead! Use that language about your friend, and partner. Are you in love with her?" He demanded.

Now I really wanted to go, but Gabe still had my keys. So, I walked over to him and put my hand out. He turned over my keys. I turned to leave. All I could think about was that I wanted to get as far away from the Cosimo's as possible and never see them again.

"Naw, Gabe. I'm not in love with her. She's like my sister, and I care about her. She's alone and sweet. She's not meant for you, you have other obligations, so stay away from her. I mean it."

I pulled the door to my car open and got in. Then the beautiful Raven-Haired Girl from the bar came out. "What is goin' on out here, Zack? Why is everyone yellin' in the parkin' lot, for the whole neighborhood to see? Papa come on." The woman cocked her shapely hip to one side and and tapped her heel on the pavement.

She put her hand on her hips, and the men shut up.

"Syd-a-ney didna know that we were all fam-a-ly. Zack didna tell her, she just found out, and now she is mad." Salvatore shrugged as if he had nothing to do with it.

She rounded on her brother, "Four years and ye neva mentioned your family or Papa.?" She was walking toward me now. "Gabriel, is this the girl that ye were tellin' me about, and ya didn't tell her you're a Cosimo? Really, Gabriel?" Her attention moved to Salvatore. "Papa did you tell Nonna that Sydney didn't know ya were Zack's Grandfather? No, a course, not. Yeah, I'm leavin' too. You, men." She looked over at me smiled. "Hi! I'm Maria, and I'm Zack's half sista."

Emphasizing the half.

I shut my door and started my car. It made a terrible noise, and then smoke started coming from under the hood. I just laid my head down on the wheel. I wanted to cry, but I didn't want the Cosimo's to see. I grabbed my purse and a few other things. I got out and started walking to the Intracoastal bridge.

"Aw, Syd, where are ye goin'? I'll drive you home." Zack looked worried.

"I'm walking to Palm Beach Hattie's, and I'll get a cab. I just want to get away from you and your family." Then I stopped, and I turned around. "How could you Zack? It's like you guys were babysitting me. Why? Just tell me why."

"Aw Syd, I wasn't doing that. God, you were just a kid when I met ya, and you were so alone. You needed a friend. I just didn't want to see you get hurt by some guy getting ya drunk and then takin' ya home. Ya know? You were very young and naive, so I told Papa to watch out for ya. I didn't realize he was sitting with you every Friday. I had nothing to do with Gabe. Did he touch you or something?" He stopped and looked behind. "I'll kill him if he did."

I didn't answer. I was too mad to say anything. Zack looked like he felt bad.

"Look, I was coming here to tell ya, and introduce ya to my sista Maria. I thought maybe you guys could be friends and hang out. She's movin' down here, and ya could keep an eye on each other. She doesn't know anyone but the family." He shrugged with his hands in the air.

I was starting to soften towards him until that. "Oh, so she is just the new babysitter since you moved to Miami huh? Yeah, I don't need one thanks, Zack." I was pushing my hand in his chest making him take a step backward. "I don't want to talk to you right now. Okay?"

I turned and kept walking til' I reached the end of the parking lot. Over my shoulder, the fireworks went into overdrive.

Maria yelled at Gabe, "Are you changing your plans? If you ever want her to speak to ya again, you will get her car fixed. Then, think of some way to let her know that ya wanted to be with her. Take her somewhere or something." She looked at Salvatore. "Papa, you tell Nonna or I will. Zack, what were ye thinking, are you in love with her?" she demanded.

"Na Maria, you know I don't like girls like her. She's sweet, nice, thoughtful. She's alone. Her family was really bad to her, and her fiancé died. That's all."

Zack turned around and looked at Gabe. "You did this, Gabriel! Why are ye even here? Why aren't you with Frederico in Italy? Don't you have responsibilities? I was going to tell her tonight, and you came in and fucked it all up."

Salvatore weighed in at this point.

"Zackary you have no right to talk like that to Gabriel. He truly likes her, and she likes him. The truth is that we all made a mistake. Come, boys, let's go call Marco and get the car fixed."

*****

Dinner arrived about an hour later. It was Zack. I let him in. He was hanging his head.

"I didn't come here to bully ya, I just wanted to tell you a few things." I stepped aside and let him pass.

"I didn't know how old you were until that big trade, and you were drunk. I saw it would have been easy for me to take advantage of ya's and I didn't like that. I didn't want some guy to rape you or something. So, the next day, I called my Grandfather and told him to keep an eye out for ya's. I thought he would tell Tony and like step in if he needed to. That's all." He flopped down on my couch and ran his fingers through his hair. "I didn't tell him to sit right by you and eat dinna or not to tell you he was the owner. But I did tell him not to tell you he was related to me, and yea I didn't tell ya. I was just tryin' to look out for you." He leaned forward and rested his elbows on his knees. The rolled up cuff on his dress shirt barely covered his elbows.

What he had just said hit me. They had been protecting me, and I should have seen that. I was only 22 and living on my own for over four years. Zack was right. He was looking out for me, like a brother. My anger started to melt away.

"What about Gabriel? What is his excuse?"

"Don't blame Gabriel. He didn't know anything. He just wanted ya to like him for himself. He didn't even know that you were my partner until Maria told him. Papa didn't tell him that you didn't know he was the owner. Okay? He didn't know anything. Papa said to be respectful, and he was. Wasn't he?" Zack's eyes bored into me waiting for an answer.

"Yes, he was. He hasn't even kissed me." I smiled and sat down in a chair.

He took my hands into his. "That is what family does Sydney. They protect you, not hurt you. That is what we were doing to you. You just didn't know it. I don't know what was wrong with your family, but they should have protected you. My family is very protective; they will neva let anyone hurt you. You just have to say the word, and they will make him wish he was dead. You're my friend and the best partner anyone could ask for." He smiled and punched my in the shoulder.

At this point, we were both smiling so he continued, "Did you know that ya helped make me over a million dollars in four years on just your trade picks? You're an amazing trader, and you know I don't say stuff like that."

No, he didn't, and he had never said that to me before.

< Forgive them. They only did it to protect you. It was well intended. >

< I guess he was only looking out for me, but what should I do about Gabriel? >

< I'm sure you will hear from him soon. >

< You're a big help!>

Zack sat there for a few minutes, looking at me. I felt like I needed to say something when the image flashed into my mind. I didn't get a lot of them, but this one was very clear -

Zack holding me while I cried on my bed, telling me it was okay and that no one was going to hurt me.

"Thank you for looking out of me, Zack. I have a hard time letting people help me."

I didn't want to get hurt, so I just keep everyone at arm's length. I had been doing that to Zack for years. He had let me have my space, like a good friend. He deserved the same in return.

I invited him to eat dinner with me. It was Penne Alla Vodka, with bread. I didn't have any wine, but we ate and chatted away. I cleaned up and put everything in the kitchen. When I came back to the living room, he looked ready to leave.

"Going home?"

He nodded so I gave him a big hug, "Thank you for being my friend, Zack."

"Syd, can I have your keys? We took your car to be fixed, but they need them to do all the work?"

"Yes, thank you. I was going to take care of it, but you are still looking out for me?"

"Yea. Well, I know a guy, and it will be ready by Tuesday. Someone will bring it by for ya's. Okay? Look, when Gabe shows up, give him a break will ya? He just wanted you to like him for him." Zack pressed his lips together as if he was holding something back, but I didn't ask what it was.

He kissed my forehead and left. I didn't know what I was going to do about Gabriel, but I was tired and wanted to sleep for a week.

My car arrived on Tuesday, and just like Zack said, it was fixed all right. All the dings and bumps were gone and painted over. My seats had brand new covers and floor mats. My windows were tinted. They put new tires on it. I had a DVD changer under the passenger seat. It was clean and detailed. When I asked for the bill, the guy told me it was taken care of. So, I called the shop, and a man named Marco got on the phone and told me that the bill was paid in full. I asked him who paid it, but he told me it was the Green-Eyed Cosimo, Gabriel.

I wanted to call him, but I didn't know what to say. What he had done to my car was more than I would have ever done. I took it for a drive. It was perfect.

CHAPTER 29

HERATHINA

Log entry 1,786,256.17 ATD

Poseidon shifted me to a village high up on a mountain, in the mid-region of the planet. They don't have a name for the village. It's tiny. There are only ten families here and the mountain was called Olympus.

They've begun building a shrine to me. I appeared out of nowhere, so they've assumed that I'm a Goddess. No matter how many times I tell them my name is Herathina, they cannot say it and call me Hera. I tell them that I am a person just like them, that I'm no different and that I'm not a God, but they still believe that I must be a Goddess.

I can understand how their primitive minds might believe that, seeing how I can control the forces of wind, water, and fire. My empathic abilities allow me to understand people's feelings. I can perceive their actions via their emotions. I appear pre-sent to them. They aren't simple minded. They have not encountered the same ideas that I have, therefore they don't understand them, but I believe they can learn and at a rapid pace.

Every time I think about Poseidon with that woman, it makes me sick. He claims to have married her in some human ritual ceremony, and I'm sure that his children have been born by now. I've tried to discover who they are, but everyone who follows Poseidon is blocking me. It's like trying to listen through the water. The only thing I keep getting is the name Herakles.

I finally contacted Athena. She was reluctant to speak to me but happy to be in contact. She informed me that Poseidon's human wife had two twin boys, and indeed, the eldest's name is Herakles. She also informed me that she's pregnant again with twins. Two boys that are unheard of amongst our people. For us, it is always a boy and a girl.

How is it that he is justifying all of this to the High Council? Poseidon cannot dreamwalk the council on his own.

My last dreamwalk with the High Council was just before Poseidon shifted me here.

A sickness fills my belly with every thought of him defiling that human. These are not the parameters of our people. We swore an oath of non-interference. Not only is he married to one, but he's also procreating with one. He's polluting the gene pool.

Log Entry:

I have dispensed with the date. There is no point. I may be here indefinitely. If I am ever allowed to rejoin my people, I will start counting again.

The village that I've become a part of is quite picturesque and everyone here is mild mannered. They work the fields and tend their goats and sheep. Most of the women tend to stay around the home and hearth. The men trade women like they would sell their animals. They are not unkind. Women are valued.

I have begun to train the women in better ways to manage their village, while still being in line with their civilization levels. I am teaching them about cleanliness and child care. I'm hoping that by providing them with this kind of information, it will lower the infant mortality rate. Children die so easily here from disease and just plain filth. If more of their children live, then perhaps, they can bring their level of civilization up.

When the High Council said to have limited interference, I believe this is what they were talking about. We're studying their genetic evolution, their civilization's evolution and teaching about cleanliness is a step on the evolutionary trail. This will be a huge step in some cases. These people have already figured out that peace is a better way to survive. They understood that intermarrying between villages allows for healthier offspring. It also helps keep the peace.

They have instituted marriages between the tribal leaders. In a lot of cases, I noticed that the chief's daughter is usually married to the chief of the next village over, in an effort to help keep the peace. This works as long as no one wants to kill their family.

Log Entry

I haven't heard much about Poseidon or the rest of my shipmates. There is a city that many of the traveling merchants whisper about. They say that it is highly advanced and the people living there are also. They have special powers, amazing tools, and vehicles that propel them through the air and in the sea. It can only be Alethea.

The city that they talk about is named Atlantis. They say the people living there are Atlanteans. It must be Poseidon and Alethea. This planet has not reached a level of civilization to have what people are describing. Many of the people ascribe these stories passed around by the traveling merchants and bards as just fantasies.

Fantasies they may be. However, I know the truth of them. I've also heard of a rise of power in the West. The power they refer to is a man they call Pharaoh. It seems he can rise from the dead. They call him a God and his wife a Goddess. They're describing sounds like someone from Alethea. But why would you purposely allow yourself to be mortally harmed then bring yourself back to life, just to have people worship you as a God?

When I look around this planet, I wonder if staying in this village is helping these people, or am I harming our project in its entirety? I am known as the Goddess of Mount Olympus, what if Alethea is hearing about me in return?

We came here to answer how we evolved into what we are? What was the trigger that caused us to become smarter and to be able to control the powers and forces? There has to be an answer. This is a place where we could find in time.

Yet every time I tune in and listen or dreamwalk, the emotions of the humans wash over me. They aren't all coming from the human. I feel my fellow Themian's filled with uncontrollable lust, hate, rage, joy. It is an outcome that no one could have perceived. They seem incapable of handling it to the point of mania. I can only describe it as insanity. They've become drunk with emotion or infected. My people never craved anything before except knowledge.

Since the Great Division, there wasn't such a thirst for power that echoed at the edge of our civilization. It should have died and yet here we are. The quest for power has reared its ugly head yet again.

Log Entry

Our village has grown tremendously in the last several thousand years. I know that some will think that staying here and helping these people was a waste of time, but I've found it rather fulfilling because I've learned a new respect for life. Everyone here lives such a short time. Life is so precious. I treasure everyone that I help bring into this world. From their first breath to the last, I cannot say I am untouched.

No matter how often I tell them I'm not a Goddess, due to the fact that I don't die or age, I can never convince them. Their mind simply cannot grasp the concept. My physiology is foreign to them. They think because I look like them, I must be one of them. If not, I must be a God. There is no other answer.

Most of what happens here revolves around the harvest and the seasons. There are very little changes, other than the faces and the names, yet I have watched the course of rivers change along with the coastlines. However, there is one item of interest. The chief of a neighboring tribe, Onus, has died. I don't know if it was on purpose or not, but his son has assumed power.

The whispering started immediately. One of the herdsmen from a neighboring village wandered onto our land. He took the midday meal with us and told how the warlord destroyed a nearby village. He went and cut down half of their warriors while they were asleep. Then, he dragged the chief from his bed and challenged him to one-on-one combat. He killed him by cutting off his head and dismembering his body. In the end, he raped his wife in front of the entire village, and he killed all of the chieftain's children, leaving no one to usurp his rightful place.

The murmuring began in our village. Many of the women were afraid to leave their huts. I was plagued day and night with petitioners. Some asked for me to tell their future, others just wanted a blessing. They sit outside of my hut, waiting for my proclamations. The very young girls would come inside to clean and care for me because they want to train as a priestess to me. They claimed that becoming an acolyte to a Goddess would protect them. Most just beg the Goddess to protect them. Limited interference, that is what the High Council said, so no matter my feelings for these humans, I cannot fight a war.

Log Entry – It had been many hundreds of years since my last entry.

A traveling merchant crawled into our village today. He was burned and bleeding from the many cuts on his body, and his clothes were nothing more than rags. Most of his body was covered with soot from a fire. The scorch marks on his skin were peeling back and filled with maggots. One of his beautiful brown eyes had been practically gored out. The hair on that side of his head was burned back to the skin and covered in blisters. I'm not sure how he actually made it to us.

I did my best to clean his wounds. I wanted to nurse him back to health. He became delirious as his eye swelled and blackened with fever. Red veins reached their deathly fingers down his face and neck, and all he could say over and over again was, 'He killed them. He killed them all', but he would not give me the name of who he spoke of. However, in my heart, I knew there could be no other. The scourge was in the countryside. No one would believe that someone would kill everyone in the village except for the young boys, women, and children. This man's constant thirst for blood and power was all that drove him.

Efron called me to counsel in the morning. The merchant had died in the night. I heard him in his death throes. Jorhan stood with dark brows shaking his head. "You are a patient Goddess, Hera. Without you, we would be lost to this scourge that comes to our village."

"Efron, you know I cannot fight a war for you. It is against my mandate. I love your people, our people, but I cannot shed blood for them." I remarked, repeating the same words from a week ago.

His tired shoulders slumped in defeat. "Hera, I know it is not your way, but can you do nothing for us?" His eyes peered up at me hopefully and pleading.

"If offering myself in any way will save your people one drop of blood. I would be happy to do it. But if the rumors are to be believed, this warlord will not be satisfied with just one drop. Only an ocean can fill his desire for power."

Efron's shoulders lifted and lowered. I could see the labor of his breathing. His time in this world was short. Soon, Jorhan would become chief, and this burden would pass to him.

Log Entry I've forgotten the date.

The latest of the warlord's atrocities have reached our village. The women raised their hands wailing night and day. Three-days prior there had been a terrible storm. Thunder and lightning preceded the rain, the likes of which I had never witnessed before on this planet.

Thunder was used to conceal him as he crept up to each sentry slicing their throats and bringing the silent death. After all of the men on watch had been dispatched, he entered the village's main path, flanked by his best warriors and standing in front of the chieftain's hut. The rain began to fall, running in rivulets down every pathway. He bellowed for the doomed leader to face him. The older man exited his hut in full battle dress. His chest was covered with a leather tunic of brigantine and he carried his weapon of choice and a shield.

Raising his arms in a battle cry, the thunder struck, and the bloodthirsty warlord threw his spear. As the sky lit up, the spear embedded itself into the chest of the chieftain, and a bolt of lightning struck the metal haft. The village filled with the sizzling sound of cooking flesh and burnt hair. The chieftains head lit on fire as did his hut. It consumed his family, for the rain was not enough to douse the flames.

Every man, woman, and child fell to their knees at his feet. In their eyes, he became a God.

His name reached my ears "Zeus. The man's name is Zeus. I feared for my life, Goddess, so I too showed him obedience. Forgive me. I have no desire to worship him, but if he can command the very lighting from the sky, how am I to stand?"

The woman lowered her eyes to the ground. Then, she tore her dress in the front, letting it fall and exposing her breasts. She had knelt in front of me by the fire. She reached her hand in and took hot ashes, spreading it over her head and arms.

"He killed my husband and son. Then, took my baby and bashed his head against a tree."

Tears filled my eyes as her despair filled me. The terror from her experience was palpable. She continued.

"Many women were raped. Even the young girls that were not yet ready for motherhood."

This is the third such village he has taken, wiping out all who would oppose him. He's a merciless butcher. I cannot imagine what form of man can carry around such barbarism in his heart.

A messenger arrived today. I ascertained by the way he arrogantly strode into our village that he was from Zeus. He gazed around gauging our preparedness for war. Our people are not warriors. They are farmers and herders. They work the ground. They carry sticks. They use a bow and arrow for hunting animals, not men.

"Efron, whatever this messenger says you must begin preparing your people. War is coming." I counseled.

The painful rattle inside his broad chest worked on my ears as it rose, seeking out the precious breaths of air but finding very little. He laid his hand gently on my arm, "My Goddess if the rumors are to be believed there is no way we would stand. All ideas of winning a war against Zeus must be thrown away as folly."

"What are his demands?"

"This warlord demands tribute. The first-born daughter of every chief in every village." Efron coughs and blood lay in his hand.

Our chief does not have a daughter. There were only two sons, one of whom has died, leaving only his oldest son, Jorhan. Without a Chief's daughter to turn over to this War Lord, we have no tribute.

Jorhan whispers, "Without tribute, there will be war. He says he will come and kill everyone in the village."

I cannot allow these people to die. I've been here for generations nurturing them, training them, teaching them, living with them. These people are truly good and wonderful people with amazing ideas.

After much deliberation, I developed a plan.

I stood before Efron, "I offer myself. I cannot let these people die simply because the Chief did not have a daughter."

He shakes his head to deny my offer, but I lay my hand on his chest and meet his watery brown eyes. He dips his head and agrees.

"I will play you as my daughter and turn you over as a tribute. Jorhan will take you to this Zeus." Efron coughs out his answer.

It is many days journey to the other Village. I could have taken myself there. I would have made it in a shorter time, but the only way for this to work was with Jorhan. When we reached the top of the rise, and I could see down into the village, I told Jorhan I wanted to make camp.

My last night of freedom under the stars. He has no idea that I could free myself easily at any time. No human can ever hold me as a prisoner. There's nothing that this warlord could do to me to harm me. I have the power to be free.

Jorhan hung his head. "What will you do?" Now was the time. If everything went as planned, I could save them all. "Under no circumstances are you to endanger yourself."

CHAPTER 30

SYDNEY

When I got home, he was waiting at my door. Gabriel was wearing a gray suit which fit him to perfection in every way. His shirt was open at the top, and he had a way of making it all look casual - he was a God. There were flowers in his hands. I almost couldn't see anything else for staring at his green eyes. They were boring in my mine.

"Gabriel."

"Sydney, I… I wanted to say I was sorry…. I didn't mean to deceive you. I just wanted you to see me for who I am, not who my family is," he was talking so fast, almost like he wasn't even breathing, "I didn't know about the rest, please forgive me. I would have told you my last name at any time if you had asked me. But you didn't, and I don't even know your last name, but I like you very much. I..."

I looked away before I replied "O'Dear. It's O'Dear. Gabe, I like you too. I..."

The next thing I knew, his arms were around me, and his face was so close. My mouth ran dry. I forgot what I was going to say. His eyes were still staring into mine, and I could feel his breath on my face. I looked at his lips then back to his eyes. My heart sped up. I wasn't sure if he was going to kiss me, but I wanted him to very badly.

"I want to kiss you. Can I?"

I didn't think about it, I just said, "Yes"

His mouth was on mine before I could take a breath. His lips were soft and demanding. I pressed my body tightly against his. I don't know if he teased my mouth open or I teased his, but we were both tasting each other hungrily. I was ready for more. I wanted more. However, he suddenly pulled away.

"May I see you on Friday for dinner?" Gabe's eyes glimmered with hope.

I was a little dazed.

"Yes"

"6:30, okay?"

"Yes." I replied.

He kissed my cheek and left.

I spent the week wondering what I should wear on Friday. It was like I was one of those little girls at the mall. I was going to buy a new outfit when Friday came, and Gabe called me at about 4 o'clock and said to wear something casual.

Problem solved!

The Stock Market closed, and I got a shower and threw on tan shorts and a white tank top with penny loafers. I put my hair in a ponytail and some light makeup.

Gabe showed up at 6 o'clock in jeans and a white t-shirt with penny loafers. I laughed when I saw him. He smiled too. His kiss grazed my lips very lightly.

"Let's go have some fun."

He reached his arms around and squeezed my ass, then we left. I liked that very much but didn't say anything. I just smiled.

He drove an old man's car. It was a Lincoln town car. It was a luxurious model with leather bench seat, power everything, and a v-8 engine. He reached out with his long arm and wrapped it around my waist. In one move, I was across the bench next to him. It was like being in a fifty's movie.

He headed South on I-95 and drove to Hollywood, Florida. After thirty minutes, he took one of the exits, turning into a giant parking lot with an equally large building. The sign declared 'Fred and George'. I'd never heard of it, but it was an arcade/sports bar. There were carnival games, virtual reality games, video games, and midway. We played everything. Gabe won me several stuffed animals, and it was thrilling. I played skeet ball and won lots of tickets. I was good at the coin games and received more tickets. We ate hamburgers and fries and drank beer and stayed there until 1:00 AM. I was tired when I got into the car, but Gabe pulled me over to him, and I felt at home there.

The drive back took longer than I thought it would have. He walked me to my door, leaned in, kissed my face, and pulled back.

"Would you like to come in?"

His lips spread into a wide grin. Even the shadows of the clouds couldn't block out the glare from his smile.

"I would very much like that, but I'll call you tomorrow." He turned and left.

Damn it.

I was tired of light kissing and leaving me waiting. I wanted him to stay and really kiss me.

<It took you almost nine months to kiss Adrian, and you knew him your whole life. You have only known this guy for three months, and you want him to kiss you and stay??>

< Well, I want him to kiss me a lot, yes. The stay part.... I waited for Adrian, and I lost my chance. I don't want to make that mistake again. >

< What if this is a mistake too?>

< Then it's mine to make. Adrian told me to be happy and get married to have a family. I want to do that. How am I going to do that alone, huh? >

< He didn't mean you should do it with the first guy you met. >

< This is the first guy that I don't compare to him. I miss Adrian, and I always will. That will never change. But Gabe makes me feel things that I haven't felt since Adrian. I don't miss Adrian quite so much when I'm with Gabe, and I like him for who he is not for who I wish he was. Argh? Why are you arguing with me about it?>

< Beautiful Girl, I won't try to dissuade you anymore. Be happy! He takes his time so that he can get to know you. He likes you and wants it to be more, so be patient. >

< Thank you!>

The voice was jealous. I don't know how this is possible, but I heard it loud and clear along with dejected resignation. I hurt him somehow.

< I love you, Beautiful Girl. I will always be here for you. Nothing can change that>

< I love you too. You're my best friend. I didn't mean to yell at you.>

I felt him pulling away. He hadn't been with me all evening. It was a gentle pressing in the back of my mind. I found it comforting in a way.

Waiting all week to see Gabe was like Chinese water torture. I could hear the clock ticking and every notch on the clock took forever.

The next week we went go-karting and of course, I received a light kiss. Then, he took me to a giant bookstore where we stayed for hours. I bought 20 books. They were so many that I couldn't carry them all. Before he took a few to help me out, he laughed at me when he saw me juggling all those books.

He was going to leave again, so just like that I wrapped my arms around him and tilted my head back. I ran my tongue over my lips to tempt him. His eyes followed the motion with a single-minded stare. A hungry need had enveloped me. He leaned in and brushed his lips over mine. I tiptoed up into his embrace, pressing my lips fully onto his. He returned my hungry kiss. His arms were clasping me tightly to his body. But a second later, I was released.

A vision flashed over my eyes. He furiously wanted possession of my body. I felt his arousal bursting through his pants and into my mind. I knew that his mouth wanted to keep tasting me all the way down.

So, what's the problem?

His forehead creased while his eyes were searching my face. His hand caressed the side of my face, then he said, 'good night' and departed.

Argh!

He was holding back so much. It was driving me crazy. Every time he left, I was hot with desire. This time was worse because I could feel how much he had wanted me too. Why didn't he succumb to it? I wanted him, and he knew it.

One Sunday he took me to brunch at one of the Hotels on Palm Beach. After brunch, we lounged on the beach, sunning our bodies on the sand. His chest had a light smattering of brown hair just covering his bulging pecs. The fur made a thin trail down his abs, disappearing below the waistband of his shorts. I enjoyed watching the water flow in rivulets down his body making his shorts clinging to his groin and revealing everything.

I inquired if he needed any tanning lotion. He assented, and I massaged it into every part of his rippling back muscles as deeply as possible, brushing my breasts against his back here and there, hoping to tempt him in some way.

I wore my neon yellow bikini, knowing it made my skin appeared bronzed to perfection. I invited him to rub sun lotion all over my body. He did just that but rubbing the cream on me was wreaking havoc with my self-control.

CHAPTER 31

SYDNEY

We had been dating now for six months, and he had only really kissed me three times. The rest were just light kisses. I felt like if I didn't do something, we would stay in this phase forever, but the voice had said to wait, so I was waiting.

Gabe was sweet, and we laughed all the time. I wanted to be with him every second of the day.

It was a Friday night when Gabriel came over with several bags of groceries and wine. I opened the door more than excited to see him and was surprised by the image I had in front of my eyes.

"What are we doing?"

Gab raised an eyebrow at me and smiled. "I'm going to cook that dinner I promised you."

He was carrying so many bags that he had to use his foot to close the door. I was hypnotized by the moment, so I sat down at the breakfast bar, resting my head on my hands.

"Well, what are you going to make?"

"Chicken Piccata, with Risotto and Insalata."

"That sounds great, what can I do?"

I was starving but eager to learn and help. He grabbed the cutting board and my French knife and began chopping an onion.

"Peel some garlic. I'm going to need some bowls, flour, milk or an egg and some lemon juice. I brought everything that I need, so look in the bags. Oh, and open a bottle of wine, we can't cook without some vino."

The flash that preceded a vision was becoming easier to detect. The list of everything he had brought was suddenly there. It was a lot of food and wine. Was he planning on feeding an army?

He took some chicken breast and began slicing it thinly. As I watched him cook, he started telling me stories about his family.

"They always cook, and Sunday's a big family day. Everyone helps. We always have opera playing, and Papa sings along in Italian."

I didn't want him to stop talking so I just stood there and listened to his every word.

"Do you play any opera? My family doesn't play any instruments, and I have never been around a musician. What do you play? You don't talk about your music much." He stopped and looked at me waiting for an answer.

It was one that I hated to discuss, but he was right, I didn't talk about it. I always connected music to Adrian, and I needed to break out of that.

"I play the piano well and a few others not so well. I mostly play classical, but I love musicals. I haven't thought about playing opera. But I'll play something for you."

I got up and went to the piano. I didn't want to play Phantom even though that was my best. I played Memories from Cats instead. "I have to warm up so give me a few minutes to run through a few things then I'll play. Okay?"

"Si, Maestro!"

I laughed. He always made me laugh. I wasn't the master, but if that is what he wanted to call me, I was okay with that. I warmed up with Boree' no 1 and 2 from Bartok, then Ivan Sings by Aram Khachaturian.

I was sure that Gabriel didn't know any Andrew Lloyd Webber, but I was going to teach him. 'Memories' is a sad, gut-wrenching song about the end of life, the wish for love and acceptance at the end. I felt the pain of being alone and the long nights, the wish for youth and the desire to be loved. I could and had felt all of those things in my life. When I played music, I wanted to be touched and loved too. I felt the tears falling from my eyes, wishing that everyone understood how it felt to be alone in the moonlight and hoping for the comfort of the day or a friend. I spent all that time alone wishing that someone would touch me or love me. So, it flowed from my fingers to the keys, and I roared with the emotions that came over me. As I hit the una corda pedal, and the sound softly sailed away from me, I looked up at Gabriel. He was entranced with the music. He smiled and shook his pan.

"You play like you know what it means to feel that kind of loneliness and pain."

"I do." I didn't take my eyes off of the piano.

He didn't say anything but kept cooking. I wanted to say something, but I wasn't sure where to start. How do you tell someone about your life story? Or how sad you were before you met them?

"Gabe, how come you don't talk about your parents?"

"They're dead. They died when I was ten. My dad traveled for business, and my mother went with him. I stayed with Papa and Nonna because I had school. They left for Italy. Twelve hours later they were dead. It was a plane crash."

I didn't add anything. I let him continue.

"My mother was from Tuscany, my father from New York. My dad went to Italy for work, saw my mother, fell in love and didn't leave until she married him. He was there for a year. I think it took him that long to convince my grandfather and grandmother to let her marry him. She was an only child, and they wanted her to stay in Italy. I'm just glad that they died before my mother did. I think it would have broken them. I didn't know them very well, but I read letters that they sent to my mother, and they loved her very much."

I moved into the kitchen and put my arms around him and laid my cheek on his back. There were no words for my loss of Adrian. I am sure I wouldn't find any for his. Holding him felt right. Like my life could be this way. He turned around to face me.

"It was a long time ago, and time heals all wounds. It really does. I have Papa and Nonna and of course, Zack and Maria. That is all of my family."

I stepped back to leave the kitchen, but he pulled me to him, kissed me and then released me. "Don't want dinner to burn."

I set the table, and we sat down to eat. There were no candles or music. It was peaceful and quiet with the sounds of the waves lapping at the shore. The food was terrific; he wanted to know if it was better than the restaurant's. He was very proud of his cooking, with good reason to be proud. I cleared the table then he inquired, "Do you want to go for a moonlight walk on the beach?"

I smiled. "I would love to."

I locked up, and we went. He took possession of my hand, and we walked barefoot. The white sugar sand was still carrying some of the heat from the day in it. There was a gentle breeze, and the waves were rolling in and out in a peaceful rhythm. We walked for a while up and then down the beach in companionable silence. It felt natural. After a while, he stopped and turned to look at me.

"Sydney, what do you want to do with your life?"

It was a question I had been asking myself repeatedly for years now. Money wasn't an issue. I could work anywhere. Travel was high on my list of things to do. But there were others, such as family and children. However, I didn't think I was capable of changing the world.

< You could change the world if you had the desire. >

< *Private conversation. I'll talk to you later.* >

While I was musing Gabriel, I responded. "I want to travel and see the world. Europe, places that helped change the world and humanity. You know, such as Greece."

As I replied, I realized that I wanted more than that. I wanted to understand as much as possible. Why do I hear a voice in my head? How can I find things without ever having been there? Why do I get visions from another person's mind? Why does it seem these gifts are stronger when I drink? I avoid people, yet I am drawn to some, why?

I began to analyze Gabriel. I looked into his darkened green eyes. My eyes shifted from one feature to another. What powered Gabriel?

"What about you Gabriel, what do you want out of life?"

His answer was swift, unflinching, "You! That's all I want or need."

I found my arms wrapped around his neck, pulling his lips to mine. His body leaned in, pulling me closer. My heart was pounding out of my chest. Our lips met somewhere between. Desire swept through my loins. His tongue pressed into my mouth, which was opened and hungry for his kisses. His body pressing against me filled me with emotions that I wanted to see to the end. I wasn't going to settle for a simple kiss tonight. He released my mouth and kissed my ear, then my neck working his way down to my shoulder.

A moan escaped from me. His mouth was back on mine, and I was hungrily kissing him back. I put my hand on the side of his face. I felt his hands pushing me into his pelvis. I could feel how much he wanted me. I wanted him, too. I was wet and ready. I pulled him along with me back to my condo.

When we got to the front door, I wasn't sure if he was going to stay or leave. I unlocked the door, and his hands were still around me. I was facing away from him, but my back was pressing against him. He was following my every movement kissing my neck, then nibbling.

I moaned out, "Gabriel." He swung me around, picked me up, and carried me through the door, kicking it closed as he went.

He was strong and powerful. He stopped, looked into my eyes and asked me with a whisper

"Are you ready for this?"

I hadn't been thinking about anything but how much I wanted to feel him in every way. I had waited before, and I missed my chance. I wasn't going to do the same this time.

I whispered in the same manner, "Yes, I want you!" I looked straight in his eyes. I couldn't look away.

He kissed me again then he added, "I never want to be without you."

I heard myself making small sighs of contentment. Gabe chuckled, his hands were still clutching me to him. In the end, I drifted off into a deep, satisfying sleep. Sometime later, I awakened to hands running up and down my body.

We didn't leave the condo for three days. Thank God, Gabriel had brought food, or we would have starved to death.

As we were lying naked on the bed, eating leftovers I asked him, "Did you plan this? You brought a lot of food for one dinner."

The laughter boomed out of him, "I never do anything without a plan. I planned everything in my life but you."

His mirth was infectious, so I was giggling too. "Well, what's your plan now?"

The jovial laughter faded away.

"Now, I just need to talk you into marrying me and traveling around the world. I have to work, and I can't stay here much longer, but I wouldn't leave without you."

I shot up in the bed. My eyes grew with the information he'd just imparted. "Marry you?"

"Yes, then I have to tell my family. I love you, but if it's too soon, I'll wait."

He had moved away a fraction from me, but I snuggled closer to him turning his face back to me.

"And if I say yes?"

His face glowed from the inside just as if a fire had been lit and eyes as green as the hills in Ireland smiled back at me.

"Is that a yes?" He asked.

"Yes, I want to spend every day with you I…. I love you." I squealed.

The moment I said the words, I knew they were right. I loved Gabriel. Kind, funny, thoughtful, planning Gabriel. He hadn't asked me about my past or parents, but there was plenty of time for that.

"I don't know where my pants are, but I was going to ask you before I made love to you."

He de-tangled his body from mine, and found his pants. They were in the living room by the front door. I snickered because they were a long way away from the scene of our erotica. I was just glad they were inside the condo and not out.

He pulled out a ring, but it didn't have a centerpiece. It was a wrap around.

"I know that you were engaged before, and he died. I am not trying to replace him. You wear his ring every day. This way, you can wear both." He offered it to me.

Tears pricked my eyes. He had thought of everything. I choked back a sob, as he fit the two rings together. His ring made the first into a forget me not flower. He slid it back onto my hand. It was a little heavier. I could never look at it again without thinking of both my loves. Gabe gathered me into his embrace, hungry for my kisses.

CHAPTER 32

SYDNEY

Gabe wanted to get married as soon as possible. He wanted to go to the Justice of the Peace and then have a party after at the restaurant. I was in complete agreement with him. I dreaded the idea of letting him out of my sight. I was petrified to lose him like I did Adrian. I was in a hurry.

Right away was my vote! He said two months, and we settled on one month. Gabe needed to leave and go to Italy after the wedding, so we used it for our honeymoon. Passports take a month to process, so that was really the deciding factor.

I called Tobias and Trish. Gabe took care of Zack and his family, he moved into my condo with me. I gave him a closet and some drawers. He didn't need too much space because he had a flat in Rome, and he'd been traveling light, sleeping at Papa and Nonna's.

Three weeks later, I got my passport information back. They couldn't issue my passport because my birth certificate had been altered, and I needed additional paperwork for that.

What the fuck were they talking about?

I looked it over. It appeared normal to me. I didn't want to tell Gabriel. He had work he needed to do in Italy. He had been waiting all this time for me. I was loathe to let him leave without me. I felt the panic rising when I thought he might go without me. I couldn't be parted from him. I had to clear my mind and focus on the problem. I just needed to contact Vital Statistics in Oregon, and they should have what I needed.

I called the next morning. They didn't have any record of a change to my birth certificate. I was pacing, racking my brain for what to do. There was no way in heaven and earth that I was going back to Oregon with my hat in my hand to ask for help from my father. How else was I going to get what I needed?

< You need a private eye, a gumshoe, a Pinkerton. >

< A PI, yesss. You're brilliant. >

< Your father had family, right? >

< Yes, I have an aunt. I bet she would know something if she wasn't crazy. >

< Langtree will get you a good one. Call him. He's retired now, but he'll do it for you. >

< Thank you! >

Langtree did do it, he was as usual, perfect self. The PI's name was Jason Knight.

A little cheesy.

He was charging $350 a day plus expenses, and he was guaranteeing results with pictures. He didn't think it would take more than a few days to a week.

It was a very long three days. I was on edge the entire time. Gabriel was on the phone most of the time, so he didn't notice or thought it was all wedding jitters.

Jason called, "Miss O'Dear?"

Who did he think was going to answer my phone?

"Yes."

"Jason, here. I did find the problem. Vital Stats gave you the adoption certificate and not the original, or the notice of update form."

What is he talking about, adoption?

"Who's listed as my parents?" My mouth had gone dry. What was this all about?

"Father unknown, mother Mary Rhiannon O'Dear, unmarried."

Mary was my father's sister's name, but I didn't think she had any children. I only remembered seeing her once. I think she had the O'Dear looks - dark hair, blue eyes. Not like me at all.

"Miss O'Dear…. Miss O'Dear?" he asked.

"Yes. Sorry, Jason um, yea, mail that birth certificate out right away. But I want you to find Mary O'Dear. I would also like to know if she had any other children, with pictures, okay?"

"It's your dollar. I'll get right on it." He rang off.

After thinking about it for a while, there was only one person I could call to get a few answers - my grandmother on my mother's side. That is if she was still alive and would talk to me.

Then, there was the letter that my father gave Harry. I could open it.... but I was not going to.

Fuck him. I never want to see or hear from him again.

I pulled out my old phone book and found grandma's number. I sat there and stared at it. Did I really want to open this can? She would call my father/Edward and tell him. But then again, she might not know anything either.

I didn't know if I wanted Gabriel to hear about this yet. I hadn't told him about my family. I didn't even know where to start. He had been raised by people who loved him. I was not sure the idea of childhood being anything else but happy, had ever occurred to him.

I had never talked about it to anyone but Adrian and Trish. But Adrian just seemed to know and understand. With Adrian, it was easy. It wasn't like I was keeping anything from Gabe. I just didn't know where to begin. If I did, would I be able to stop, or would I get hysterical and frighten him off? Also, could I tell him about the voice and the visions or the finding things or my dreams?

< NO, don't tell him about any of that. That will scare him off. >

< What? Shouldn't I tell him that there's a voice in my head that tells me when to buy and when to sell? Yea he'll just think it's my gut talking, not you.>

I was snickering.

< Yea, don't tell him that. What if he tells someone else? The government is always looking for people like us. I can hear people, and you can find them. What would they do with that? No amount of money could save you if they want you. Think, Beautiful Girl! >

< I didn't think about that. But what about my family? Should I tell him about that?>

< You can tell him as much or as little as you want about that. That is not going to change your life anymore. It's in the past. But your gifts, those can and will change your future. I just want you to be safe. There are more bad people than good ones out there. Think what would happen to you if a genuinely evil person got their hands on you.>

< All things that I don't want to deal with right now. Why can't you just focus on her and find out what I need to know? >

< It doesn't work like that. I can only pick up what people are thinking at that time. To find out everything, I need to have touched them. >

< Do you know everything about me? >

< You and I are different. We are connected. We are special. I only hear what you tell me.>

< So, all those times I was being beaten, did you hear that? >

< Yes, every bit…. I felt it too. I am tied to you and you to me. >

< You feel everything I feel? >

< You mean sex? No, I can block things out too, so can you. >

< Ooh, I so you haven't touched me?>

< It doesn't matter; I can't hear you unless you let me. >

< Have you or haven't you touched me? >

< Yes. >

< Yes, you have? Or yes, you haven't? >

< Yes, I have. >

< When? Where? Why didn't you tell me? What is your name? Hello?>

He was gone. I could feel him pulling away, like a wave pulling back from the shore. I rode the wave that pulled me back into a place that I didn't know. It became a roller coaster ride with ups and downs. In the end, I was slammed into his mind. His body was tense and filled with a new fear. He was arguing with someone.

She had an ethereal beauty. Her body had a youthful vigor, but her eyes held age and wisdom. Her voice was heated and her cheeks flushed, but I couldn't make out what she was accusing him of.

His mind became filled with feeling both morose and lonely. He longed for me! She screamed.

"You were talkin to her? You can't do that." She yelled.

Then it started to fade. I was falling back, down, falling, slamming into myself. My body was shaking, and it was all a jumble in my mind. I was entangled with his mind, he sighed.

< DON'T DO THAT AGAIN!!! >

< *I'm sorry. I didn't mean to intrude…. I… Are you okay? She was admonishing you.* >

< YOU CAN'T DO THAT, Beautiful Girl! I….. Stay on your side. I can't let you in ever. That is the way it is. I can help you, but not often. It's the only way to keep you safe. Please, I can't explain. >

He left, but I didn't follow this time. Every extremity screamed with icy burning. I didn't know that mind travel was so cold. My teeth chattered. I wrapped my arms around myself to conserve heat.

It was just a feeling, but somehow, he was familiar. It was itching in the back of my mind, but I couldn't place who he was. She had a familiar look to her too. Her eyes had that clear quality of blue, of seeing you and through you.

It was too much. My body eased to the floor, and my eyes closed. It was all black, but not empty. The dream began.

*****

Blue, Azure, Sapphire, the kinds of blue that only exists in the warm waters of the tropics. It stretched to the horizon where it met the warm, aquamarine blue of the ocean.

The dream always starts the same and I ride it like the wave to my voice. In some ways it feels the same.

Though I can't see the entire island, I instinctively know it is perfectly round. In the center of it is a mountain. Its apex is rounded, dome-like. The wind buffs my hair as I move closer to it. The salty dryness of the ocean is replaced by the humidity of the tropical rainforest before me. The entire mountain is covered in the variegated shades of green. Large-leaved plants trail down the slopes. The scent of the flowers surrounds me thick, drugging my senses.

In the center is the shining white palace. The massive plain pediment is held up with large Doric Greek-style columns. The building grows out of the side of the mountain and seems to be held together with stars that glisten in the sun. I raised my hand to shield my eyes from the blinding glare it was reflecting back at me.

My gaze finds the cloud of mist lingering at the base of the building. A torrent of water pours from the base. It gives the illusion that it floats on a cloud. It is too far of a drop to see the pool at the bottom. Every plant glistened with dew from the watery mist in the air.

Rings appear to surround the mountain. Watery rings or channels frame the island. Every ring is connected to the other. Bridges connect everything, and it all had symmetry to it, balance.

The roar of the waves rocks me with its rhythm. I could almost taste the salt on my face. The wind is gently caressing my skin and throwing my hair around my head. I could just make out her murmuring. It came in rhythm with the waves. She whispers to me. I cup my hand around my ears, straining to hear her words. All she has to do is say it one more time.

I could just make out the woman as she spoke in her calm manner. She has the translucence of a ghost. Her reddish gold hair waves in the breeze, her eyes are large and blue with a dark ring.

*****

Gabriel was patting my face as my eyes fluttered open. "Syd, are you alright? Wake up, sweetheart!"

~ 410 ~

I wanted to shoot up, but my arms were heavy, as were my eyes. The weakness was overwhelming, so I slipped back into unconsciousness.

CHAPTER 33

SYDNEY

The package that had arrived was rather bulky. I didn't expect him to have sent so much information about her. Mary has been in a mental ward for the last twenty years. What could she have possibly been doing?

"Mary Rhiannon O'Dear suffers from Delusional Schizophrenia; she hears voices, and one of them is in love with her."

She told them, and they locked her away at seventeen. I continued reading.

"She managed to escape from care several times though they couldn't figure out how. After being in care for four years

and under heavy lockdown for forty-five days with no outside contact, she became pregnant.

Birth of a girl on March 22, 1975. Custody was turned over to Mr. and Mrs. Edward O'Dear on March 25, 1975. No further children. She is still housed at Cedar's Hospital."

She has been languishing there ever since. The doctor's notes had a few interesting tidbits:

"Mary says she doesn't have delusions. She is convinced that she is simply special and different. She claims to talk to a man named Njord. After looking it up, I found Njord Viking. He was God of the Sea. She is convinced that he is in Noatun. It's his world. She doesn't have a special education in Norse Gods, so I'm not sure how she would have found out about this one. Or, why she chose him and not Thor or Odin."

That stuck in my mind, the voice had said that to me several times, different and special.

The picture was no help at all. She looked like an O'Dear. All family members had black hair and blue eyes. She had the dark rings in her eyes too.

Such a striking combination.

He had sent several recent pictures along with a few older ones. The oldest one was just before she was admitted. Her thick dark hair was parted on the side and held there by a beret. Her eyes were filled with innocence and hope, and her full lips were parted in a shy smile. The blue of her eyes startled you with their clarity, the rings ten shades darker than the rest. It was unusual.

The hope of finding a resemblance was lost. I was blonde with the O'Dear eyes, but I was taller than the rest of the women in my family. Not that I was that tall. I was skinny. Some called it willowy. The O'Dear women had curves. The only thing we had in common was our eyes. Oh, and hearing voices, apparently.

There was only one real revelation for me. She was a twin. I had been led to believe that my father, Edward, was older. He was, but only by a few minutes. Mary, my mother, was his twin.

Most of the research that I had uncovered about PSI abilities involved twins, but they both had abilities, not just one. I had made a list of all of my abilities: Clairvoyant, Telepathy, Psychometry.

Edward never let on that there was anything different about him other than the fact that he liked to beat me.

Was she the whore he was referring to all those times he beat me? Did he think that I was just like her and going to have the immaculate conception?

He had said he failed before, how? She must have trusted him, and that bastard betrayed her.

Of course, I could read the letter. Nope, not going to happen. It will be the last thing I do before I depart this world. Edward O'Dear and whatever he wanted to say to me can just wait. I ain't dyin' yet.

The most important part of the package was my birth certificate. Now, I could get my passport and leave.

CHAPTER 34

HERATHINA

Log entry – my bracelet no longer keeps the time correctly and I see no reason to bother with Themian ways.

Before Jorhan and I reached the village, we stopped, and I told him,

"No matter what happens, you have to stick to the plan. We have to make sure that this warlord makes our deal the way we want it to happen."

He nodded his head and as he did that, the muscles in his jaw worked over the bone.

There were no sentries on guard; it would not have been difficult to enter unnoticed. Not only was this warlord overconfident and arrogant, but he was also lazy and stupid. If I had known that he was so lazy, I would most certainly have brought a war party. We could have wiped out everyone putting up a fight. They would never have known we were coming. But that was no longer an option, so I let Jorhan take me to my fate.

There was a hut set off to the side, away from the main housing. It had an enclosed area around the back. It resembled a holding pen. I was assuming that this was where all the women were kept.

Jorhan immediately deposited me within the tent. There were between twelve and fifteen women inside, most of them very young. One girl appeared younger than fifteen. She whimpered quietly in the corner.

Two women approached me and knelt down. "We are your servants if you can save us from this evil." Their heads bowed.

The red-haired one raised her face. "I will never leave your side."

I asked her name.

"Sybil. I will do anything not to become enslaved to that warlord. Or, become one of his concubines."

Many gathered around with their heads nodding. I looked at them and said,

"If you wish to return home, listen to me."

Murmuring filled the small space. I raised my hand to quiet them.

"Is there any fabric lying around?"

I explained my plan. They all agreed they would do anything that I asked. After that, I parted the tent flaps to watch Jorhan's show.

*****

Jorhan reached the center of the village. There, the workers of the village had begun construction of a stone building. They had used white stone with veins of gray through it. The front had a platform with a raised portion in the center. Upon this pedestal sat a stone chair.

"Where is this warlord that demands my sister as a tribute?" His bellowing reverberated off the stone edifice.

A large man stepped from behind the chair. His black hair flowed over his shoulders and down onto his chiseled back. He let a lazy smile roll over his face as he cocked an eyebrow.

"Here I am. Who are you to present yourself in such an arrogant manner?" He sat down in the massive chair with easy grace. Self-assurance filled his every move.

"Arrogance is not a trait that I suffer from." Jordan stood his ground with his head held high and his eyes boring into the barbarian sitting on his throne.

The smile vanished from his face, only to be darkened by rage. "What is your name? I demand to know your name!"

Glee filled Jorhan's face. I was right, Zeus is quick to anger.

Jorhan replied. "My name is Jorhan, and I am the son of Efron."

"Where is your father? I demanded tribute from the chief, not his son!" Zeus relaxed back into the stone seat. He wasn't dealing with the chieftain merely a son.

"My father is probably dead by this time."

Zeus freed one of his daggers from his boot and began to toy with it. "Where is your sister? I want to see her."

Jordan raised his voice. He wanted to make sure that it carried over the entire to the village, as I instructed. The stone structure in front of him was excellent. It bounced the sound of his voice behind him spreading it throughout the village.

"She's with the other women. If you wish to have my sister, you can take her as a wife. Otherwise, I will take her home." He crossed his arms in satisfaction.

"Take her?" he stuttered, "How dare you to speak to me this way? You have offered your sister as a tribute. I will take her and use her in any way I wish."

Jorhan clenched his teeth. I had been very explicit. He had to keep his head and not let his opponent bait him.

"What is your name?"

"Zeus, my name is Zeus. Lest you forget it. Perhaps I should have it branded it on you."

Jorhan replied, "Zeus, I did not bring my sister here as a tribute. I came here to make a treaty. My sister will only remain if you marry her. If you do not marry her, I will take my sister and go. If you don't allow us to leave unmolested, there will be a war between our people until the end of time."

"I could eliminate your village in one day. Without blinking an eye." This threat carried a heavy weight.

"I'm sure you could Zeus, all by yourself against just me and my village." He scratched his chin, shaking his head thoughtfully. "Yes, you might decimate us. However, I call upon the other chieftains here. All of you. You, who brought your daughters. What will you get in return? Nothing? He said, 'bring your daughters and give them to me as a tribute or I will bring war on you', but he doesn't guarantee you peace. I'm here to negotiate a better deal."

There was a lot of grumbling in the background. All of the chieftains were talking amongst themselves. Dorr shuffled forward.

"I agree with Jorhan. There should be another deal. There are many of us and only one of you. I will happily leave my daughter here as tribute to seal a pact. However, I agree with Jorhan you will not make my daughter your concubine, slave, or your servant. She will become your wife, or she will not stay at all, and there will be war."

Zeus shifted uncomfortably on his stone chair. He did not anticipate they would ban together. He realized the error of his plan, but it was too late. He should have had each chief bring tribute separately. Not all at once. Now they realized that banding together will get them what they wanted.

Jorhan saw his opening and struck. He put his hands on his narrow hips, puffing out his shoulders and arms to better display his strength. "I will swear an Oath of Allegiance for all time. I will not take up arms against you. You shall not take up arms against me. For any who break this pact, we shall ban together and destroy them, down to the last man, woman or child. I will take none into my village. I will show no mercy to betrayers and oath breakers."

Zeus scratched his chin in contemplation. The other chieftains stamped their feet in the acknowledgment. They agreed this was a good deal.

Zeus realized he'd been backed into a corner. He could not get away, he had to make a choice or be destroyed. He moved out of the chair, taking up his full height. He wanted to look down at every person there. They all had made it clear whose side they were on.

"I will agree to your terms. We should have a scribe record them. Now bring out your daughters. I will choose my wife."

Zeus' warriors led us out in a line. All were heavily veiled to stand in front of the assembled. The chieftains and people backed away, allowing an opening to form. We stood in a straight line facing the stone seat.

"What is the meaning of this? Remove those veils. I wish to see their faces." Zeus was angry.

Jorhan raised his hand "No. You shall choose your wife based on your observations and not based on their beauty. You must choose wisely. I have seen them. Many are beautiful. Use your mind because a good woman's beauty fades. Intelligence never goes away."

Zeus angrily surveyed down the line of women. Then immediately picked out anyone with small breasts and narrow boyish hips.

"Send the children home. I have no desire to marry a boy."

Every single one of the women he pointed out, removed their veils. Returning to their fathers, the young girl who'd been weeping was immediately chosen. Her weeping turned to cries of joy. She dropped her arms around her father.

A lump formed in my throat. I knew she would not be chosen. My anger for Zeus boiled below the surface.

How dare he treat women like this? We're not possessions. We are people just like men. Every bit as intelligent and strong only in different ways.

There were also a few plump women.

"I do not wish to marry the fatted calf." His words were cruel and cutting, but I know that one of the girls was happy to go home. She had someone she wished to marry from her village. She had no desire to be the wife of a warlord. She was happy to be the wife of a simple farmer.

Zeus finally left his chair and began walking up and down the line. One of the daughters was extremely short. She barely came up to my breast.

"You! You're too short. I have no desire to have a pixie as a wife." He sent her on her way.

That left only three of us. We clasp hands as a sign of solidarity. Sybil's hair was flaming red, a color that was rare in this part of the world. Zeus didn't like it.

"I have no desire to be married to a flame."

She walked over to her father. He pulled off her veil. Her father clasped her shoulders from the side and squeezed. She whispered something in his ear, and he shook his head.

Zeus was a man with beautiful gleaming black tresses. They waived in the wind. He possessed piercing blue eyes. The kind that seemed to stare right through you. His broad, muscular shoulders and strong tree trunk legs gave him height and stature. Humanity was not known for its size. I towered over most men. But not Zeus. I had to tilt my head back to look him in the eye.

Women were not tall. I was considered a Goddess mostly because I was larger than life, and I had abilities.

He stepped over to Atea.

"Go home to your family! I have found my bride." Then he pulled my veil off to reveal my honey-colored curls and my dark-rimmed blue eyes.

Jorhan clapped his hands. "Well done, Zeus! You have chosen my sister. Bring your holy man to let us have our wedding ceremony."

"We don't need to be married today. No preparations have been made for a wedding feast." He waved his hand around, gesturing to the open area in which we stood.

"You can have your wedding feast on the morrow or within the next month. My terms are that you marry my sister today. You must consummate the marriage within the next twelve moon cycles, and you may not take her by force. You must win her. If you cannot do those things, I will bring the largest army I can scrape together, and I will lay this village to waste, killing every man, woman, and child. It will be your fault."

Zeus sat back into his seat, lifting his head. He indeed seemed scared. He knew that Jorhan could talk everyone into joining him. No one wanted to see their daughter or sister ravaged by a heartless killer.

Zeus leaned over to one of his warriors. He covered his mouth with the back of his hand and exchanged a few words. The man disappeared into the crowd returning a few minutes later. He had a Wizzin old man in tow. He had white tuffs of hair stuck up in every direction, and he wore an interesting bone necklace and several seashells. He was held up by a stick, heavily carved with runic type symbols.

The old man's name was Storni. He stood before us and instructed men to bring the log. Their village had a tradition of jumping over a log to seal a pact or marriage. He waved the stick around, then mumbled and moaned several things. He did a dance, chanted for a few minutes, and then he waved his hands in an urging motion. We were to jump over the log. Zeus seized my hand and immediately jumped over, pulling me along with him.

Before my feet even reach the ground, he wrapped both of his arms around me and planted his lips over mine. His kiss was hungry, greedy and harsh. There was no gentleness in his touch. His fingers dug into the tender flesh of my arms.

I stood stock still. It was my first kiss. When he finally released my mouth, I slapped him across the face. Many in the crowd laughed. He raised his hand to hit me.

Jorhan immediately raised his voice, "I said you would not take my sister by force."

Zeus grabbed my arm. His blue eyes were flashing as he stared Jorhan down. "Your sister needs to learn her place. A woman has no business striking a man."

Jorhan chuckled, "Obviously you've never met a real woman. A real woman would never allow a man to take whatever it is that he wants, like a child. Zeus, meet a real woman, my sister, Hera." Many in the crowd immediately knelt down to the ground.

"So, she does exist." He quickly hid the awe that had filled his voice, and his eyes devoured every part of me and continued, "You are the Goddess of the Mountain, the Queen of Olympus, the one they all speak of."

I nodded my head, and an evil smile curled his lips, "Then, I have gotten my heart's desire. Now, I am, the King of Olympus."

I school my face to hide my disgust.

CHAPTER 35

SYDNEY

Balmy air poured through the doors to the Fort Lauderdale Airport, warming me to the core.

God, I missed Florida with all its sunshine and humidity.

I spread my arms wide and embrace the sun.

"It's only been a couple of years. Did you miss it that much?" Gabe was smirking at me like I was a child.

"Yea, it's where we fell in love, why shouldn't I? Anyway, it's been ten years."

Okay, that was a little cheesy, but I loved the beach and the sand of Florida. Europe was amazing, but not the same.

There were so many things you could do in Florida that you couldn't do anywhere else – Disney, the Keys, treasure hunting, diving, sailing. I could go on for days. The energy here was great too. People were running everywhere, speaking several languages.

Maria pulled up to the curb in a cargo-van, Cosimo's plastered on the side. Gabe piled our luggage in the back, while I settled the twins and hopped in the front. I leaned over to kiss her.

"Are you happy to be back?" she asked.

I nodded my head. I wasn't sure why Gabe had wanted to come back. When he asked me to pack up and go, I didn't say no. Why would I say no? Every day with Gabe, from the first moment he asked me to marry him, had been a dream come true, even when I told him I was pregnant. It was perfect.

The twins were more than I had expected. It wasn't really a surprise, though. After all, I was the child of a twin.

Tristan and Isolde the most unlikely of twins. Both so opposite. The only thing they had in common was their hair.

Tristan had blonde hair and blue eyes, just like me. His eyes had the piercing quality and the O'Dear blue but no dark ring. He was the type of boy that got into trouble but always for a logical reason. Tristan examined everything, working the issue from every angle possible before he made a choice. He waited for Isolde always. I think Tristan was the wiser of the two, but you weren't supposed to say things like that about your children.

He informed me one morning, at the early age of two, that his breakfast wasn't appropriate. His face held all the seriousness of every adult man I had ever done business with. That was the first of many such instances. Isolde was the only person able to make Tristan loosen up and smile and laugh.

Isolde was more like Gabe with sandy blond hair and green eyes. She was quick to laugh. She jumped before looking with the blind trust that Tristan would be there to save her. Where Tristan was serious, Isolde was jovial. Life was one big joke or party to Isolde. She hated school, even though she didn't have to work very hard to get good grades.

I still hadn't figured out why Gabe wanted to come back. He clearly had a plan but as to what ...well, that was that the real question.

Gabe jumped into the back seat next to Tristan and tapped Maria on the shoulder. The van jolted into action. Maria had never learned the finesse of driving. She was all gas and go. It was a ride to remember. The only comparison that came to my mind was stock car racing.

I was terrified she would actually hit something. At the speed she traveled, we were sure to become road rash, with nothing left but chewed-up parts scattered all over I-95.

Maria's face took on the look of ecstasy. She lived for the speed. She missed her calling. She should have taken up racing. However, the van was a poor substitute for a Ferrari.

The van shifted to the left, then the right. The main exit for the Miami airport was a bottleneck from eight to two lanes. She accelerated to pass a hotel van. It wasn't a competition for anyone but her. I covered my eyes to hide the scene. There were three cars all jockeying for the two lanes ahead of us. She jerked the van hard to the left into a lane everyone else had abandoned, slamming her foot into the gas pedal. We jumped forward, and I was pushed back into the seat.

A low laugh issued from the seat next to me.

"No one beats me, ya bastards."

We flew onto the connecting highway, as it too merged with I-95. Driving in Miami/Dade was always an adventure no matter who was driving. Most of South Florida didn't speak or read English. The signs didn't mean anything to 80% of the population. They had no idea what they said.

When a sign said I-95 they thought it was the speed limit. If a sign said min 40, they thought something would happen in forty minutes. Express lanes were a joke. 'Carpool' - they didn't understand why you would put a car in a pool or why there were pictures of circles in a car. It was a free for all.

Heaven forbid you had a flat or needed gas. You were better off driving on the rim and buying a new one or calling a friend to bring you gas when you ran out. If you took an off-ramp in the wrong area, the locals might very well carjack you, then kill you and dump your body in the Everglades.

Maria jumped from one lane to the next, without hitting her brakes. The closer we got to the Golden Glades interchange, the tighter my grip on the armrests was.

I turned my head and gave Gabe an imploring look, begging him with my eyes, 'Please make her slow down'. He gave me a half smile while raising his shoulders. The forward motion of the van was cut in half, making me tilt my head forward touching the rearview mirror. I whipped my head toward Maria.

"Sorry Syd, don't want to hit someone, right?"

Who is she kidding? Hit someone? What about killing them?

I settled myself back in my seat, and I foolishly glanced up at the road. She was slowing slightly because we were entering one of the big turns of the cloverleaf, something the Golden Glades is known for. Between the turn and the rise of the road, it was too much for Tristan.

"Mom, I feel like I'm going to be sick," he put his hand over his mouth.

"Oh God! Gabe, grab the bag on the floor and give it to him." I wanted to climb in the back and let Gabe move up here, but at this speed, that would be suicide.

"Hold the bag close to your mouth, honey. If you get sick, it will go in the bag, not on your clothes. Okay?"

He shook his head, smacking his lips every few minutes and swallowing. Tristan was not prone to motion sickness. If Maria couldn't make someone car sick, no one could.

I could swear she never hit her brakes through the descent from the cloverleaf. But after a few minutes, I opened my eyes. I could feel the light pumping of the brakes and my eyes landed on a toll booth. We had reached the start of the Florida Turnpike. I didn't know if I should be happy or worried. The speed limit here was seventy, but Maria would do over ninety. At least the toll booths slowed her down every so often.

The line for the fast pass was not as fast as one would think. We practically came to a standstill.

Thank God!

The machine beeped, and she hit the gas, jarring me back into my seat. Making several sudden rights and lefts, she maneuvered around cars, buses, trucks, even a few other vans, leaving a trail of honking horns and road rage.

The only people who wove through the traffic better than Maria were the crazy crotch rockets. A bright red Ducati blew past us like we were standing still.

"Oh, no, you don't!"

Gabe reached out and put his hand on her arm. "Family first, love."

She huffed but slowed down. For the first time, we were doing the speed limit. I mouthed 'thank you' to him. He put on his 'all is right with the world' smile, pulled his arms up, lacing his fingers together and leaned his head back, closing his eyes as he went.

I glanced at Tristan, and he winked at me and balled the bag up. Both the men in my life were trouble.

Maria pulled up to the curb in front of the restaurant.

"I have to run in, then I'll take ya's home. Okay?"

My condo was still rented, so I was not sure where she was going to take us.

She bustled out and leaped into the driver's seat. Turning the car around, she headed to the back of the plaza, but instead of parking, she pulled up next to the marina.

"Welcome home!"

I was looking around and all I saw were boats. "What are you talking about?"

Gabe had already gotten out and started unloading the van. I rounded on him, "What is she talking about, home? Gabe what is this?"

He turned his back to me, and his shoulders took a big sigh. "Remember I told you I wanted to go sailing, well..." He turned to face me and put both hands on my arms running them up and down. "Well, right behind you is our new home, a floating condo."

I could feel how dry my mouth had become from hanging open. He propelled me toward the dock.

The boat in front of me was a massive brand new 56-foot Marquises Fountaine Pajot Catamaran. It was a mass of white and blue. Frozen in shock, I sputtered several times.

Issy pushed me out of the way to dash aboard to the floating "condo."

"Daddy, can I open the doors and go inside? Pleeease!"

Tristan took purposeful strides to gain purchase on deck. He plopped himself down in the captain's chair, smiled, put his hands on the wheel turned and announced, "I'm ready. Where to, Captain?"

I know my astonishment shown. I couldn't shake it.

Gabe jumped on the deck, and in two strides, he opened the sliding doors to the salon. The main deck had a large teak table that folded down to make space to move around. The captain's chair was a front/back one. You could swivel the backrest forward or backward depending on what direction you wanted to face. It was all covered by a hard-topped

Bimini. The Bimini came with walls to enclose it for heavy weather and screens for the hot, muggy weather.

The salon had two seating areas. On one side was a dining table with tattered banquette seating for eight. Opposite it, was another banquette in need of love and a cocktail table seating for four. Across from the cocktail area was a wet bar/prep kitchen and across from the dining table was the navigation station. All the wood was worn and needed love. There was a companionway on either side of the main salon.

Gabe took my hand and led me toward the Nav. Station. I reached out to grasp the railing as I stepped down to my new home. To the left was a berth with a large bed. In front was a settee and desk with a few upper cupboards. To my right was another berth.

"There are two more berths on the other side with a kitchen down. I have already contracted to have all the woodwork redone. We can redesign any way you want. There are two more crew cabins in the back near the engines. We can convert one to a workshop and the other for food and storage. I will change it in any way you want to make you happy."

The silence was thick in the air. I was still trying to take it all in. I didn't want to say anything just yet.

I turned and went down the opposite companionway, gave the kitchen a cursory once-over. I mean the galley. Both kids had already moved their cases into their rooms. Tristan raised his head and smiled. He was happy. Isolde hopped up from Tristan's bunk and hugged me, then ran back to hug Tristan. The boat shifted under me.

"Mom, close your eyes and listen to your inner voice. This is our home." Tristan's words chilled me to the bone. Inner voice. He climbed down off the bunk and led me to his bunk. He then took his hands, to slide them over my eyes to close them. "Sit down, close your eyes, and you will see."

"Come on, Issy, let mom be alone for a few moments. Don't worry, mom. We'll be up top. Come up when you're ready."

It felt silly to sit there with my eyes closed, but I did it nevertheless. I could hear the water from the intercoastal lapping at the sides of the hull. The light shifting of the boat was lulling.

*****

I had learned it's a vision, not a dream. It is always there in the back, lurking. Over the years, I had found it easier to tap into the vision. Every iteration, I learned something new.

Filling my lungs with air and slowly releasing it, I relaxed into it.

Blue, Azure, powerful, clear, all-encompassing. The sky so large it gives you that feeling of insignificance. I am high in the air, floating. The sky meets the aquamarine of the ocean, divided by an island, an unnaturally perfect circle shaped island. The mountain sitting atop of it is covered in the mixed greens of the tropics.

The shining white palace is growing out of the side of the mountain. Water spills from the base of the palace and falling into the basin, creating a moist mist.

As the vision fills my mind, I strain to listen. I know it's coming. I need to hear it this time. Air blows over me, pushing my hair back. Mumbling, her voice is there, but is indiscernible. She calmly speaks, but it is just out of reach. I am leaning into the wind. It stops blowing just for a moment. 'Repeat it. Just one more time I know, I'll hear you.' The wind picks up to a roar. I can't make it out.

Yes.

*****

My eyes cleared, and the tunnel and the fog dissipated. Tristan is holding my hand.

"Yes, Tristan, there is your answer."

The boat shifted. I knew it was the right choice. I'm not sure what prompted Gabriel to buy this boat, but I needed it too.

CHAPTER 36

SYDNEY

Being on a boat was like living in a dinky shed in the middle of an amazing garden. Everything was super compact. You lived with so much less but gained so much more. Oh, and there was a learning curve for everything.

Gabe didn't want to take any chances, so every change that was going to be made had to be made before we left Florida. It wasn't like he had bought a leaking mess; the boat was watertight. We just had a few problems....

The first night on the boat we ate at the restaurant. In the morning, I put water on to boil for coffee. I walked away from the stove only to hear a pop, then a loud whoosh as the pan burst into flames. Feeling the heat from the flames, Issy began screaming and a black spot formed on the ceiling.

The shut-off for the gas was under the sink. Everything on the boat was small. Every crevice of every cranny, including the space under the sink, was filthy. Dust and grime covered the bottom of the cupboard. As I rubbed my shoulder and hair into it, contorting my arm, I reached around and behind the stove encountering cobwebs and several creepy crawly things. It was hot back there. My hand grasped the nozzle for the shut-off valve, but my fingers slipped off. Clasping at it again and turned it with all my might, it slowly creaked to the side and off. Needless to say, the stove didn't work.

"What the hell is going on up here?" Gabe asked.

"Mommy is trying to burn the boat down." I threw a scathing look at Issy.

"The stove is a death trap. We'll have to get a new one." I grabbed the potholder and the kettle and went out onto the deck to light up the gas grill. One way or another, I wasn't living on this boat without a cup of coffee, and I wasn't going to spend my first morning scrounging for one somewhere. If this was our new life, I was going to embrace it wholeheartedly. The grill lit like a dream and boiled water for coffee. After that, all became right with the world.

It wasn't just the woodwork that needed to be repaired or sealed. The big issue was that a lot of the electronics in the boat were out of date. It was an analog boat in a digital world. Everything needed to be updated and rewired. We needed an SAT phone. We added a Wi-Fi antenna to the main mast that was hardwired into the boat. The refrigeration had to be replaced with something that was more energy efficient. There was no solar power, so we had to go and buy panels, inverters, and batteries, and they all had to be wired into the systems.

About the only thing on the boat that was good was the VFR radio, but even that needed the antenna wiring redone. The boat didn't have an autopilot. We needed to purchase one and install it. Also, we needed a water maker for desalination because no one wants to run out of water.

The funny part was that the boat didn't even have a radar of any kind. We didn't have a plotter or a GPS. The truth was that if we put it to sea in this state, the only way we were going to figure out where we were going was a dead reckoning in the stars. I wasn't even sure there was a compass or a Sextant on board.

Everything was giddy to Gabriel. This was all fun. He was having the time of his life. I was scared but eager to learn a new way to live and travel. I didn't want to rain on Gabriel's parade. He'd been working hard every day since long before I met him. He deserved to have fun and to be happy, and I wasn't going to stand in his way, which just meant I had to conquer my fears. I guess I could look at this time as a way to find my limits.

Every day had its own rhythm just like the waves. We got up to make coffee, went up on deck, checked our emails, and read whatever news was available via the Internet. The kids would eat breakfast. I generally just had coffee. We would go over what we needed to do that day, such as what new things on the boat needed to be fixed, and then we would decide if it was a two-man job or a one-man job. Being on a boat wasn't a solitary existence. You had to work together as a crew.

There are tons of people who live on boats alone, but a great deal of them never put the boat to sea alone. Solo sailing is not as common as people might think. Sailing is all about your crew and your boat, and you have to know both well. You have to trust each other. I learned more about myself, Gabriel and our relationship in the first month by just living on the dock.

Gabriel and I had never argued or even had a major disagreement in our entire marriage. The first month on the boat, I think we bickered every day. Most of it was bullshit about little things. It took me a while to get the swing of things and to realize that every day was going to be a new challenge. Every day was going to be a different kind of exciting. And yet, every night I got to lay down in my bed in my own cabin safe in the knowledge that my children were on the other side of the catamaran in their cabins. This was my new home, and with the sound of the water lapping against the side of the boat slightly rocking, sleep was easily attained.

After several months of repairs, we were finally ready for our first sea trials. The idea of doing anything other than motoring up and down the intercoastal still scared me.

"Look, I'm going to find someone to help us. I know you don't know how to sail. I'll get somebody to help me teach you."

I read a ton of books. In theory, I understood the basics of sailing. It was the practice part I severely lacked. That and the fact that I couldn't tie a rolling clove hitch to save my life.

*****

It had to be some kind of a joke. Gabriel hired a man to help us learn how to sail. His name was Captain Ron.

Captain Ron sounded exactly like the kind of guy you didn't want to have on your boat, just like in the movies. When he first arrived, he smelled like bourbon, and I couldn't tell if it was his breath or his clothes. He was jovial, with reddish cheeks and a potbelly. He had long white hair trailing down the back of his head and a bald spot on top. To be honest, he reminded me of George Washington. The only difference was that Captain Ron was without the uniform and the regal stance. I kept picturing him on the deck of the boat staring off into the distance like he was crossing Delaware. Every time I did this, I started snickering uncontrollably, so I'm pretty sure he thought I was crazy.

He was a crusty old dog, but cleaner than I expected. The name was a little deceiving. He wasn't a pervert, he was just an old sea dog. He'd obviously seen better days and was down on his luck, so he hired out his captain's abilities. I think it was the only way he could sail.

I will say this about Captain Ron; he was a whiz with electronics. He managed to rewire several circuit boards. He helped us redo the entire electrical system and figured out a few ways to save power here and there in the entire boat.

"There are only a couple of things you guys are going to need: One is some really good charts and local knowledge."

What the hell is local knowledge?

I think he read my mind because he continued, "Local knowledge means wherever you go, the first thing you do is to go to the nearest place you can and buy the local charts. Then, you talk to the locals. They'll tell you where you can and can't sail and the best places to avoid. The rule of the sea is this simple, 'don't be a dick'. Don't be a dick! If you can remember that, you'll be just fine at sea."

I couldn't help but start snickering again seeing George Washington standing on the bow of the boat saying, 'don't be a dick'. This just made me laugh every time.

"You got a joke you want to share with the rest of the class there, Miss Sydney?"

I really didn't want to share with the rest of the class. I know I needed to stop picturing him as George Washington. I just couldn't. I was waiting for him to take his wooden teeth out at any minute.

"Sorry, Captain Ron, not trying to be rude. I do enjoy your company, and I know that you're extremely knowledgeable about seamanship. Thank you for your time and effort." I took a deep breath, hoping that I had smoothed it over well enough.

He cocked an eyebrow at me. "Well now missy, I do believe that you have a private joke that has something to do with me."

My face must have turned twelve shades of red. I could feel the heat radiating off of it. I was so embarrassed he'd caught me. I was expecting that any minute I was going to get a flash with exactly how he saw me. But it didn't come.

"I know I remind a few people of George Washington, and I know you're probably snickering about it every time you look at me. Go ahead! Get it out of your system. Say it out loud, if you must, so we can move on from here."

I was mortified. Clearly, I wasn't the first person to see the resemblance. I felt like such an asshole. How do you reply to something like that when you're caught like a middle schooler?

"Captain Ron, I am so sorry. You do look like George Washington, and I have been snickering about it. I know I'm wasting your time, please forgive me. I really didn't mean any disrespect."

I was expecting a disapproving look or some scoffing or something but, instead, he just burst out laughing.

"Were you picturing me crossing Delaware? I get that one a lot. You know that no one ever thought I looked like George Washington til' my hair turned white? Then, I started growing it out just as a lark. I even curled it one year and dressed up in an officer suit for Halloween. You know I won the first prize that year? What really put them over the top was when I pulled out my wooden teeth."

I started laughing so hard I thought I might cry.

He was right. After I got it out of my system, it was never a problem giving him the courtesy he deserved and listening to everything he said. He was an excellent teacher. I don't know really what my problem was, but I just couldn't seem to get the hang of sailing.

Apparently, I wasn't the best student. He told me I was a control freak. I understood all the concepts of sailing, tacking, coming about, reefing. I got it. I was just distracted continuously. I constantly was consumed by the fear that one of the kids would fall overboard and drown. I was also terrified we would run into a hurricane, even though it wasn't hurricane season.

Most of my fears were utterly unfounded and irrelevant. I was worried we would run aground, but we had a depth finder. I was worried about the weather, but as Captain Ron had pointed out, we had paid for Weather Service, so we got a daily weather update. Also, we didn't go out on days when the weather was terrible. I wasn't sure if I was ever really going to get the hang of it.

"Sydney, I think you're going to get this. I think you're too distracted, so I know what we're going to do to fix it. First, we put the boat to sea. Then, I'm going to tell you how I'm going to fix your wagon. All right, little lady?"

I didn't think we were ready to go to sea. Gabriel seemed to know his way around, but I was still having problems figuring out what to do and when.

"Do you really think we're ready to go to sea? I don't even know if we have enough provisions."

"Well, tomorrow we're going to go, and we're going to work on provisioning." He moved his attention to the children "You hear that Issy, Tristan? Tomorrow's class will be Provisioning 101. Main staples is what every boat should have, and we will have to do an inventory of your goods. We need to make sure that whenever you put to sea, you have enough food to get you where you're going plus three days. Also, Mr. Tristan's going to help me stock up all the fishing supplies."

My trepidation was still pretty high, but Captain Ron had been living at sea on a boat for the last forty-five years, so I figured he oughta know a thing or two.

Provisioning was pretty basic - fill your freezer with as much cheese and meat as you can, stock your fridge with as many fresh vegetables, eggs, and milk as you can, chicken stock, beef stock, vegetable stock. Don't buy it liquid. Dry flour, sugar, powdered milk, powdered eggs, things like that. If it is dry, it would last longer and take up less space. Everything that you buy needs to go into a container. You have to take everything out of the original wrappers. When you're at sea, you don't have space to carry a lot of trash, and you can't just dump it over the side. So, when you go grocery shopping, you have to unpackage everything. For example, cereal comes in a box and a plastic bag. You don't need both. Take the plastic bag out of the box, then empty the plastic bag into a plastic container, seal the container throw away the box and the bag before you put to sea. That's how everything is. Canned food isn't that big of a deal. Glass is actually a good thing to take to sea because if it breaks and you throw it over the side, it will eventually get ground back into the sand it came from.

Everything was like this; it all had to be broken down to its lowest common denominator. You simply couldn't haul all the shit. We got three tablets. One for navigation, and two for school. This way, we didn't have to haul any books. There were plenty available digitally on the pad. As for school books, I have gone ahead and bought a homeschooling program. I had no idea if I was actually going to use most of it, but it was there, and I could use it as a crutch til' we figured it out. Gabe's idea of homeschooling was just winging it.

I finally figured out what it was Gabriel was doing. There's actually a name for it. It's called unschooling. That's a fancy way of saying I'm not going to do shit and try and educate my children anyway. Gabriel's message was pretty simple whatever the kids wanted to talk about or learn about was what he spoke of that day. They would come up with a subject, and he would speak to them until their eyes glazed over. After that, they go fishing or swimming, rinse and repeat. That was Gabriel's version of education.

My version of education was pretty simple. Sit down at the table and open your books. I write the date on the top of every page I want you to do. You do them, and you ask me for help if you can't figure it out yourself. If I needed help with anything, I would ask Gabriel or look it up on the internet. A lot of the homework I assigned my children was reading. Read, read, read. After you were done with a reading, I wanted you to write about it. This is one of the best ways to learn. Reading helps set it in your mind, and writing it down makes you remember it. It's pretty simple. We worked on the map with the kids together, Gabriel and I, both took turns.

Every swell of the blue-green in the ocean had a crest of turquoise aquamarine. Soft white sea foam was floating around sometimes on a crest being created by the crash of the wave. The constant sound of moving water was lulling and hypnotic.

Our first big sail was crossing the Gulf Stream to the Bahamas. Captain Ron said we should get to know Cape Town. He also said it was a perfect hangout spot for Cruisers, which is what we had become. It was a term for people who lived on their boats and sailed around the ocean like gypsies. I liked the nickname, and it inspired me to convince Gabriel to name our boat 'Gypsy.'

Every boat comes with a name. It doesn't mean you have to keep it. They say it is bad luck to change the name of the boat. Captain Ron said, "You can change the name of a boat, but there is a ritual and yea have to follow it."

According to the legend, every vessel is recorded by name in the 'Ledger of the Deep,' and Poseidon or Neptune knows them personally. To change the name of a vessel without consulting Poseidon meant to invoke his wrath. A ceremony was used to appease the God of the Seas.

The first thing that must be done was to purge its old name from the 'Ledger of the Deep' and Poseidon's memory. This involved wiping out every trace of the old name and reciting a short ceremony to remove the name from Poseidon's records.

You couldn't just change the boat's name and call it good. First, you had to get rid of everything that had the boat's name on it. If you couldn't get rid of it, you had to white the name out or remove it in some way. This also included the life rings.

There wasn't much on the boat to begin with that had its name on it, so that part was easy. Really, all we had to do was scrub the name off the back of the boat. And take the paperwork down to the local office and have the name changed legally.

"Boy, don't you take that new paperwork back on the boat. Go over there, and you leave it in the car for when we're ready. I'll let you know." Captain Ron was vehement.

It was kind of funny. This was a serious side to the seaman, but for the rest of us, landlubber folks, it seemed like he was a little crazy.

He took out some metal dog tags that had the old name of the boat written on them. "Gabriel, did you get me that nice bottle of champagne I asked you about?"

Gabe had a sly smirk on his face. He pulled out a bottle of Dom Perignon and turned it over to Captain Ron.

"Now Gabriel, I want you to go over to that bar and invite about ten people to come over here and tell them you'll buy them a drink. If they ask why, tell them what we're up to."

Gabriel rub both his hands together with glee, tapped Tristan on the shoulder and said, "Let's go!".

They disappeared across the street to the tacky bar. About five minutes later, he came back with a couple of guys and several girls of varying ages and with differing levels of drunkenness. They did a lot of hooting and hollering on their way over.

As they assembled on the dock, Captain Ron cleared his throat, and they seemed to settle down. He popped the bottle of Champagne and held it up as an homage facing the ocean breeze.

"Oh, mighty ruler of the seas and oceans, Poseidon, to whom all ships, pay homage. We implore you to expunge for all time from your records and recollection the name 'Rogered' which has ceased to be an entity in your kingdom." Half the crowd fell out laughing. Captain Ron cocked an eyebrow at the crowd, and they settled down. "As proof thereof, we submit this ingot bearing her name to be corrupted forever be purged from the seas." He threw the metal tag from the bow of the boat into the ocean.

"In grateful acknowledgment of your munificence, we offer these libations to your majesty and your court." Then he poured half of the bottle of Champagne into the sea from East to West. The remainder, he passed amongst the assembled rabble that Gabe had dug up.

When the rabble settled down again and the bottle was finished, he started again. He repeated the process of opening another bottle and hefting it aloft in reverence.

"Oh, great ruler of the seas and oceans, Poseidon, to whom all ships, pay homage. We implore you in your graciousness to take unto your records this worthy vessel hereafter and for all time known as..."

Before he could say the name, my eyes blurred. I heard her whispering softly in my ear. "Calypso." I yelled it out as my eyes cleared, "Calypso."

Captain Ron stopped and sputtered. He glared at me, opened his mouth to say something closed it and then continued. "Guarding her with your mighty trident and ensuring her of safe and rapid passage throughout her journeys within your realm. In appreciation, we offer these libations to you and your court." He poured out two coffee mugs. The rest he offered up to the sea from west to east.

He handed out the mugs, one to Gabriel and one to me. I drank mine down and relished it. I thought it was over, but the captain continued, cracking yet another bottle of Dom. I wonder how many bottles a boat needed to get a new name. The answer was, as many as Captain Ron said it needed.

"Oh, mighty rulers of the winds, through whose power our frail vessels travel the wild and faceless deep, we implore you to grant this worthy vessel Calypso," he had paused, stared me down then continued. "The pleasures of your bounty, ensuring us of your gentle ministration according to our needs.

He turned North, poured out a generous portion of Champagne into a cheap glass and flung it that way. "Exalted Ruler of the North Wind, grant us permission to use your mighty powers in the pursuit of our lawful endeavors, sparing us the overwhelming scourge of your scalding breath."

Turning West, he poured out more Champagne and flung to the West. "Exalted Ruler of the West Wind, grant us permission." Yadda, yadda.

Turning East he once again flung champagne. Repeating his requests.

Finally facing South, he poured and flung to the south.

Of course, with the remaining champagne began a suitable celebration in honor of Poseidon and Calypso, our new boat.

Captain Ron pulled me aside after a few rounds with the bottle.

"Why did you change her name? It is a good name, but to invoke a Goddess for the name of your boat, you ask for her protection."

I liked Captain Ron. He always surprised me with his knowledge. "I don't know. It felt right somehow. I don't think she will mind."

< I think she will be happy to watch over you, Beautiful Girl. >

< I think so too. >

CHAPTER 37

HERATHINA

Log Entry – Zeus's village.

The marriage ceremony was over, so he drew me to his hut. Compared to the other homes it was a palace. There were numerous chambers. The first was an antechamber crowded with a low table, bolsters and cushions all over the floor. He ushered me through. There was a blur of color and a sense of luxury. The last room was a bedchamber.

A raised platform, dominated the center, covered by furs and woven fabric. Cushions littered haphazardly around as I surveyed it. The walls dripped with woven fabric in local designs. What portions of the walls I could perceive contained decoration with local ores. There were no specific patterns.

"So now I have you. You are my wife. What should we do now, wife?" His eyes glittered as they raked over my body.

"Perhaps you could tell me something about yourself? We could use this time for me to get to know you as an individual, as a man."

He made a harsh dry laugh, turning his back on me to fiddle with an object on the table, "Would you like wine? Perhaps it will calm you."

I appreciated that he was expecting the wine would lower my sensibilities. It was a ploy. "That sounds lovely. Shall I call the servant girl to serve the refreshments?"

He turned, flashing his smile at me. "Yes, one of those women who've sworn themselves to you?" he asked, "You assumed I wasn't aware?"

Every man believes himself clever. "Aware of what?"

"The women in the tent were in a twitter over you, because you had a plan." He snickered.

I didn't care. If it made him feel superior, I was willing to grant him that. "I knew you had spies. I also knew that no matter what, you would choose me. Just think of how much respect you gained from the other chieftains. They assume you applied your mind and not your cock."I forced a smile on my face.

He tipped his head back and guffawed with amusement, "You are a fascinating woman, Hera. Is being the Goddess of the Mountain as much fun as it should be?"

"Being considered a God or Goddess is not fun. It's a great responsibility. People believe in you and listen to you. They will give their lives for you unnecessarily if they think there's a purpose for it. It is a great burden. You treat it lightly as if you have won a lottery. It is not something to be thirsted for. The lives of other people are precious. I never wished to be the Goddess of the Mountain. I never told anyone I was the Goddess of the Mountain. I am Herathina and nothing more. It is your people and others like you who made me the Goddess of the Mountain. It is not something I wished for. Do you wish to rule alongside me, helping me, or to become a God? To do any of that, you must win hearts and minds before you can rule them."

"I won hearts and minds, it was easy. I terrified them."

Bile rose in my throat. His eyes glittered with the power he wheeled.

"Ruling through fear is not the only means to rule. The moment these people recognize they have nothing to fear from you or fear you no more, your authority will come to a bloody end. However, if they love you, they will do anything and everything in their power to defend you, to protect you and enforce your laws. The only way to win their lives is by fair treatment and to lead fairly and justly."

He shook his head. I chose that moment to clap my hands. One of my maids waited off to the side. She parted the curtain between the two rooms, "My lady?"

"Please bring my husband and me fresh wine. We also wish for a small plate of food and perhaps some sweet incense to burn."

She lowered her head as she backed out of the room, closing the drapes behind her.

He didn't even look at her. "You have taken to your role of chief woman?"

He's baiting me.

"I've been the Goddess on the Mountain longer than you or any of your people have been alive."

He was at my side. His shoulders were wide as a wall blocking out the light from the candles. The musky scent of a man floated around him and I found it alluring.

"Will you not give your husband a kiss?" His eyes spoke of experience wooing women, but I was not one of his goat herder's daughters easily pressed into an intimacy I didn't want.

"Have you done something to earn one?" I stilled, schooling my face into bland indifference.

"Will you not give it? Do I need to earn it? I'm your husband, and I demand you kiss me." His voice reverberated around the room. It was a command. His attitude revealed himself. He was used to having his every command obeyed.

"Zeus, all your bravado, everything you showed those chieftains out there, that will not help you with me. I will not be bullied. You heard my brother. You are not welcome to take me by force. It will cause a war. Perhaps you've tried the stick so maybe now you could try the carrot?"

Just then, the girl returned, and we ate in silence. You cannot force someone into love. I suppose he could've forced himself upon me. The threat of the chieftains' waging war was more of a driving force than his wish to bed me.

"I'll bed elsewhere." A huff escaped as did he.

"You don't need to."

"If you think I'm going to lay in that bed like I'm your brother, you're mistaken." He plucked up the wineskin turned and left the room. I heard him shifting things around in the outer chamber.

I laid down on the bedding, and it smelled faintly of him. I let sleep overwhelm me.

Disoriented and awake, I didn't know where I was. It came crashing on me. I was married to a warlord monster, the butcher of women and children.

In the dark gloom, I heard shifting and moaning. Following the sounds, my eyes found Zeus laying on a mound of pillows. He must've procured them from the antechamber. He looked young. All the woes of humankind were swept away with sleep. Without his pinched eyebrows and gnashing teeth, he had a sweetness to his face. I got up from the bed and crept across the room. I caressed his mane back from his brow to calm him. Then, I climbed back into my bed.

Nightmares mean you must have regret. Does he have a conscience?

Days went on much as they did before. He did not force himself upon me. Every night he piled his bedding on the floor, then moved them back out by morning. I do not think he wanted everyone in the village to know he's not sleeping with me.

"You need not sleep on the floor. We can share the same bed."

"I already told you my sentiments on the matter. Welcome me to your bed with all that it entails. Jorhan said not to take you by force. I will not be regarded as a cuckold. Welcome me as your husband, or I'll sleep on the floor."

I did not want to hurt his pride, perhaps he was right. I did not desire to share a bed with any man, or at least I thought.

His people had feast days like all societies do. Those special remembrances and reverence for Gods, it was a planting feast. There was a great celebration with much drinking and eating far into the night. There was dancing around the fire pits. There were many marriages. Nine months from now many children will be born.

"Are you not drinking my wife?" Zeus doesn't understand that we are not the same species. Overindulgence of alcohol is not a problem for Themians. It does not alter us physiologically the same as humans.

"Yes, I am. The wine is lovely." I carried a smile on my face at the light-hearted joy most people felt. If the harvest was good, the winter would be easy. I allowed the emotions of the humans to wash over me. It was a drug I had learned to enjoy. However, if I let it take me too far, I may never let it go. It is a balance I must keep at all times.

"I drink to celebrate the harvest, celebrate the planting of the harvest for it will strengthen us." His hand grips his cup as he waves it toward the village center. "Will you not bestow a blessing on to our village, great Goddess of the Mountain?"

I couldn't tell if he was mocking me or seeking to entice me. He rose up banging his metal cup against his blade, "The Goddess of the Mountain wishes to give us a blessing."

The music ceased as the throng quieted down. The only noises were of small children crying or giggling and the crackling of fire pits, so I needed to say something.

"I wish merely for a favorable harvest of fruit and of man. May we grow ripe and become fruitful in the coming season. May we grow with love and may the many blessings of the mountain be upon all of us."

I took back my seat. Zeus also sat down. I could see the longing in his eyes. His desire.

What was I to do with this husband of mine? A slow smile broke over his face as he reached for my hand. Clasping it, he brought it to his lips. His eyes never left mine as his lips brushed the sensitive top skin of my hand.

The evening darkened, and the moon rose so I took my leave. As I entered my bedchamber sounds followed me. Zeus was drunk. He'd followed me but did not bring his bedding.

"Will you not give me a kiss, wife?"

He looked vulnerable like a man not knowing what to do.

Am I toying with him? Will there ever be something between us? He is human, and I am Themian. The council was clear, limited contact. Yet, I am married to him. Even without physical intimacy, this is wrong. My reasons for being here may be honorable, but is my interference?

The conversation went round and round in my mind. There will never be a correct answer. If we are higher beings, then the intervention of any kind was wrong. If we are equal, then what I do is irrelevant. Although humans are less developed, they are not less intelligent. The only discernible differences I could find were my mental abilities.

What if I removed his past deeds and only looked upon him, the man? From the moment I met him in the flesh, he was attentive to his people. Kind to the old and young. Worked hard in building his villages. These were admirable qualities.

I had not kissed him since our wedding day, many months ago. His blue eyes sparkled with the candlelight. The color was common among my people, but rare in humans. The flash of it took my breath away. A flush rolled through my body. It began in my chest and flowed out, reaching up my neck to engulf my face. I was aflame, and heat covered my surface.

"I would be happy to give you a kiss on this blessed feast-day." The words were out of my mouth before I could stop them.

Why had I said that?

In two strides, he was in front of me and instead of seizing me as he did on our wedding day, he leaned over, dangling his face towards mine. I could see his blue eyes boring into me. My heart sped up. His face was close and his lips a breath away. I looked from his lips to his eyes. He touched me on the side of my face, cupping my cheek in reverence. I found I was leaning in. He gently brushed his lips across mine, pressing ever so slightly, and then pulled back.

That is when I realized my hands were touching him, clasping him. I caressed the side of his face in return.

What is this feeling that tears through me?

I wanted him to kiss me again.

He whispered, "So, you're not so indifferent as I thought?"

I caught my breath. My chest rose and fell with the quickness of it, "I cannot be indifferent."

His eyes tore through me as did a fire of desire, "Shall I get my bedding?"

I didn't understand how to answer. I was unsure if I was ready for what he was implying. My heart was beating wildly. I wanted him to touch me again, and I knew where this would lead.

Is this the level of emotion Poseidon has with his human? Does Cleito evoke passion like this? I can't deny I want him. His lust washes over me in waves, but underneath that is love. He loves me. How can he love me? I can't comprehend it, but only a fool would push that away. Is this what mates feel?

"No, come to bed, husband." The whisper left my lips to hang in the air. I won't look back.

Log Entry

I believe I've fallen under Zeus's spell. Do I love him? A fluttering fills my chest and belly at the site of him. It's a chemical reaction I know this, but it twists me up inside, causing forgetfulness and loss of appetite.

Not exactly sure when it happened but somehow in the middle of this, I think I have fallen in love. Or is it lust? I know who and what Zeus is. He has a way about him that is endearing. He makes me feel special. Amongst my people, we are equal. The same, no one different from another. Yet with this human, I'm highest, first. He treats me like a possession, yes. A prized possession. To him, I am the most precious thing in his life.

CHAPTER 38

HERATHINA

Log Entry

Athena contacted me. My recall to Alethea has finally come. Poseidon and his machinations are at an end. The High Council has to take action. I'm confident they have established our mission here is a complete failure. I cannot perceive what the ramifications of Poseidon's horrific actions will be, but I have a suspicion it's something none of us ever expected.

How do I justify to Zeus? I must leave, and he cannot come with me.

Athena informed me I would be shifted on the marrow with no guarantee that I'll ever return. I finally find someone to be with, and now I'm to be transported away.

The secret of Zeus must be protected for assuredly I'm just as culpable as Poseidon and his cohorts. It tears at me. Is this what Poseidon felt when he met Cleito?

I turned my back to Zeus. It is unavoidable. I must tell him.

His chest rises, filling with air before he exploded, "I must go with you. We cannot part ways. Don't you understand if you leave me here while you're off with the other Gods how that will make me look?" His ego knows no bounds. He is more worried about his grip on the people than my safety.

"If I take you, they will kill you. You must stay, don't you see that? Every person here depends on you to lead them. They need you." I offer my feeble excuse.

He moved like lightning to my side. "I need you Hera, without you by my side, I appear weak. The other chieftains will see it as an opportunity. They will make a move."

I can't face him. He is right. They will. His pleas fill me with tears. My chest burns. I want to stay. This life has become mine. It is simple and easy. Here I have a place, a home. I have never felt the level of acceptance I have here. But that is not possible.

I am all that keeps the other chieftains at bay. I don't know if it's his lust for power or his lust for me, or because he's finally found something he wants, other than destroying everyone or ruling them, but he seems to have changed recently. He is softer and kinder somehow.

Shaking my head, I can't follow those thoughts. I will be shifted whether I want to be or not.

"If we don't make a good showing when I leave, they will move on you. The plotting will begin in earnest. We are a united front for all of Greece. The King of Olympus must give me his leave to visit my family. I will ask for your leave. I will show obedience to you."

This is the best way. I placate him and give him the show of power he needs. His head lowers as his eyes glisten. He wants me to bow to him. He can't turn from that. His tongue circles his lips as they dry with his desire. "I will publicly give you leave. Will you bow to me? For all to see, wife?"

I have him. "Yes, Zeus. I will beg your leave in front of all."

His hands reach for me. Relief fills my heart as I give over for the last chance at his physical touch.

*****

I walked to the center of Zeus's dais. Carrying only a cloak over my shoulder, Mica shifted me. One moment I was standing in front of all the village, and the next one, I was on Alethea. I never even had a chance to ask for leave.

My eyes light on the front of a massive temple. Built over the top of the pediment stands a statue. It is dedicated to Poseidon. When I left, his chariot had flying horses, now they are Hippocampus, horses of the sea. He carries with him a three-tined fork. I have seen humans fishing with such a device. They call it a triton. But that is not what strikes me. It is the ecstasy in his countenance. The sheer joy. I have never witnessed Poseidon with such an expression, yet the artist must have seen it for it to be here. He is dressed in full battle gear, one hand gripping the reins, the other one is thrusting into the sky carrying the Triton as a prize or a weapon. The artist has caught the look of wind sweeping his hair back. He stands with all his glory gazing down on us as he rides to battle.

The sheer idea that humans have been worshiping him as a God, bringing him tribute and building him temples, disgusts me on a level I cannot explain, but can I claim to be different?

In the Citadel, only one member of the High Council is present, Hermes. All the rest remain back on home-world 12. Athena sits beside him, along with Apollo, Artemis, and Isis. Osiris is missing. A young boy stands next to Isis with his hand on her shoulder. He is present to support her. I hear the whisper of his name before his mind slams shut, Horus.

People from our mission project are sorted into two groups. A few others and I were on one side, but most were across the room from me. I know precisely what the sorting is about - those who broke their oath and those who have not.

Hermes stood for his proclamation. "What has been done here, on this world, is a travesty in the highest order and it shall not be tolerated. Not only did you taint the gene pool of the humans, but you decided to start ruling them is if you had a right to enslave them to your will. The price you must pay is all your offspring; the Nephilim will be butchered."

A shutter ran through the room, and my entire body vibrated with the emotions rolling over me.

The harrowed look on Poseidon face is almost more than I can bear. He spent his entire life working towards our people's ends. He was the reason for our discoveries of Science and Mathematical facts. He never once wavered from the belief of finding a mate, only to come here and fall in love, or so he claims, then have his offspring butchered.

Tears sprang to my eyes. I ached for him and his loss. His head hung down in defeat, and his handlers loosened their grip. He slumped on his knees to the floor, hunching his shoulders. The great Ancient One had been broken, but I took no joy in his fall.

One among us mentally screamed with glee. Apollo and Artemis shared a look. Apollo stood up and addressed the council.

"I, Apollo, along with my sister, Artemis, will go forth. We will do the High Council's bidding. If anyone must put your offspring to death, it will be us. I will cleanse the planet of their taint. All who have reproduced children with humans their children will be put to the sword. My sister, Artemis, and I will go on the great hunt. We will flow across the sky until every one of them is found."

My stomach lurched. I never once believed that Apollo had such bloodlust in him. I could see the sorrow in his eyes. Artemis, on the other hand, reveled in the glory of the hunt. She was hungry for the hunt. She was a consummate predator always looking for the proper prey. The animals here weren't challenging enough, but she had found something that would be, hybrids. I could taste her lust for it. Bile rose from my rolling belly to fill my throat. Her eyes turned to lock on me. She smiled as I tightened the shields of my mind. She wanted to hunt down the Nephilim and kill them. I could not call her out on her bloodlust. I had far too much to hide.

I could not allow the scrutiny of someone tiptoeing through my mind to see my true aims. Stilling my tongue to her bloodlust, I gulped in the air to clear the gage in my throat. Thinking of her killing even the babe in its mother's arms caused me to sway.

Her eyes glowed with the thrill. Themians are beautiful on the outside, but today I have seen the deep ugly that rots at our bones.

Hermes raised his hand to still the room.

"Bring in the human."

Narcissus drug a dust-encrusted rag across the floor. I blinked several times to clear my eyes. It resembled an animal. Matted hair the color of dung filled with dry leaves and bramble lifted up to reveal a woman I knew on site, Cleito. She hadn't aged a day, her skin was covered in filth, but it still carried the glow of youth. Her eyes flashed with hatred. It hit me harder than falling through ice into a mountain lake. I shivered with it. Her eyes lit on mine.

She was swift as she lunged. Both of her hands raised, fingers curled like the claws of the cat she resembled. "You evil bitch, I'll kill you!"

Apollo slammed his fist into the side of her face, and she fell to the ground.

"She knows too much about us. She cannot be allowed to leave Alethea. She will spread stories about us, telling the humans of the people from the stars." Narcissus pulled her up to her knees as her head lulled to the side.

Swallowing, I surveyed the room. Heads nodded all around. The word that floated around was 'death'. My head shook, but the words wouldn't come.

I can't stop them.

Hermes nodded his head. Apollo raised his sword, and in one swift motion, he thrust it into her chest.

The cry that filled the room was echoed from my throat with Poseidon's. His two handlers switched to using both hands.

"Hold him! He must be judged." I lost the rest of Hermes words.

Poseidon's mind raced out to every Themian in the room. My eyes were open but frozen in fear. "You have taken everything from me. You will not take my freedom."

The Citadel had always dampened our powers. Something about the crystals in these rooms caused the lessening of our abilities. Poseidon had overcome that. His mind forced us to our knees as he rose into the air.

His hatred focused on me. "You, Herathina! You will pay for this."

His body angled down as he dove for me. My heart burst in my chest.

I can't die like this. Not now.

I dove to the side as his foot hit the floor, cracking its tiles. The field in the room broke with it releasing everyone from the trance.

The wind took Athena into the air to meet Poseidon. A flash of steel followed her.

"Mica, my shield!" There it was on her arm, along with a shining helm. It was the warrior in her I had always felt below the surface. Athena raised her sword to strike only to find an empty space. Poseidon rode the wind out of the temple and beyond. The only thing that remained was the echo of his voice.

"I'll be back. You will all pay. Of that, I promise!"

Log Entry

Isis chose to return with Hermes. The rumor is she's become mated and wishes to accompany her mate on the next project when it is announced. I'm assuming that the boy is one of her offspring, which is why the High Council has allowed him to attend her in the Citadel and not put him to death on the spot.

Where is his twin? Why is he a single child?

I push those thoughts to the side. I have no time to worry about the drama of others if I am to protect my own.

Hermes proclaimed that Alethea must be moved. The continent which it sits next to, along with all its villages, the very idea of Atlantis, will die. Part of Poseidon's punishment was to destroy the very world he'd built.

Athena is to take over the lead on the project. She is not the oldest member, however. Apparently, she has shown herself to be an excellent leader in times of strife.

I've been given the option to return to my previous location or to move on to somewhere fresh. Making sure to school my face and guard my mind, I informed them I would be happy to go back to the area now being called Greece and to continue studying the human population there. I've watched them for the last several thousand years. My close study could garner the answers we seek, or so I've led them to believe.

CHAPTER 39

SYDNEY

He had lied. It had all been a lie. Because he didn't want to be here like this. His face was sunken and frail. The parlor of his skin had yellowed as his life went away. I felt his pain in my heart torn into a million pieces.

There were tubes coming out of his body, every one of them filling him with drugs, but not hope. One was a pain killer, another was a blood thinner. There was also saline for hydration. His hand was covered in the tape that had been there long enough it was peeling up at the sides. The oxygen tube over his face was flowing into his nose. It was air for the dying.

He is dying.

His eyes were the only part of him that was the same anymore.

How could I have missed this? I should have asked more questions. When he got that boat and said, he wanted to run off and sail, it was him shirking his responsibilities, and he had never done that. I should have known Zack didn't want to take over. Gabe had made him.

Zack, you fucker, you knew all along, and you never said a word. I hate you! You call yourself my friend.

My eyes flash to the wall. Zack was in the next room, and I wanted to go kick the shit out of him. A good meat hook to his asshole would have made me feel better.

A hand gently squeezed my shoulder, and tears quietly found their way down my face. It was Tristan, reliable Tristan.

I could tell by Gabe's breathing, he was close. I was holding my breath every time he stopped. Every part of me burned with a deep ache. I hadn't moved from this seat in days. Sleep is elusive to the watchers of the dying. I didn't even want to use the restroom for fear of leaving him alone.

He had refused all resuscitation orders. He didn't want anyone trying to bring him back. He'd signed a living will and left it with Zack the week he bought the boat. Zack was his executor. He told me he wanted to be cremated and spread in the ocean so he could travel the ocean that he loved forever. The knot in my throat never went away.

I could hear Issy crying softly in another room.

"Tristan go get your sister! We need to be together. Bring uncle Zack too." My eyes dried with the heat behind them. I turned away from the door to look at Gabe. He opened his eyes, then smiled.

"Hey, good looking! I love you! Don't you ever forget that. Where are my kids?" His eyes searched around the room slowly and lazily.

"They're coming. Tristan went to get Issy."

Issy rushed into the room, taking her place on the other side of the bed. Tristan was next to her, holding her back. She desperately wanted to hug her daddy one last time.

"Good, we're all here." He reached his hand out to the kids. They both took it eagerly. "Tristan, take care of your sister and your mom." Issy choked back a wail. "Zack, remember what I told you. Watch out for our family. Issy, don't do anything silly. Listen to your mom and Tristan. I love you all. I lived a great life. Being on the boat for the last few years was exactly how I wanted to spend my time."

He closed his eyes, and I leaned over to kiss his lips. Breath left him, his chest didn't rise again. I heard the crying from across the bed, as I laid my head down on edge.

A roaring scream grew inside me. I felt it rising from the bottom of my diaphragm climbing its way out of my lungs and issued from my lips. As it rose, the lights flickered, and the room began to shake. Gabe's bed vibrated. Windows rattled in their frames. Creaking tore the air as I raised my head, staring into Tristan's eyes. I tilted my head back. The entire building rocked violently from side to side. Zack came to my side wrapping his hand around my shoulders.

My chest heaved with the fire burning inside me. My head filled with napalm.

"Sydney, we need to get out of this building."

I stood up, still crying, while the rocking continued.

"Mom, he's gone!" Tristan shouted.

My eyes shifted to Issy. Her green eyes were different. My eyes darted back to Tristan's. They had the ring, and Issy's eyes had it too. A new scream filled me, ripping out of me.

The shaking ramped up, and a crack ran up the wall behind Tristan and Issy. Tristan reached out, laying his hand on top of mine and Gabe's. I could feel his strength flowing into me. Issy pulled Gabe's hand from mine.

"Mom, stop! You still have us." Issy wailed.

Issy was right. My crying slowed as did the rocking. Tristan came around the bed wrapping me in a hug. I took Issy's hand pulling her around into my embrace. Zack held us all for a moment.

"Gather up ya things. We need to get out of this building. It doesn't look safe." Zack's deep voice commanded.

Zack was right, of course. I would never see Gabe again. He was gone. It was just a body.

< He's gone, Beautiful Girl. The building is unstable. You need to take the kids and get out. >

< *That's what I'm trying to do!* >

I ran around the room picking up everything that I could think of and shoving it into a bag. I was about to walk out but stopped. Taking three determined steps back to the bed, I looked down at Gabriel. I lifted his hand and pulled his wedding ring off, kissed his cold hand, and left.

In the hall, the building shifted and shuttered with every shuddering breath I took. Zack had a hand wrapped around Issy's arm to keep her upright. I stumbled, and Tristan grabbed me as we hurried to the stairs. There were four flights of stairs between us and the questionable safety of the street.

A lump formed in my throat and the building groaned with me. Every emotion I felt manifested itself in the real world.

The cornucopia of screaming grew the further down we went. Zack and Issy had gotten ahead of us. On the second floor, a piece of the stairwell fell in front of me crashing into the railing. The stairs shook with the impact. The walls reverberated with my shock. The chunk tumbled and blocked off the stairway.

I screamed, "Zack, get her out! We'll meet you at the flat." My voice came out raw over the screaming around us. He glanced back at me. His face was pinched with worry, but he gave me a curt nod. With Issy in tow, he darted into the crowd.

I had done this. I didn't know how, but it was my doing. That meant that I could do it again. Reaching out, I put my hand on the giant piece of rubble blocking my path.

< Feel the weight in it and imagine it's a feather. Shift it slightly, so no one notices. It will give everyone enough room to pass. > The voice urged.

< *Okay. Here goes nothing.* >

I pictured a feather in my mind and pushed. It went through the handrail careening into the other wall on its way to the ground floor. Shock rolled through me.

< Maybe with a little more finesse next time, Beautiful Girl. >

< *Next time, you come and do it.* >

He didn't take the bait and was not amused. I could feel the fear of bleeding through.

"Mom wake up! Let's go!"

The press of bodies behind us threatened to push me down the stairs, crushing us. My feet stumbled under me running while dust drifted down from the ceiling. The screaming grew louder the closer we got to the exit.

The crush of human bodies at the door was unbelievable. The panic of the masses overwhelmed me. My blood was already pumping with adrenaline. There was no way to get out that door, so I turned my head searching frantically left and right. My eyes seized on the glass window of a gift shop. Shifting directions, I pulled Tristan past the writhing mass. As I had expected, the gift shop had an exit to the street. Retching the door open, I heard glass breaking as we ran away from the building.

"We need a taxi. Can you see one around here?" I was swinging my head around, desperate to find a way to our apartment building.

What filled my eyes was nothing short of a horror. Every car on the road was stopped. People were standing around, staring down into the cracks in the street that were radiating out from the hospital.

There was a police officer on a megaphone yelling at everyone to leave the area. Panama City was in chaos, and it was all my fault.

I reached out and pulled Tristan toward the road. We would just have to walk all the way if necessary. "How far do you think the walk is?" Tristan asked.

"Five miles, give or take. I don't really know, but we may have to walk it. The further we get from here, the more likely we can get a cab. I'll call Zack and see where he is." As I was digging in my pocket, I realized that I had no phone. My purse was in my backpack which I gave to Issy.

"Fuck! Do you have your phone?"

With his eyes like a deer in the headlights, Tristan shook his head.

"Great! Well, I don't have any money either, what about you?"

Reaching into his back pocket, he pulled out a wallet, "Ten bucks. That could get us there if we get a good driver."

He was right. It would get us there, maybe.

Looking around at the road with the network of cracks everywhere, I cringed. There was no way to make this right. The road was blocked with cars sitting idle as far as the eye could see. The road curved about a half mile ahead, so there was hope.

Tristan kept sticking a finger in his ear and shaking his head. As we walked by a truck, the driver laid on the horn. Tristan immediately covered both ears with his hands, cradling himself in pain.

"Tristan, are you OK? Tristan?" I was rubbing his back. He stood up and shook his head again.

"Sorry, I didn't expect the noise, and it's so loud." I could see the tears in his eyes.

I stopped and hugged him. I could hear the quivering in his breathing. Every breath was shuttering. I didn't want to let go of him. I shook too. The burning in my chest rose, as did my grief. The glass in the car next to us rattled. The vehicle shuttered with me.

< Sydney, breathe! You have to stop, Beautiful Girl. You can't lose it in the open. Breathe. >

< He's gone! Just like Adrian. >

< Stop! You have to get Tristan to a safe place before you lose it. You don't want him to see you like this. >

< Yes, survival mode. I can do this >

< Yes, you can. Just breathe. I'm here for you. You are not alone. >

< Okay. >

The rattling receded as I calmed. Pushing the pain back with one swift mental motion, I locked it up in a little box in my mind. I pulled Tristan's arm as I strode with purpose in the direction of the apartment.

Rounding the curve in the road didn't bring any relief. The road was not as cluttered with cars. Most of the taxis didn't want to take a fair. A couple acted like they did not understand me which was total crap. My Spanish was just fine. The kids are much better at Spanish and Italian. But none of the drivers weren't taking any rides.

"I think we should leave the main road and cut over a few streets." Tristan's idea would have been fine in Italy but not here.

"No, I don't know what the area is like off the main road around here. It's not safe, we're gringos. With all the chaos, a few nefarious fellows might get the wrong idea and kill us. What's the rule?"

Ever since the kids were little, we'd been traveling. We had to make rules.

"Don't go where you don't know. I know mom, but I just feel like we would be okay."

I didn't like the sound of that. "Are you willing to risk your life and mine on it?" I needed him to really think everything through. It's not like his sister was ever going to do that. He needed to look out for her.

"No, I'm not willing to risk you. Can we turn off on the next major road we come to?" He asked with determination.

That was smart so I shook my head in agreement.

We walked on, to the next crossroads. It was a good choice. There was a cab driver who waved us over. We climbed in, and he took off on every side road to be found in Panama City.

We made it to the apartment not long after Zack. The building looked untouched by the "earthquake." I just wanted to lay down and die.

Issy ran to us, wrapping her arms around us. We all began crying, but I had to hold back. I couldn't let it take over again. The voice was right. I couldn't lose control.

I lowered myself and the kids to the floor. I knelt there, holding them. The burning in my chest threatened to consume me. I had to keep pushing it back.

Isolde wept openly. There was no comfort for her. Tristan had silent tears sliding down his face. Otherwise, he was stiff, keeping his head close to Issy's. I had to get up at a point because my knees couldn't take the hard tile anymore. I left the kids holding one another and headed to the bathroom.

"Yes, there was an earthquake. It hit at the same time Gabriel died…. Sydney? She's in bad shape. I've neva seen anyone cry like that. Maria can't ye come here please? … No… yes, I'll try…okay. I love ya's too… okay, bye." Zack sniffed a few times, and I heard muffled steps coming to the door.

I ducked into the bathroom. It was so much worse than he could even imagine. My eyes moved around the room. The toilet seat was up. I hated that, and it slammed down.

God, what am I going to do?

My hair was a mess, so the hairbrush just flew into my hand.

Fuck that's new.

*****

I woke up screaming. I could still feel the building shifting underneath us. Don't know what I was more afraid of. My power or life without Gabriel. Sitting on the bed, I was drenched in clammy, sticky sweat. My mind was a wreck. Every time I got upset things started to fly around the room.

So far, no one had noticed. I wanted to keep it that way, but I didn't think it was possible in a city with a population density of 3.8 million.

Every time I looked at Zack, I just wanted to murder him. He'd known, he'd known all along. I always felt he was my friend, but blood comes first. That's the Italian way. They're all like that. It's all about the family. Gabriel had been the head of this family for a long time, now Zack was.

I sat down at the breakfast bar and gazed out the window behind Zack, "Zack, I'm going to take the kids and go back to the boat. I just don't like this building at all. I don't like living here. I haven't lived in a building in a long time. I'd just feel better on my boat."

"Sydney, ya can't go on like this. You wake up screaming, and you're hiding in your room. Then, you get up and leave the room suddenly." He stopped and made me look at him, "Are ya trying to get away from me? You seem to be avoiding me specifically. I'm trying to help you…" His hazel eyes followed my every move.

I didn't answer so he continued. "Look, why don't you pack up the boat? Or we will get a captain to sail it to Florida.

Put the kids on a plane, send them to Maria. You go too, or stay here with me. But you can't keep going on like this."

I'd heard that, but I just couldn't do it. Leave the boat or send the kids to Maria.

I didn't feel safe being around people. I didn't feel safe being in the city. How was I going to make Zack understand it wasn't him? It really was me.

"I'm not avoiding you, Zack. I'm just trying to survive. I'm not sending my kids to Maria. I can't be separated from them." I will never be separated from them.

"Look, just promise me you won't leave without telling me. Can you do that?" He pleaded.

"Yeah, I promise I won't leave without saying something first. Promise me you're not going to ask a ton of questions. I don't want to make any big decisions right now. You are Gabriel's executor, you handle it." I moaned and gulped back my pain.

I turned and walked out of the room before he could say anything. I didn't want to have a big discussion or argue. I just wanted to get the hell out of that building.

"Tristan, Isolde gather up your things! We're going back to the boat. Don't leave anything behind."

They scrambled to pack.

"What about Uncle Zack? Are we just going to leave him here alone?" Issy crossed her arms.

"Uncle Zack has been living alone his entire adult life. I think he'll be just fine without us." I barked back.

Tristan didn't seem surprised. He turned away, maybe to hide his feelings. He'd always played it close to the cuff, keeping everything tightly under control. Something was different now, but I couldn't put my finger on it. His eyes definitely looked different. Everything I feared was gripping me like a vice, holding me tight with fear.

God, please don't let them be like me.

I entered the room I called my bedroom. I grabbed my bag as it started packing itself. Everything was flying into the backpack. A couple of items even came from the bathroom. It took me a total of three minutes to gather everything that I had at Zack's apartment. I was just happy that I hadn't started flying through the air in front of everyone.

As I walked over and put my bag by the front door, Zach became agitated and burst out, "You're leaving now? You're going back to the boat right now?"

"Yes, I told you. I don't want to stay here. I don't like this building. I don't like this apartment. I want to go home, and the boat is my home." I returned then griped the handle of my back pack with white knuckles.

Zack was standing in front of me. "So, you're just going to leave?"

The doors rattled in their frames. I tried to calm down. "No, not just going to leave. I made you a promise. I said I wasn't leaving without telling you. I'm leaving the building and going back to my boat. I'm taking my children with me. You can come if you want, but I'm not staying another minute in this building"

Why couldn't he understand that? I just wanted to get the fuck out of this building.

I could feel the vibrations in the building. The more upset I got, the more the vibrating continued to rise. Soon the vibrating would become shaking, and shaking become cracking, cracking turns into Earthquakes, and I didn't want to cause any more earthquakes.

Take a deep breath, Syd. Calm down!

Issy's eyes lit up, and she ran over to Zack wrapping her arms around his waist. "Yes, Uncle Zack, come with us. Come stay on the boat. It'll be nice. We're all sad over Daddy. We should be together." She hiccupped and shuttered, "Mom doesn't want to be here so let's go to the boat. We can all be together there. Don't be alone!"

His eye bulged out of his head. I could see he was on the verge, but I didn't really want Zack to come with us. I only invited him so that he wouldn't get suspicious. I had to get the fuck out of the city.

I had to get away from people. I didn't know how to handle this new power. I couldn't be around people while I was learning to control it. I didn't know if I'd be any safer at sea, but it would be safer for everyone else.

Tristan bent over stuffing clothes in his bag, his head whipping around. When he stared at me, his eyes were wide with fright. Slowly he stood up straight with stiff shoulders, and he turned toward me.

"Mom, is there anything that we need to get before we go to the boat? Food or supplies of some kind?" Strain colored his voice.

"I can't think of anything right now. Let's just get to the boat and see the lay of the land. If we need something, I'll send you or your sister out for it. Okay?"

He didn't answer. He just shook his head, but I couldn't tell if he was acquiescing or not. I took my eyes off of him only when Zack started talking.

"Awe Syd, I'm not coming to the boat with ya. I'm just not a boat person. I'm one of those Land Lovers. You know that. I'll come to see ya's in a couple of days. Okay?"

I knew he wouldn't come, so I nodded. I tiptoed up and kissed him on the cheek. He gave me a brief hug and cleared his throat. I could hear him working on his breathing trying not to cry.

I grabbed my backpack and headed for the elevator. I heard Issy sniffling and Tristan mumbling goodbye in my wake. We loaded up onto the elevator and hit the street. Tristan waved down the first taxi he could.

The train ride back to Cologne was a blur of green. I only saw it through the tears that filled my eyes.

"Do you want to tell me why you were in such a hurry to leave Uncle Zack's apartment?"

My heart rate jumped, Tristan couldn't know anything. I can't hear him, and he can't hear me.

You're just getting paranoid, Sydney.

"What is there to say? I didn't want to be in a tall building. There was an earthquake. There will be more aftershocks. The building codes here aren't the same as America. Do you really think they build them better here? Do you want to change it? I don't know about you, but I feel safer on the boat."

Judging from the raised eyebrow he was sporting, I wasn't sure he bought it, but it didn't matter. We were out of the building. On the boat my word was the only one that mattered. He snatched up his bag and headed down the gangway to his berth.

Issy was still lingering in the salon. She was shifting from one foot to the other, and she had something to say because her eyes glistened with moisture.

"I love you, Issy! Is there something I can do for you, sweetheart?"

"Mom, did you ever feel like you were going crazy? That you didn't fit in your own skin?" her eyes darted around the saloon as her fingers worked a knot into her shirt.

"Yes, sweetheart. It took me a long time to feel comfortable in my own skin. It's just hard when you're young and someone you love dies. It does get easier, just might take a long time. You're never going to forget."

The tears trailed down our faces. I felt the boat shift, and I moved to her wrapping my arms around her. She wept. I didn't want her to feel alone in her grief.

It was getting late, and we all kind of wanted our own space, so we went to sleep.

*****

Blue, Azure, carnelian, none of those colors could adequately describe the brilliance of the sky that loomed ahead of me. The sheer vastness of the curvature of the Earth. Following that curve, the indescribable blue of the sky met with the aquamarine turquoise of the ocean, both divided by an island. I could just make out the curve that formed the island. It had a curiously shaped mountain in the center.

It appeared to be a mountain, but after all these years, I began to believe it was a pyramid. Pyramids were pointy at the top. This one was rounded. It was covered in tropical rainforest's foliage. I could see all the various types of palm trees reaching towards the sky all around the island and down the sides of the pyramid mountain.

Jutting from the side of this curiously shaped mountain, there was a building that resembled an acropolis. Shining perfectly formed and proportioned temple. There was something different this time - a statue. It looked Greek. It was a man in a chariot, carrying a trident. I could just make out the veins of the marble in the vast pillars supporting the pediment. It was a misty dew floating around the base of the building caused by a waterfall. How could anyone build a building on top of a waterfall, especially one of that magnitude?

Waves pounded on the sand of the island, but the pounding turned into the wind blowing and the blowing became the whispers. She was going to talk. I had to listen.

Maybe I'll hear it this time. I know it's important. Straining, I close my eyes, desperate to pick up any sound. The murmuring starts, and the wind rises. I can hear the tone of her voice. Soft, authoritative, just under the rule of the wind. I can feel the pressure of the wind on my face and my body like it's pushing me back. Her voice becomes louder.

What is she saying?

And then, I can hear it. She says, "You're almost ready!"

*****

And then, it was gone. I was awake. My whole body was shaking drenched in sweat. The tears flew down my face and neck, reaching my chest which felt like it was in a vice. If Gabriel were here, he would hold me, and he would tell me I was safe. But he was not, and he was never going to be here again. The pain raged through me, and I could feel the boat rising up.

Breathe, Sydney, breathe. Calm yourself. You have to calm down. Can't let this take over. Oh my God, don't hurt anyone. I don't want to hurt anybody.

< I don't think it's a good idea for you to be around civilization right now. >

< *I'm dangerous.* >

< Yes, a little bit. You know you need to go. Find a beach to hang out on. Somewhere away from other people where you can practice and learn >

< *My kids, I could hurt them. I know I would never hurt them. I'm actually more likely to hurt someone else for them. You're right, I need a few days to get things together, and then we'll go.*>

CHAPTER 40

SYDNEY

"I need you and Issy to do a full inventory of all our food stocks. Start running the water maker full time because I want a full tank. I'm going to go out and buy two more five-gallon diesel cans. Tristan, do you remember how many gallons of diesel we have in the tank?"

"Daddy said we had fifteen gallons left when we pulled in." Issy choked on her statement.

"Are we going somewhere, mom?" Tristan was no fool, for a fifteen-year-old, he was pretty sharp.

"You know the rules. Always be prepared. Uncle Zack wants us to go back to Florida. We should be ready for that or anything else. We have been off the boat for a couple of weeks." I stopped only to check the look on their faces and continued, "Tristan, start washing everything down, checking hatches and turn the engines over. Issy, I want you to double check all the lines and all the sails. Spinnaker everything."

"Mom, that'll take days." Issy wined then huffed while throwing herself down at the saloon table.

"Yes, it will, so you better get on it. Nothing helps grief like work." I barked, then swallowed and took a deep breath.

I wandered up on deck to survey the lay of the land. I needed to step away from the boat and the kids. The more I looked around, the tighter my chest felt. The more it clenched, the choppier the water of the marina became.

I quickly grabbed every diesel can on deck. There were five, and every one of them was empty. I lashed them all together with a bungee cord and headed towards the fill-up. I knew there was no way I was going to be able to carry them back. Maybe I should have just taken the dinghy, but that was a lot of weight on that little boat.

I'll figure it out.

The diesel fill-up wasn't far away. I was kind of hoping for a longer walk.

There were three Panamanians and one Antillean hanging out there. The Antillean filled all my gas cans. Then, in broken English, asked me how I was going to get them back to my boat. I replied in Spanish that walking was the only way to go.

Panama is a male-dominated society. Which in this case was helpful for me. One of the local Panamanians came over with a wheelbarrow, loaded all my gas cans up, then told me to lead the way.

He was nice enough to load all of the cans onto the deck and help me lash every single one of them down. I tipped him two Balboas, and he seemed pretty happy as he went on his way.

I have never been much of a drinker, and with Gabriel gone, I didn't see any reason to drink whatsoever. That, and the fact that I was deathly afraid that if I did drink something I would lose control. And at this stage, it could turn into a catastrophe.

Issy finished the inventory faster than I expected, and it fit in with my plans just fine. The sooner we got everything done, the sooner we could leave.

"Okay, Mom. We don't have eggs or milk of any kind, dry, canned, or otherwise. We're low on pasta, and if we're going to have any sauce, we need to get canned tomatoes. We don't have any meat. We've got maybe three pounds of flour. We need a mess of fresh and dried vegetables. Canned anything would be a good idea at this point. We should probably grab a bunch of fresh fruit, and as much lemon juice and lime juice as we can get our hands on. Overall, we've still got a lot of staples. Worst case, two weeks' worth of food on half rations if we don't catch any fish."

Her assessment of our larder was about as bright and cheery as a murder scene.

"Go help Tristan with the boat, and I'm going shopping. I'll be back in three or four hours. Clean up the salon. I want everything spic and span. It will keep your mind busy." I offered and gave her a tight smile.

She heaved a sigh and slumped her shoulders as she headed off to help her brother.

I was actually kind of optimistic. At this point in time, I felt like we could leave the next day. Maybe. I promised that I wouldn't leave without telling Zack, so I decided to call him at dawn. I was glad we'd docked the boat in Cologne because it would take Zack hours to get here, and we would be long gone by that time.

Gathering up all the supplies we needed was easy. You only had to go to one store. That is, if you didn't care about the price. I hit the ATM machine and took out the max amount of cash. I figured I'd hit it again in the morning before we left. We always kept about a grand of cash on the boat to begin with, but I wasn't sure where we were going. I knew I should have waited a day or two more, but I was too afraid to sleep. Too afraid to do anything.

What could happen if I let go for a second?

I pulled up in the cab to the roar of our engines. Tristan had just turned them over with all the gusto that Yanmar engines are known for.

"Mom, everything looks good. Everything is in order. All the electronics are in good working order. We don't have any leaks. I checked the rubbers on all the seals for the hatches. They're good too. You can hear for yourself the engines are fine. Freshwater tanks are full. Solar batteries are fully charged. Looks like we're good to go, that is if we're going anywhere."

Stupid was not a word I would use to describe either of my children. I would say headstrong and stubborn. In Issy's case impulsive, but never stupid.

"Great. Go get the rest of the stuff out of the cab before he decides to drive off with it, and thank you."

Isolde was down in her cabin. I could hear her singing softly to herself. It was a lullaby she made up as a child. She sang it when she was sad.

I think they knew we were leaving in the morning. I didn't say so, and they didn't ask. Dinner was mostly composed of three people pushing food around on plates trying to avoid the big white elephant in the room.

"Both of you, get some sleep! We're getting up early in the morning."

I hugged Issy. She sniffled a few times then turned and fled to her cabin.

"I know we're leaving in the morning. Issy knows it too. I don't know where we're going. I don't even think you know where we're going. Are you sure you want to do this, Mom?" Tristain asked from the shadows of the lower hall.

I stared intently into his eyes. They were that startling blue, the kind that stared right through and into you. They made you feel like they could see to your very soul. But his were different now. They still had that clear piercing quality, only now, there was a dark ring around the outer edge, just like mine. There were other things about him I had noticed. I couldn't put my finger on it. Somehow, I felt like he had grown bigger in the last few weeks. He'd always been a serious child, thoughtful and contemplating. But there was a new stillness to him like he was listening to something.

It was a path I did not want to go down, and yet I knew I had to travel that way. He had changed. Something had changed.

My change occurred when my father beat me - trauma. Whatever happened to Tristan and, I think, to Isolde, may have come from the trauma of losing Gabriel, or maybe a combination of losing their father and almost having a building brought down on top of them. It was something to think about later when we were away from here and all the people I could potentially hurt.

I needed a good night's sleep. We couldn't put to sea if we were all tired.

"Tristan, you need to trust me. I think we might go to the Zapatillas Islands. They're almost uninhabited and just remote enough for us to be left alone for a little while."

He shook his head as I hugged him and held him tightly for a few minutes. He was so much bigger than I was now. He leaned his head down on top of mine, and I couldn't tell who was hugging whom. My little boy was getting so big. I could feel the emotions turning inside of me. I had to stop it. I had to push it back. I ended the hug stepping back. I squeezed his arm gently and turned in, as did he.

*****

Carnelian, Azure, Tanzanite, Sapphire. Trying to find the right shade to describe the sky was an impossible task. I know because it's been over twenty years and I still can't find it. It was a dream, none of the colors were real, but I could feel the spray of waves on my face. The salt burning my eyes and lips. The wind pushing hair away from my face and whipping it around behind my head.

It felt like I was flying or floating, maybe levitating. I had to refocus. I saw the ocean with the aquamarine, turquoise, that indefinable shade that is constantly changing. Why is it I couldn't find the right words for the colors? They were so bright and vivid.

The mountain didn't look the same. I could see it clearly now and it had sides, but it was covered with vines, palm trees, tropical foliage of all kinds. A millennia worth of growth and the top was rounded. Thrusting from the side of the mountain was the shining White Palace - an Acropolis. Standing on the top of the marbled pediment was the statue of a half-naked chiseled man in a chariot being pulled by water horses with one arm holding the reins and the other arm thrusting a giant triton into the sky. He had a look of unfettered ecstasy like he was ready to join a battle. There were several smaller statues around the top of the pediment. I didn't pay much attention to them.

My eyes were drawn to the man. It took a great deal of effort to tear them away. Something about him was familiar. The cut of his face or the shape of his eyes.

I could already feel the misty dew that floated around the base of the Acropolis. The fresh water from the falls kissed my face and moistened my clothes.

I rode the falls all the way down to the base where there was a massive pool. It looked like it would be refreshing to swim in. The area was surrounded by flowers, and their heavy scent filled the air. My body began to pull back. I was lifting, pulling away. That was the closest I had ever been to the island. The further back I went, the louder the roar of the wind became. I knew she was going to speak, and I had to listen.

This will be the time, I know it.

The further back I pulled, the smaller the island became. The colors of my world shifted from the dazzling blues to the dinghy browns and yellows. I wasn't looking at an island anymore. It was a map.

The edges were curled with age and everything had a sepia tone color to it. As if it might have been made out of vellum, or heavy leather. The island was perfectly round, and it didn't show a mountain in the center, but a pyramid. A four-sided pyramid with a building projecting from the base. The map key in the top left corner had a signature. The writing was heavily scrolled with the flowery script of the time in Spanish with a name - Juan Ponce de Leon. There was a date at the top 22 de Junio 1497 Isla del Calypso.

"Look for Calypso. Come find me. You're ready."

CHAPTER 41

HERATHINA

Log entry

Before leaving Alethea, Athena informed me that I would need to make an in-person report every hundred years to track the progress of the humans I'm watching. It was necessary for them to determine whether I was to be returned or moved elsewhere.

That was a polite way of watching. They needed to confirm my emotional objectivity. Few have been granted the privilege of human contact. Most oath breakers returned to the home worlds or were confined to the ship.

Log Entry

I was shifted back, but it was to the village I originally began my journey in. Jorhan was happy to see me. I visited all my old friends and saw the new children that had come into their lives. It is more of a homecoming than I could have wished for, better than the one I had perceived.

"I will personally escort you back to Zeus's village," Jorhan insisted, after many assurances of my happiness and description of Zeus's treatment of me.

"That is not necessary. I can return on my own."

My protests fell on deaf ears. I was to return with two young men from his warrior class, both determined to become my own personal guard. It's silly. As if I would need a guard. If I wanted to fight someone off, all I had to do was call the forces. I could overpower them with little effort on my part.

Jorhan does not understand the use of the forces. He understands the use of human force. But if it makes him feel better, I'm happy to accept the young men. The exchange of genetic material is important to the villages. It will brighten the genetic aspects of the entire region.

Genetic aspects…I have a secret. I cling to it, like a hungry dog to a bare bone. I cannot bring myself to speak it out loud. I can no longer hold to the hope that I am wrong. It is confirmed every morning when I wake. My fear drives me to hold to it, even from Zeus.

I'm pregnant.

The end

KILLING GODS II

CALYPSO

https://amzn.to/34nM35C

If you've enjoyed what you've read here please give it a little

love and leave a review or feel free to follow me on Amazon

Or send me an email slmason1889@gmail.com or follow me

on Instagram @s.l.mason_author

For the most up to date information on the Killing Gods

Universe or These Hallowed Hills visit:

Quickquillpublishing.com